PRAISE FOR TRAC

'I was left absolutely traumatised
Beautiful, heartbreaking, uplifting .

—*HELLO!*

'A pacey read . . . A great book to take to the beach!'

—*Daily Mail*

'I was entranced from the very first page and couldn't put it down until I had all the answers. Tracy weaves a seamless tale while offering brilliant descriptions and raw emotions.'

—Angela Marsons, author of *Child's Play*

'A must-read for fans of psychological suspense. Tightly plotted and intense, this novel will have you looking over your shoulder and peeking under your bed. Filled with twists and turns, it will keep you flying through the pages to the shocking end.'

—Heather Gudenkauf, *Before She Was Found*

'*Wall of Silence* is wild, a "whodunnit" rollercoaster. The story launches with a bang with one of the most original openings I've read. Tracy Buchanan has crafted a novel where the plot literally thickens with every page turned and new secrets simmer as the reader is pulled deeper into her cast of characters' web of lies and silence. I was captivated from page one, entertained throughout, and shocked over the final reveal. Loved it!'

—Kerry Lonsdale, *Wall Street Journal* and *Washington Post* bestselling author

'Secrets and lies abound in this complex and chilling mystery. I was totally shocked by the ending!'
—Lesley Kara, *Sunday Times* bestselling author of *The Rumour*

'A darkly addictive read that draws you deep into the tangled web of secrets that lie at the heart of the Byatt family.'
—Lucy Clarke, bestselling author of *The Sea Sisters*,
a Richard and Judy Book Club choice

SECRETS BETWEEN FRIENDS

OTHER TITLES BY TRACY BUCHANAN:

SECRETS BETWEEN FRIENDS

Tracy Buchanan

Text copyright © 2022 by Tracy Buchanan

Published by Lake Union Publishing, Seattle

www.apub.com

Amazon, the Amazon logo, and Lake Union Publishing are trademarks of Amazon.com, Inc., or its affiliates.

ISBN-13: 9781542032223
ISBN-10: 1542032229

Cover design by Lisa Horton

Printed in the United States of America

To Aunt Laura
See, I said I'd set another book by the sea!

Prologue

20 Years Ago

There is something almost hypnotic about the sight of his body being carried away by the sea, especially when it's a body as perfect as his. Beautiful dark hair spread out around a pristine, pale face. The sea, his new lover now, lifts him gently, so gently it is as though he is sleeping as his arms bob above his head, the huge moon watching like a concerned parent. The waves softly twist him around. Suddenly, reality hits as once divine memories turn to dust when I catch sight of the back of his head, bloody and clotted.

Is he dead, truly dead? A confusing mixture of grief and relief rushes over me and as though in response, the sea turns violent, ripples of ocean transforming into hungry, angry hands clutching at his limbs as they are pulled, finally, beneath the surface.

I double over with the pain of it. How can this be happening? I sense eyes on me and turn to look up at the manor. Its black spired roof looms over me, a wary guardian watching and waiting, much like the shocked face I see in a lower-ground window now. She beckons for me to come back inside. But I'm not sure I want to. In fact, for a moment I wish the manor would crumble and fall to the sea below, the memories clutched within it disappearing beneath the waves. But like the sea, it can never be destroyed. Like the sea, it grabs at us, twisting and turning all of us so violently; even if it did crumble away, it would always be there: the bittersweet weeks that led us to this day. But unlike the body below, we who remain don't have the gift of sweet oblivion. Instead, we must stay behind and endure what we have done.

Our secret. This secret between friends.

Chapter 1

Now

When most people think of the picturesque fishing village of Easthaven, they envisage the view depicted on its postcards, taken from the sea and sweeping up towards the ten rows of pastel-painted cottages that trickle down to the promenade below like a gorgeous melting pot of ice-cream flavours: subtle mint and eggshell pink, sweet lilac and haze blue.

But I've always preferred the view from the top of the long cobbled path that cuts through the centre of that melting pot. It's how I start each day in fact, parking my Royal Mail van at the bottom of the hill before marching up the path so the van becomes just a red spot on the horizon. Sure, it means an uphill walk, but that's easy enough for someone who spent her school years competing in rock-climbing championships.

I pretend to myself I come here first so I can get the best morning shots for my Instagram account, 'The Jolly Postie' as I've called it. Each day, I post a scene from my postal round . . . anonymously, of course. If people do enough digging, they'll figure out it's me, seeing as I'm the only postie covering Easthaven. But I don't want to make it too obvious; last thing I need is the people on my old postal round getting wind of where I am now and posting rude comments. As soon as that starts, the account will be closed. It'll be a shame though, I'm at over 500 followers now!

But no, the truth is, I start my round up here because it's where I get the best view of Lakewell Manor on the cliff above. Though it's surrounded by mossy high walls, I find if I stand on tiptoes in just the right place, I can catch a glimpse of the overgrown gardens and mossy grey walls of the building within, which haunts my dreams each night. Sometimes, I'll see part of the garden wall has crumbled, or a window has cracked. And that's all I need, confirmation that it's no longer as strong as it once was. Confirmation that the march of time will one day mean it is finally gone.

But today, something is different. There's movement within the grounds. Several people flooding in and out of the manor carrying boxes, some with hardhats on too. I almost stumble as I strain to see better. Maybe it's finally going to be knocked down? Or worse, has it been sold to new owners looking to renovate Lakewell Manor and return it to its former glory?

I feel a shiver of horror as I contemplate that. My friend Lester will know. The sooner I get this round out of the way, the sooner I can visit his patisserie and see just what he knows. So I quickly go to the first house on my round, my hands trembling as I slip several letters into the postbox there. *It'll be fine, Liz,* I tell myself. *It'll all be fine.*

'A word please?' a voice calls out above me.

I look up to see a woman leaning over the balcony closest to me. Tilda Beashell lives in a sunflower-coloured cottage, ironic really considering she's the least sunny person I've ever known. She used to be in the year above me at school and revelled in the fact that her father was a local police officer. He was actually lovely, a complete contrast to his daughter. Her husband, Toby, is also lovely. I've never understood how the two of them can be together. I often overhear the way she speaks to him, treating him like a piece of rubbish that needs taking out. And yet he's the one who pays for her expensive boutique dresses. I say *expensive* because I overheard Toby shouting at her once about a credit card bill. And who can blame him? In the three months since I've moved back to Easthaven, I've recorded in my notepad that she has received seventy-two clothing deliveries (I'm presuming they're clothes from the feel of the packages). Looking at the labels on the packages, the shops they come from sell dresses at an average of £60 per dress. That's £4,320 spent on clothes in less than three months! No wonder Toby gets so angry, poor man.

'I saw you on our Ring camera, you know,' Tilda snaps down at me now. 'I don't appreciate you sniffing around our front garden.' She gestures angrily at the small lawn to the right of their house, surrounded by a white picket fence and accessed by a small matching gate.

Damn. I didn't realise they have a Ring camera. 'I appreciate that must have looked strange, Tilda,' I say with a forced smile, 'but your bird feeder had fallen off the branch.' I point to the pretty driftwood feeder hanging from the only tree in their garden. 'I thought it best to hang it back up before the seed spilt all over your lovely lawn.' Of course, it's a lie but how could I resist when I heard them arguing the other day? My feet were walking into the garden before I had a chance, desperate for a discreet peek through the window.

'I would have noticed it soon enough,' Tilda retorts. 'You had no right doing it; our lawn is private property. Any more trespassing and I'll be talking to your manager.' Then she storms into the house, slamming the French doors behind her. I feel a sense of trepidation in my stomach. This day has *not* started out well. Sure, I've grown used to the odd confrontation over the years, it's part and parcel of what I do, excuse the pun. But I don't like it when they mention my manager. I need to be careful, especially with the custody hearing coming up in two weeks. I can't give my ex, Scott, any more ammunition for getting full custody of the kids.

I take a deep breath and walk to the next house, getting my notepad out as I do to jot down an update: *10.32 a.m.: Told off by Mrs B re: bird feeder. Mrs B threatened to tell manager. BEWARE.* I tuck my notepad back into the pocket of my shorts and continue with my round, hurrying along each row. Usually I'd take my time, much to the jokey annoyance of my boss, Greg. 'Oh look! Liz is the last one back from her round again!' he'll often say. Fine, let him. I've already told him there's a reason I've been doing this job for over ten years now: I understand being a postie is a *community* role, on a par with being a vicar or a schoolteacher or any array of other essential community roles. If he can't see that, that's his problem.

As I draw closer and closer to the sea, gulls swoop above my head and the heady scent of seaweed and salt tickles my nostrils. But something else stirs too. Anxiety as Lakewell Manor looms closer, and the worrying thought that it may be revived. When I've finished with the cottages, I rush towards the promenade. It stretches along the sandy coast, stopping at the private road with its steep incline towards the cliff edge where the manor sits. On the promenade itself are several shops and the patisserie, a large grassy expanse behind it where families like to picnic and play football.

I walk along the promenade and peer towards the manor again, tummy turning over. I never dreamed it would be occupied again. I honestly thought (hoped) it would one day be knocked down to make way for more villas like the ones that sit at the bottom of the cliff. I quickly deliver post to the row of small shops and restaurants, before heading into the patisserie at the end. It's the closest building to the large green making it an ideal spot to catch beach goers and picnickers fed up with their home-made sandwiches. It used to be a typical seaside cafe with pale-blue walls and driftwood tables. But when Lester took it over five years ago, he channelled his French roots to give it a Parisian vibe with an assortment of red and white bistro tables organised in an L shape around the front and side, the white walls graced with mirrors and Art Deco pictures. He'd always dreamed of running his own place since I knew him when we were kids, serving the creole and French food he learnt to cook from his mother. And now he's doing just that! I'm so proud of him.

Though in different classes, we used to go to the same school and grew to know each other while sharing the village newspaper round. He was like me, from a rougher part of Easthaven, living with his single mum in a house that had been converted into two flats. We'd spend our rounds chatting about his dreams to run a posh restaurant in London, and my dreams of being a journalist. When I moved back here three months ago, we took off where we had left, falling instantly into our old, easy friendship.

I walk in to see him dancing to some music playing from his radio, his tied-back dreadlocks bouncing as he jigs. His face lights up when he sees me. 'Hey, postie,' he says. 'Time for tea?'

'Only if you have some gossip to entice me to stay,' I say, walking up to the counter and handing him his post. 'Do you know what's going on at Lakewell Manor?' I'm trying to sound casual. Lester knows nothing of its past, nor my role *in* that past. I want to keep it that way.

'Exactly what I was waiting to tell you,' he says, his blue eyes sparking with drama. 'Tamsin Lakewell is back in Easthaven!' I have to grip on to the counter to stop myself from stumbling as my legs turn to jelly. She's back. Tamsin is back. 'You look like you've seen a ghost,' Lester says with a laugh.

She might as well be a ghost. She is as fascinating and as terrifying to me as one. My old best friend, Tamsin Lakewell. The beautiful, talented girl whose family has owned the grand manor on the cliff since the 1800s when it was built. The same girl who somehow decided that I, a quiet nobody who lived in the roughest estate in Easthaven, was worthy of being her friend. The last time we saw each other, she said she would never set foot in Easthaven again. So why is she back? What could possibly have possessed her? If I'd had the money and choices, I would never have returned. But sadly I have neither.

'I thought you'd be happy to hear the news,' Lester says. 'She was your best friend.'

I blink, trying to focus on his face. *Pull yourself together, Liz.* 'Yeah, course I am, but I haven't seen her since she left twenty years ago,' I reply.

'None of us have.'

'Do you – do you know why she's back?'

He sighs. 'Her mother died.'

I suddenly get an image of Tamsin's lovely mother with her huge smile and short strawberry-blonde hair. 'Oh no, she was lovely.'

'Yep, I remember. Crazy to think Tamsin's a published poet now. Do you remember all those times we'd see her writing her poetry in the garden through the manor's gates when we used to deliver the papers together?'

'Yep, I remember. Right,' I say. 'Better get on with my round. See you tomorrow.'

'Sure thing,' Lester says. 'You can report back if you get to see the mysterious poet.'

'I doubt it,' I say. 'I don't have any post for the manor. But I'll let you know if I hear any goss. Have a good one!'

I walk out of the cafe, the sea wind on my back, the heat of the late spring morning on my face as the soles of my walking boots thud on the wooden slats of the promenade. I can feel my heart thumping against my chest as I pass the 'private road' sign marking the start of the exclusive cliffside road, and climb the increasingly steep incline. I head towards the villas first, delivering their post. There are three of them, each built seven years ago by Douglas Gold, the local property mogul who himself occupies the last villa with his family. Lester once told me Douglas had tried to buy the manor from Tamsin's mother years ago. He was hoping to knock it down to make way for a fourth villa. But she refused to sell it. I bet Douglas didn't like that. He was used to getting his way. He was the same at school, an arrogant bully who enjoyed using the fact that his father was one of the wealthiest men in the town thanks to his antiques business to throw his weight around. He even once shoved another kid down the stairs after they tried to stop him bullying another child, and he was caught spying on the girls through a hole in the changing rooms. Somehow, he managed to wriggle his way out of all that, just like he did most things.

And now he's my landlord, I think with a sigh. He'd taken over the lease of my mother's house from her previous landlord a few years back as he bought up more and more property in Easthaven. On the day I moved in with the kids, he'd been waiting for me by my mother's gate. 'Promise to behave?' he'd said, the gold in one of his front teeth shining.

'Of course,' I'd replied.

'As long as I continue to be paid on time and your kids give me no hassle, you won't have to worry.'

Worry. The way he'd said that had made me shiver. Polite but with an edge of malice that I knew too well from our days at school. It just made the whole experience of having to move back in with my mother even more onerous. I shake my head as I approach the Gold residence. Their villa is built in exactly the same way as the other two, a vast white two-storey building with a circular entrance protruding from the front with a balcony above it. Except the Golds have added 'embellishments' including two gold – yes, real *gold* from what Lester told me – lion statues facing the two pillars in front of the house.

Luckily, most of the time Douglas isn't in when I deliver his post. But when he is, I often catch him watching me from one of the vast windows, eyes drilling into me like he knows all there is to know about me. Maybe he does. Men like him usually do know more than they should. What disconcerts me the most is the high gold telescope that stands beside him. It was the same telescope that sat in the window of the vast house his parents owned by the Easthaven Hotel at the other end of town. Douglas was keen back then on telling anyone who listened that it was worth a fortune as it belonged to his grandfather, a 'great war hero'. I sometimes see Douglas's teenage son, Aubrey, looking through it, watching the mother in the villa next door sunbathing. Like father, like son. I thrust their post into the letterbox, always desperate to get away from that villa as quick as I can, not just because of Douglas's menacing presence but also its proximity to the manor. I pause now, peering up towards the manor. Is Tamsin in there right now? I wonder if she looks the same, acts the same? Despite that awful last evening we spent together, I can't help but remember her with fondness. She *had* been my best friend, after all.

I suddenly feel strangely drawn there and before I know it, I find myself walking up the cliff towards the manor gates. I haven't come this far since that fateful night twenty years ago. As I look at the huge, black iron gates marking the entrance to the Lakewell estate, my stomach bubbles with nerves, a contrast to the days when the sight of those gates would make it bubble with excitement.

To make matters worse, the road feels like it's on even more of a knife-edge here, looking down over craggy white cliffs to the sea below. It's calm today, a relief because I fear if the waves were too fierce and loud, the memories would be too potent. Still, they whisper to me as I walk up the road, each crash of a wave a dark bell tolling past memories.

As I get to the top of the cliff, Lakewell Manor appears in all its glory. It's always been such an imposing and Gothic wonder, a huge grand building with grey brick walls and sharp black spires. Due to the steep incline of the path that leads up to it, it really does seem to loom over the village and the people below. Combined with the vast sea to the left of it and the long, gravelled drive and once perfectly manicured gardens at the front, it's quite a sight. Even now, it is still beautiful, despite its once immaculate walls being now thick with ivy and moss. Before, Tamsin's mother, Dorothy, would have the walls cleaned regularly so the usual thrust of sea salt and air didn't discolour them. But that hasn't been done for many years and it shows, the walls so grimy they almost blur in with the black spires of the roof above. From here, I can see birds nesting within the broken eaves of one of those spires. Surely Tamsin isn't intending to move back here permanently? But then why would she have men in hardhats here?

When I get to the gates, I dare to reach out and touch their iron bars, so cool and achingly familiar. Then my eyes catch on to something. Wind chimes. Dozens of rusty wind chimes in all sorts of faded colours hanging from the trees that are dotted around the overgrown front lawn, their metal and glass pieces catching the sun streaming into the garden and bouncing light from one to the other.

A memory rushes at me of lying on the grass and looking up at those wind chimes, the sound of Tamsin giggling in the pool nearby as a firm, calloused hand took the chance to slide up my thigh. I clench my fists, willing the memories away. As I do, I hear the distant tinkle of music and catch a whiff of baking bread drifting towards me on the breeze. The house is awakening, all my senses tell me that, and the memories continue to assault me. Memories

I'd rather forget of a handsome face smiling down at me, full lips curving into a smile as blue eyes dance with desire. Then a scream, a guttural sound and the thud of a body on marble.

As I think that, I notice movement in one of the top rooms of the house and catch sight of a tall man pacing back and forth in front of the large arched window. He's wearing a white shirt open at the neck and is talking to someone on the phone, his expression irate, his fingers frantically raking through his thick dark hair. He pauses for a moment and looks down at me, and I let out a small gasp.

He looks just like Gabe.

Of course, I know it can't be him. But still, the similarities are astounding. I quickly move out of sight. Maybe this is just a nightmare? I simply haven't woken up yet and all the things I fear – the manor being returned to its former glory; the return of *him* – are just figments of my dark imagination. I go to rush away but as I do, there's the sound of smashing glass followed by a scream.

Another memory. Another scream. The sight of blood.

I quickly look back through the gates to see a woman in the distance in a long peacock-blue summer dress, holding her hand with shattered glass around her.

It's Tamsin and suddenly all those memories from the first time we met twenty-one years ago come flooding back . . .

Chapter 2

21 Years Ago

I peer up at the huge tree sitting to the side of one of the vast walls surrounding Lakewell Manor. I know I can climb it. I've climbed taller, larger trees. The question is, can I find a spot to nestle in so I can look into the manor's gardens without being seen?

But what if I get caught? Is it worth it, this stupid yearning to see Tamsin Lakewell, the new girl that moved into Lakewell Manor six months ago? She's such an enigma though and I absolutely *must* solve all enigmas that are put in my path. Mother says it will be my downfall one day. Maybe that day is today. Maybe I should walk away right now.

And yet how else will I be able to get a glimpse into this girl's life? It's not as though she attends the local school like the rest of us. Instead, she's homeschooled. Nobody really knows why. Some of the kids reckon she's agoraphobic. Others that she's dying from some terminal disease.

I bite my lip, still staring at that tree, so tempting with its perfectly climbable branchiness. I really ought to step away from the temptation. Surely it's enough to catch sight of her through those large iron gates on my paper rounds. But there's something about Tamsin Lakewell that makes me just *know* we could be friends, and boy, could I use a new friend. Scratch that. *Any* friend full stop. I mean, the whole *loner with notepad* thing is cool and everything, but there comes a point in a girl's life when she needs someone to confide in.

So that's it, I've made my mind up. I'm doing this. I look around to check nobody's watching then jump up to grab the first branch, hauling myself up on to it as the thrill of what I'm doing battles with nerves. Just two more branches and I'll be able to peek right over the wall. I let that thought guide me as I huff and puff my way up until finally, I find myself hovering on a slightly precarious branch to look inside.

Wow, Lakewell Manor looks even more impressive from here with those posh grey bricks and gleaming sash windows. It's stood empty ever since Lord Lakewell died in the seventies, but it's still maintained by local gardeners and handymen. I see them there sometimes on my rounds. I often wish I'd been alive back then to witness the summer luncheons the lord organised for all Easthaven residents. I'd love to be able to wander around the grounds while taking my first sip of expensive champagne and nibble of delicious canapés. It'd beat the cheap cherry and yucky salmon things my mother serves on Christmas Day, that's for sure.

'Hello there!' a voice calls out.

I peer down to see the very enigma herself, Tamsin Lakewell, smiling up at me. *Bugger*. I go to scramble back down the tree but then hear her voice again. 'Don't go!' I pause, knee painfully digging into a knot in the bark of the branch below. 'Surely you want a drink after all that,' she says. 'Tree climbing and spying is thirsty work.'

Is this a trick? Does she have a camera so she can take a photo as proof of spying for the police? But something about that smile of hers just now and the tone of her voice, it *speaks* to me. It tells me this is a girl who is searching for a new friend to confide in too.

So I take a deep breath and haul myself back up again, perching on the wall. Tamsin guards her eyes from the sun with her hand as she regards me, her red hair like a blaze of fire in the mid-afternoon light. 'You do look funny up there,' she says. 'Come down.'

'How?' I ask, looking around me.

'Use the tree there,' a voice shouts out from the back. I look over to see Tamsin's mother lounging on a chair by the vast pool at the back of the house. She and Tamsin look so alike with their red hair and curves. But unlike Tamsin's long tresses, her mother's hair is cut into a chic bob. She's directing this massive smile towards me, despite the fact that I'm a wall scaler and spy. I instantly feel enveloped in that smile, like the sun has popped down and wrapped its arms around me. I've heard *so* many nice things about Dorothy Lakewell, like all the charity stuff she does around the village since they moved here. Of course, my mother hates her with a passion which proves to me even more what a good sort Dorothy Lakewell must be. Mother reckons she's 'snooty' but the truth is, she's just jealous the woman has money. Not only is she the daughter of a lord and wife to a property mogul, but she also makes her own money from her fashion design business. And now she's smiling at little old me.

Reality suddenly hits then. That's me who is sitting on her wall, caught mid voyeurism. 'I'm so sorry,' I quickly shout over to her.

Dorothy laughs. 'Don't be silly, come on in. You can keep Tamsin company while I take a call inside. The tree this side is much comfier anyway. Tamsin should know, it's the one she uses when escaping.'

'You know about that?' Tamsin asks.

But I notice she doesn't look horrified, she's just smiling at her mother. I look between them, these two strange and wonderful people, and I know in that moment I want to be part of their world. No, not just *want* but *insist upon*. I climb my way to the tree

15

Dorothy is referring to and swing down from it on to the perfectly cut lawn.

'Come to the back,' Tamsin says.

I follow her around, unable to quite believe I'm here. I reach out and glance my fingers over the grand grey bricks that make up the manor as I walk along a rose-bush-lined path towards the patio area at the back. I gasp as I take in the large pool that looks out over the cliff. Beyond it is a garden filled with more rose-bushes and trees over an immaculate lawn, with steps down from the cliff to the beach below.

'This place is even better than I imagined,' I can't help but say.

'It's pretty, isn't it?' Tamsin says as she leads us to a sun lounger and pours me some juice. 'Much nicer than the townhouse in Chelsea. Mum needs the sea air; she has asthma so Dad insisted we come here.'

'Yes, nothing quite beats a lungful of seaweed-clogged air to help with things like that,' I say.

Dorothy laughs as she stands up. 'I like this girl,' she says. 'In fact, we haven't introduced ourselves. I'm Dorothy and this is my lovely daughter, Tamsin.'

I pretend I haven't been obsessed with them for six months and smile. 'Nice to meet you,' I say. 'I'm Liz. That's . . . Liz with an L.'

Tamsin and her mother burst out laughing.

'I can't believe I said that,' I say, laughing with them.

'Well, Liz with an L, I have an important call to make.' Dorothy waves at us both and heads inside.

'Your mum seems nice,' I say to Tamsin.

'She is nice. So you do the paper round, don't you?'

'Yep,' I say, taking a sip of the delicious juice she poured for me, eyes gliding to take in the back of the house with its bi-fold doors and vast modern kitchen. 'I need to pay the rent.'

Tamsin frowns. 'You pay rent?'

I roll my eyes. 'My mother insists. She is definitely not *nice* like your mum.'

'Well, I couldn't possibly afford the rent here,' she jokes, gesturing around her. 'How old are you anyway?'

'Sixteen.'

'Samesies!' Tamsin raises her hand in the air, presenting me with her palm. 'This is when you give me a high five.'

'Oh sorry, what a dork.' I slam my palm against hers and she flinches.

'You are *strong*. So I take it you live in Easthaven?'

'Yeah. Don't ask me where, it's the worst part.'

'Do you go to the school here?'

'Yep. You don't though, do you?'

She looks down and plays with a thread on her denim shorts. 'No. I have a tutor to homeschool me here.'

'Do you mind me asking why?' She doesn't answer. 'Sorry,' I quickly say, 'I'm too nosy for my own good sometimes.'

'Oh, I don't mind you asking.' She raises her green eyes to meet mine. 'It's because I hate crowds and you can't get more *crowdy* than a school, can you?'

'No, I can confirm schools are very crowdy.' I notice a notepad on the table by her. 'Do you write?'

Her face lights up. 'Poetry.'

'That's so cool. I write too,' I say, getting my plain brown notepad out of the back pocket of my jeans. 'I want to be a journalist.'

'Now that is even cooler. What sort of things do you write in that hip notepad?'

'Just observations about the stuff that goes on around town. You know, exciting things like "Amy Johnson has a new parasol in her back garden" or "Dean Jones bought a new car".'

'Well I have one for you,' Tamsin says, leaning close to me as her green eyes sparkle. 'Local girl scales Lakewell Manor's walls and finds a new friend.'

I smile. *New friend.* I like that.

Her mother strolls back out then.

'Appointment made, sweetie,' she says to Tamsin who frowns a little in response.

I wonder what the appointment is for. Tamsin doesn't look too happy about it. Her mother turns to me.

'Please tell me you'll stay for dinner, Liz with an L? Simone is going to barbecue some meat for us,' she says, gesturing to a small, blonde woman who has emerged from the house with a plate of burgers and sausages.

My smile widens. 'That'd be great.'

Over the next couple of hours, I have, officially, the best dinner of my life. Not only is the barbecued meat *perfection* but so is the company. But it's bittersweet. As I watch Tamsin and her mother, I see a life I could have had with a mother like Dorothy. It's not about the manor and the money. It's this bond I see between the two of them.

I feel sad when it's time to leave. The thought of returning home to my mother, the polar opposite of Dorothy, fills me with dread. As I wave goodbye, I notice with surprise that Tamsin seems to be suddenly angry with her mother, gesturing at the phone in her hands and shaking her head. Is it about that mysterious appointment? The last thing I see as I round the corner is Tamsin storming off inside.

Maybe their life isn't as perfect as it seems?

Chapter 3

Now

I know instantly it's Tamsin as I look at her through the manor's gates. She may have been just seventeen when I last saw her, but that long, red hair of hers is unmistakable. She's standing by a bistro table I hadn't noticed before at the side of the manor, overlooking the sea. There is a notepad on it, and a pen. A large pitcher lies smashed on the ground. We stare at one another, she bleeding, me shocked. I wonder if she recognises me. She seems not to have changed but I am so different, my once long, dark hair now short, my curves gone, the stress of the past few months taking their toll on my appetite.

'Liz?' she calls out in a trembling voice. 'I saw it was you and I jumped up, knocking the pitcher over.' She peers down at her bloody hand, confused. 'I tried to pick up the glass but then I cut myself. You remember how funny I get around blood, even the teeniest amount?'

Of course I remember. How could I ever forget? She obviously realises what she's said as she blinks, cheeks flushing as she looks towards the cellar door in the manor. Then she sways slightly before stumbling, grabbing on to the table for support, blood still dripping down her hand. The Gabe lookalike is back to striding back and forth on the balcony, talking on his phone. He hasn't even noticed. 'I have a first-aid kit,' I shout out to Tamsin. 'Do you want me to help?'

'Yes please.'

'Is the code still the same?'

'You still remember?' Another thing I can't possibly forget, imprinted on to my mind. I nod and quickly tap the number into the nearby keypad. There's a clicking sound and the gates move open at what seems to be a glacial pace. I squeeze into the small gap and dash inside, pulling the small first-aid kit I always carry around with me from my cross-body postal bag.

'You should sit down,' I say, trying not to feel overwhelmed by the memories Tamsin's peachy perfume brings. She does as I ask, lowering herself on to one of the rusty iron chairs. I kneel in front of her, noticing her feet are bare, each of her toenails painted a different vibrant colour. *So Tamsin.* She really hasn't changed. How can she have *not* changed? I feel like I became a different person that fateful night twenty years ago.

'This is so silly,' she says as she gives me a faltering smile. 'It's just a small cut.'

'Better safe than sorry.' I carefully lift her left hand, seeing she's right; it's really not so bad, just a small cut on the soft fleshy pad of her thumb. I quickly get a gauze out, pressing it against her skin to stem the bleeding. Then I replace it with a plaster, wrapping it around her thumb. She watches the whole time with a frown on her freckled face, the sun haloing around her head.

'Thank you so much for this, Liz with an L,' she says.

I smile at the memory of the first time I met her mother. Then the smile disappears from my face. 'I heard your mother died. I'm so sorry, Tamsin. Dorothy was just the best and I know how close you were.'

Her green eyes fill with tears. 'It's been just awful. Bloody cancer, of course. It's been six months now. Still feels so raw. I've worn this dress three days in a row you know,' she says, gesturing down to her beautiful maxi dress. 'It's the last gift my mother gave me.' She sighs. 'I guess I've truly seen behind the veil now.'

'Behind the veil?'

'When you lose someone you love.'

I frown as I think of Gabe. I've seen behind the veil. I lost him, didn't I? Right here, in this very place. I wrap my arms around myself as I look at Tamsin. There are too many dark memories between us. And yet we were once great friends and I can still feel the very energy that drew us together fizzing again. It's a terrible conflict.

'What are your plans for the manor then?' I try to make my voice sound casual when I feel anything but inside.

'I've been asking myself the same,' Tamsin replies, eyes flitting inside towards the cellar door again. 'The initial plan was to sell it. But I wanted to come back first to be sure that's what I want.'

'Have you been out and about yet? I'm sure Lester would like to see you; he's taken over the cafe and it's amazing.'

'Oh, you know me,' Tamsin says. 'A bit of a hermit. You're the first Easthaven resident I've seen since arriving! I haven't set foot out of the manor yet. Maybe in a few days. I shouldn't let Carl be on his own as he explores.'

'Carl?'

'My fiancé.' So the Gabe clone is her fiancé? 'We've got some renovators over at the moment so I'll see what they say about getting it redecorated and tidied up. I promised Carl we can stay until I manage to wrap my head around what to do.' She sighs as she looks down at her hands. 'It could be *weeks*, I'm so undecided.'

'I think you should sell it,' I quickly say.

Her eyes shoot up to me. She knows why I'm saying that. She goes quiet, pensively biting her lip. 'Yes, maybe I should. It – it might be good to get it bulldozed after all that's happened here. Have it all smashed to pieces.'

We hold each other's gazes. So many years have passed but I can see Gabe's fate haunts her still, as it does me.

'Smash what to pieces?' a deep voice asks.

I look up to see the man I'd noticed at the arch window strolling towards us. I find I can hardly breathe. It really is as though Gabe is strolling towards us, that knowing smile on his gorgeous face. It's not just the dark hair and perfect features though. He walks with the same confidence Gabe once did, one hand in the pocket of his dark suit trousers, the other swinging by his side with his mobile phone clutched between his long tanned fingers. His eyes are a startling blue against what my ex Scott used to describe as an 'expensive tan', as if he's got it from a yacht in the Maldives rather than a plastic sun lounger in Benidorm.

He walks to Tamsin, a wide smile on his handsome face as he kisses her on her freckled forehead. Can she not see how similar he is to Gabe? Or maybe she absolutely does and that's why she is attracted to him. I, on the other hand, found I had to latch on to the polar opposite of Gabe by going for a short, blond man in Scott. The man's eyes alight on the glass shards below and traces of blood. His smile suddenly disappears.

'What happened?' he asks in a concerned voice.

'Silly me accidentally knocked the table and the water pitcher fell off,' Tamsin says. 'I cut myself trying to pick up the shards, see?' she says, holding her thumb up to show him as she pouts. 'Liz saved the day by providing me with a plaster. You know how I get around blood.'

Carl looks down at me. '*The* Liz? Your old friend?'

I feel my blush grow even deeper. She told him about me? Then I frown. What else does he know?

'An honour to meet you, Liz.' He bows as though he is a prince. Then he looks my outfit up and down. 'I thought you were a journalist?'

'The journalism thing didn't quite pan out in the end after I got pregnant,' I say, feeling a thread of disappointment. I stamp it away, forcing a smile on to my face as I gesture to Tamsin's notepad. 'I hear the poetry thing *more* than worked out for you though, Tamsin. Two books published already with one soon to be! I always knew you'd be a famous poet one day.'

'Hardly famous! Do you still carry a notepad everywhere with you too?'

I dig mine out and wave it about. 'Of course.'

'Watching you both,' Carl says, 'I can so imagine you terrorising Easthaven with your notepads.'

Tamsin and I both laugh. But I notice our laughs are laced with nerves. It's not just the years that have passed but also what Tamsin left behind when she ran from Easthaven.

'So you have children?' Carl asks.

'Two girls,' I reply. 'Ruby's sixteen and Mia's twelve.' I avoid the *husband* bit. 'Ruby even has her own investigative TikTok channel with fifty thousand followers,' I say proudly.

'How wonderful,' Carl says, 'that journalism streak clearly runs in the family.' I notice Tamsin is staring out to the sea now, quiet as Carl makes polite conversation. His phone rings. 'Please excuse me, I must get this. But you must come over for dinner sometime, Liz,' he calls over his shoulder to me as he walks away, putting his phone to his ear. We watch as he disappears into the manor.

I know this should be my cue to leave. But I find myself wanting to hover a little longer, the pull of Tamsin's and my old friendship still strong. 'He seems lovely,' I say. 'How long have you been together?'

'It always sounds so silly when I say it but . . . not even six months.'

My mouth drops open. 'Wow. You seem so . . .'

'I know, so *together*, right? And that's how it feels, like we've known each other for years. I've been rather cynical about love ever since . . .' Her voice trails off, stopping just short of saying his name: *Gabe*. 'Anyway, the moment I saw Carl, it was bam! I just knew.'

'Where did you meet?' I ask.

'Group grief counselling. The funeral home I used offered group counselling as part of their package, so one day I just went along, rather impulsively really. It was just two weeks after Mum's death and I – I was struggling. I mean, I'm struggling now,' she adds with a sad smile.

'I'm so sorry to hear that.'

'Oh it is what it is. I've accepted the hole of grief never really disappears, I just have to learn to live my life around it.' Her face lights up then. 'Anyway, that's where I met Carl, at the grief counselling. I was thinking about making my excuses after five minutes and leaving, but then Carl walked in.' She takes in a deep breath, a huge smile spreading over her pretty face. 'I mean, you've seen him, he's beautiful.'

I don't know how to respond to that, so just smile awkwardly.

'But it wasn't just that,' Tamsin says. 'When he began talking about his mother whom he'd lost, it was almost like we'd been cut from the same cloth. We weren't only experiencing the exact same emotions but we were *reacting* in the exact same way. After,' she continues, 'when he suggested we get a coffee, I agreed. We didn't leave the cafe until it closed at nine that evening! Ten hours of non-stop talking, can you believe it?'

24

I can. Didn't we used to spend that amount of time talking?

She lets out a laugh. 'Gosh, listen to me. I must be boring you!'

'You could never bore me, Tamsin. Not then, not now.'

We smile at each other, two old friends reminiscing. But we're not ordinary friends and she knows it as well as I do. What friends share secrets like ours? Her face goes sombre again as she returns her gaze to the sea. 'Maybe boring would have been preferable back then,' she murmurs, almost to herself.

How can I respond to that? 'I better get back to the sorting office,' I quickly say, backing away, the memories seeming to match each step. 'But it was nice seeing you again.' And I realise it really has been nice. Yes, there are dark memories that we share. But mainly, there are the good memories and the fact that she's considering getting the place bulldozed gives me *some* solace.

'You too, Liz,' she says. 'I'm expecting some post here this week, actually, so maybe we'll see each other soon?'

'Ah-huh,' I say noncommittally, not really sure how I feel about seeing her again. As I walk away, I dwell on it. I'd love for us to reconnect. It just reminds me, seeing Tamsin again, how well we get on. But can we really get past what happened twenty years ago? As though to remind me, the waves crash violently down below and for a moment, I think I can see a body down there. *His* body.

But then I shake my head and the image is gone.

Chapter 4

By the time I get home later, it's two o'clock and clouds have gathered in the sky, shrouding the sun. It makes the small housing estate I now call home look even more grey. Though officially part of Easthaven, it feels nothing like it with its bland brown houses and tiny glimpses of sea. Each time I return from a round, it feels even farther away from the pastels and whites of Easthaven's beautiful seafront. It's set off the main road that comes into Easthaven, the only nice thing about it the roundabout with a pretty metal sculpture of a seagull surrounded by small lush palm trees and colourful flowers in the middle. Beyond it, the road continues to slope upwards, leading to the estate where I now live with my mother and the kids.

I mustn't moan too much though. At least I have a roof over our heads. There was a time when I thought I wouldn't even have that after losing my job last year. Scott had been renting the house we lived in so when we parted ways, it meant I needed to find a house of my own if I wanted any chance of having the kids with me. But I'd just been fired from my job too and was left with a dicey reference, meaning getting a new job was challenging.

But then I'd seen a postie job going in the area serving Easthaven . . . and the person advertising it happened to be my old friend, Greg, whom I'd met while at Easthaven Secondary's sixth form, the very same place Ruby is studying now. I didn't *want* to return to Easthaven. But I couldn't ignore the fact that my mother was sitting in a three-bedroom house way too big for her and if I wanted to stave off Scott's threats of getting full custody of the kids, I knew it was my best option. So in the end, I put my kids above my fear of revisiting dark memories and the horror of living with my mother again.

It was a miracle she agreed to us moving in. It was only my promise of helping with her care so she didn't need to fork out for as many carers and the fact that I'd be contributing to the rent that made her concede in the end. When the girls and I drew up in front of Mother's small three-bed three months ago, Ruby moaned it looked 'even more tiny and even more dull' while Mia just continued listening to her music, eyes down. We had rarely visited my mother here but when we did, it would be a depressing affair filled with stale sandwiches and biting criticisms.

I let myself in now, wrinkling my nose at the now familiar smell of damp and cheap ham from the sandwiches one of my mother's morning carers would have made her. I try not to let negative thoughts intrude as I take in the ripped wallpaper and the stained Artex ceilings. Sure, the house Scott and I rented in Manchester with the kids had been larger. But the area it was based in wasn't exactly the nicest, with regular bouts of crime, late-night parties and vandalism. At least this estate, dull as it is, feels safer, even if the house and garden is a third of the size.

'Liz!' There goes my mother's daily greeting from the living room, screeched over the sound of the TV. 'Liz! I'm hungry!'

I place my bag on the round oak table in the small kitchen. 'Be there in a minute.' Welcome to my routine each workday: get in, get shouted at, then get shouted at again. No writing poems in a garden overlooking the sea for me. I sigh, going to one of the kitchen's beige cupboards to grab some tinned soup. It's ridiculous really, my mother had her lunch only three hours ago. It feels like the less mobile she gets due to her rheumatoid arthritis, the hungrier she is. You'd think it would be the other way round.

While the soup's warming in the microwave, I quickly butter two slices of bread, placing them on my mother's tray with her soup. The tray features three cute puppies, ironic really considering she hates dogs, all animals in fact. My eldest Ruby got it for her seventieth birthday last month. She knew exactly what she was doing and I couldn't help but smile. I carry the tray into the living room. It still smells of paint from my attempts to cover the old yellowing magnolia with bright yellow.

I try, I really do.

My mother is sitting in the most expensive chair in the house, a fully orthopaedic chair that lifts and moves to help her out of it. Not that she ever uses that function, instead preferring to holler for me, or one of her carers if they're here. She's wearing a stained white blouse and black nylon trousers, the flesh around her bare arms spilling over the chair's sides. Her white hair has been combed and her lips are covered by a badly applied slash of red lipstick. As I approach her, she gives me her usual look of disdain.

'You're sweaty,' she snaps.

'It's hot out there.' I lay the tray on her lap, unable to stop myself feeling self-conscious as she wrinkles her nose. *Do I smell?* Another thought occurs to me. Did I smell when I saw Tamsin?

'Well, I'll never find out if it's hot outside when I'm stuck in here, will I?' my mother snaps. I don't bother reminding her of all the times over the past three months when I've offered to take her out in her wheelchair to no avail. There's no point. Instead, I walk to the window. If I stand on my tiptoes and peer down the road, I can get a glimpse of the rooftop of the manor. What will Tamsin be doing now? Maybe she's still sitting in her garden, writing her poetry as she once did. Maybe I ought to do that more too, sit out in the garden? It's so overgrown though, so small. But still, if I added a few colourful pots and wind chimes, I could take my laptop out there and complete my spreadsheet for the day. Sometimes, it can take over an hour to transcribe all the details from my notebook into my spreadsheet and check it against past notes. It's important to record these crucial moments. They may seem trivial to the untrained eye, but experience has taught me no small detail should be overlooked. If it weren't for my spreadsheet, Mrs Thompson might not be alive.

She was one of the elderly residents on my last round in Manchester. I knew from my notes she was a member of Diabetes UK (the postmark on the letters she received from them gave that away) and several times a week, she got a visit from someone driving an orange Mini. One week, I noticed the Mini hadn't been in her drive yet and the week was almost over. I got my answer when she received a postcard from Brisbane in Australia from her daughter, saying they'd settled in in their new home. No more regular visits for Mrs Thompson. And then one Friday evening, I realised when I was filling in my notes for the day that Mrs Thompson wasn't doing her usual pruning of her rose-bushes when I did the round that morning. She was like clockwork out there each Friday with those secateurs of hers. Luckily, I put two and two together and realised something was wrong. I biked to her home and a peek through her window confirmed my worst fears: she'd collapsed. If it weren't for those notes of mine, God knows if Mrs Thompson would still be around. People like Tilda Beashell need to realise if it weren't for people like me, chaos can descend.

This is why I never drop my routine of filling in that spreadsheet. It could save somebody's life. I think of the garden again. Yes, maybe it would be good to set myself up out there, look for a little table and chair on eBay or similar. But is it a luxury too far? I'm strapped enough for cash as it is.

'What are you looking so miserable about?' my mother asks now.

'I'm not miserable, just tired.'

'Rubbish! I know that look. You're the one who got yourself into this mess.'

I don't bother saying anything. I've heard the same lecture from my mother every day since we moved in. I've given up reminding her Scott was the one who cheated on me.

She leans forward in her chair, her stomach flopping over the tray. 'The problem with you is that you can't stop sticking your nose in,' she continues (will she ever stop?). 'Why can't you just let things be? It's like what happened twenty years ago.'

I close my eyes, pinching the bridge of my nose. There's not a day that goes by that I don't regret confessing everything to my mother that fateful night. She'd caught me crying as I let myself in and for some reason I will never quite understand, I'd told her what happened. Maybe it was born from hope that once, maybe once, she'd be propelled into comforting me.

'If you'd only kept your nose out of the Lakewells' lives,' my mother hisses now, 'then it would never have happened. You've been paying the price ever since,' she adds, eyes cruel and triumphant. 'And now you've lost Scott, the best thing that ever happened to you.'

I follow my mother's gaze towards a photo she's insisted on placing on the mahogany sideboard. It's of Scott on a boat, his blond hair lifting in the wind, his blue eyes twinkling. It's the only time my mother seems to show any softness, when talking about her beloved ex-son-in-law. She idealised him, is probably even secretly in love with him. Her face hardens. 'You'll never be happy again.'

I turn away, eyes filling with tears. My mother's right. How can I possibly ever be happy again? But damn it, I still have a chance

30

to make something of my life and leave the past behind. Didn't Tamsin? I definitely owe that to the kids. I make a decision then: when they return from school, I'm going to insist we get something to eat at the patisserie.

While I wait for them, I sit in our overgrown garden scrolling through Tamsin's website. I've often googled her over the years but nothing ever came up until a website suddenly appeared five years ago, declaring the launch of her debut book of poetry. She was definitely into the whole 'reclusive poet' thing, stating on the website she would not be available for any events, the only photo of her an illustration that looked nothing like her, frankly. I'm not surprised, she'd always been shy.

Of course, I bought her first two collections and loved each of them, as I had loved it when she shared her poetry with me when we were friends. Some of those poems featured in her debut book of poetry too, including one about our friendship from which she drew the collection's title. It was called *Remedies for a Black Tide*. The black tide was how we referred to those few days before our periods would start when we'd feel all angsty and grumpy. But somehow, being with each other seemed to lessen the darkness. I'd loved seeing it in her book and still remember every word:

Remedies for a Black Tide
For L

Moonlight steady,
Soft ripples of woe,
I feel calm as the ocean,
I feel able to cope,

But then there on the horizon,
It comes into sight,

A ripped pleat of agony,
A siren's delight.

It curls right above,
Black curtain of despair,
Then folds over me and dyes me,
Until I'm no longer there.

Then one pen-wielding hand,
Reaches down into hell
And pulls me right out
My friend with an L.

I smile as I remember her reading it out to me many years ago. I felt the same way about her, how she pulled me out of hell.

An hour later, the girls arrive back from school. I don't exactly get the reaction I was hoping for. Ruby shoots me an arched eyebrow, clearly not impressed at the idea of being dragged away from her 'work', as she calls it. She's convinced she won't need a 'normal job' and instead will make enough money from her true-crime TikTok channel – *Young, Beautiful and Dead.* She started it as part of her production and technology lessons back at her school in Manchester, focusing on the mysterious deaths and disappearances of teenagers with short, atmospheric videos hosted by her on TikTok. I have to admit, she is pretty amazing in them. They're all shot in black and white apart from the purple highlights in Ruby's black bob. I don't know how she gets that effect; I don't know how she does half the stuff she does on that laptop of hers. But it makes me proud.

'Do we have to?' she says now. 'I have a new video to edit.'

'We'll be out for only an hour or so,' I say.

'Can I have chicken nuggets?' Mia asks, sweeping her blonde hair, so like Scott's, up in a high ponytail.

'I'm sure Lester can rustle some up just for you,' I say. I walk into the living room. 'We're going out for dinner, Mother.'

My mother drags her eyes away from the TV and looks me up and down, taking in the maxi dress I grabbed from one of the boxes I still haven't unpacked piled up in my small room. Seeing Tamsin in hers inspired me. 'You look like a drag queen in that dress,' she snaps. 'I've told you before, dresses don't suit you!'

'Wow, thanks Mother,' I mumble, rolling my eyes. I should be used to her snipes by now but somehow, they still sting.

'I think you look nice,' Ruby says, giving me a sympathetic smile. 'You know, in a *mum* kind of way, anyway.' I guess I'll take that as a compliment.

'Yeah,' Mia says. 'Looking like a drag queen is a compliment anyway.'

I smile at my girls. They *can* be nice sometimes. In fact, I'm not sure how I'd have got through the past three months without them. My stomach drops. If Scott wins his case to have full custody of the girls in two weeks and he moves them back to Manchester, being without them is exactly what *will* happen. Getting the letter six weeks ago informing me Scott was applying for full custody was a shock to the system. I'd tried to reason him out of it but he cited me getting fired and the fact I'd accepted the job two hours away without consulting him. We've already had social workers visit to do a report which was a nightmare as I had to work my butt off to get my mother's house looking half decent. And now we're going to court in two weeks to hear their verdict. I have to remember what my solicitor told me though. Chances are, he won't win. He essentially threw me out of the house when *he* was the one who cheated and ruined our marriage. I had no choice but to move back home, not to mention I now bend over backwards to drive the girls to Manchester each weekend so they can see their dad as part of our co-parenting agreement.

Still, the thought of losing custody of the girls makes me feel sick. I have to make the most of my time with them and that's exactly why I'm determined that we will all have a nice dinner by the sea. I plant a smile on my face. 'Come on then, Mother. Ruby will help with the wheelchair. Go and get it from the hallway, Ruby.'

Ruby sighs and goes out into the hallway, getting the wheelchair from its spot. I help her unfold it as my mother stubbornly watches on.

'Sit up properly, then,' I say to my mother. 'We can shuffle you into it.'

But she keeps her eyes on the TV, gnarled hands clutching the arms of her chair. 'You go. I'm staying here.'

'No, you're not,' I say in as light a voice as I can. 'It's not healthy, you staying in all the time. The sun will be good for you, for all of us.'

'It's too hot out there,' my mother says.

'Not in the shady area Lester will let us sit in. Come on!' I say. 'Let's get out before the evening heat disappears.' I go to my mother and try to lift her as Ruby stands behind the wheelchair. My mother lets out a yelp of protest, and I can see Mia is trying not to laugh. It really is ridiculous and I find myself trying to hold in the giggles too. 'You'll love it when you're out there,' I say as I try to lift my mother's large body up.

'Get off me!' she says, slapping my hands away. But I continue, determined to make the most of the weather.

'Get the wheelchair closer,' I say to Ruby. 'I'm going to lift her in a minute.'

'No, you're not going to lift me Elizabeth, you stupid, ugly girl!' I flinch at my mother's words and I see Mia and Ruby do the same. I don't react. I've learnt that's the best way with my mother, ignore, ignore, ignore. I just hate the girls having to witness it.

'Wheelchair closer,' I say again to Ruby, giving her an encouraging smile as I wrap my arms around my mother's generous waist, thanking all the years of walking for my strength. 'Your grandmother's just being a bit stubborn.'

'Not one bit closer,' my mother hisses at Ruby over my shoulder. 'I told your stupid mother I do not want to go!' Ruby hesitates, clearly unsure what to do as Mia watches with fascinated eyes.

'I am *not* stupid, Mother,' I hiss as I try to lift and heave her on to the wheelchair.

She glares up at me, a look of pure malice in her watery blue eyes. 'What was that quote from your school report?' she says. '"Decidedly average".'

My eyes fill with tears. 'That teacher was fired,' I say, realising my voice is trembling. *Damn it. Why do I let her get to me like this?*

'Shame,' my mother says as Ruby and Mia exchange sad looks. 'I liked him, very astute.'

I squeeze my eyes shut and count to three. I will *not* let my mother get to me. Instead, I imagine having dinner with Tamsin like Carl suggested, laughing and smiling. The next time I open my eyes, I feel serene. 'Just shuffle your bum into the chair, Mother, and we'll be done,' I say, ignoring the look of hate she's giving me. She continues resisting, clasping hard on to the chair, showing remarkable strength for someone who claims to have no energy. 'Mother, if you can just—'

'You're useless, so weak and pathetic,' she whispers into my ear. 'Can't even get your weak mother out of her chair. Carers half your size have managed it.'

My pulse speeds up, coursing through me like fire, buzzing at my temples. *Ignore ignore ignore.* I take a deep breath then use all my strength to try to heave my mother's large body on to the wheelchair.

'I bet it was difficult lifting that dead body too,' my mother hisses in my ear. I freeze and she takes the chance to kick out her leg. I stumble back as the wheelchair scoots away so that all that's left is thin air.

My mother lands with a bang on the thinly carpeted floor, her leg at an awkward angle beneath her. She screams in pain and I look up at the ceiling, letting out my own anguished scream.

Chapter 5

The remainder of the evening is spent at my mother's bedside in hospital while Lester looks after the girls with his daughter, Eva, who goes to sixth form with Ruby.

'Keep that woman out of my cubicle,' Mother says to the nurses and doctors as I hover nearby, 'she did this!' Turns out she has a shinbone fracture ('a tibial diaphyseal fracture' as the serious doctor had described it) and she'll have to remain in hospital for the next few days. I return home in the middle of the night, picking the girls up on the way. I notice they're quiet on the drive back and can't help but feel guilty about the fact that they have to witness the dysfunctional relationship my mother and I share.

As I lie in bed, I silently cry tears of guilt over what happened to my mother and, I realise with a start, grief. I'm grieving my mother, like Tamsin is. But in my case, I grieve the mother I *ought* to have had. I've been grieving this all my life. But instead of the hole of grief Tamsin described, this is an albatross that hangs around my neck and my mother never lets me forget it. I've always known I was a mistake, the result of a drunken night at a wedding with a solicitor called Giles whom my mother either couldn't or *didn't* want to track down. Nine months later, she gave birth to me and all her dreams of continuing the family tradition of becoming a nurse were shot to pieces.

'Generations of promise and expectation stopped because of you', is how Mother always likes to round up her tragic story. When I ask her why she didn't just have an abortion, she replies: 'It's a sin to kill a child.'

The guilt of it would overwhelm me as a child. I'd ruined my mother's life! It was only when Tamsin and her mother highlighted the fact that my mother was the sinner for not giving me the love I deserved that I began to let go of that guilt. Sure, my mother had worked hard as a secretary to provide a roof over my head and make sure I was fed. But that was where the care stopped. There were no cuddles when I fell and broke my arm as a four-year-old, no kind words when I got bullied at school. No congratulations when I passed my exams with decent grades, nor fun holidays and days out.

The only time I got *any* of this was when I was with Tamsin and her mother. She really was about as different from my mother as you can be, simply bursting with love and joy. I suddenly feel a rush of grief at Tamsin's mother's death. Why were people like her taken away and people like my mother left behind? But as soon as I feel that grief, I feel guilt too. I sigh and turn my head, looking out of the open curtains towards the sea. Tomorrow will be better. As I think that, I realise part of the reason I hope tomorrow might be better is the idea of seeing my old friend again. As much as the memories from twenty years ago haunt me, all of a sudden I realise just how much I need my old friend back in my life.

My alarm goes off at four-thirty. I stretch and yawn my way out of bed. I enjoy my morning routine. All I need to do is brush my hair and teeth, have a quick wash and a spray of deodorant. I save my showers for the evening. Luckily, I've never been one for make-up; I always tend to have a tan throughout the summer anyway, so I don't need much colour on my face, and I keep my once long brown hair short so it's easy to maintain.

Each morning, it's up to Ruby to get Mia ready and walked to school. I set three alarms in the house to make sure she really does wake up. Though she does it reluctantly, she never lets me down. Maybe it's the fiver a week I give her as payment. Maybe it's the fact that, deep down, she knows if we don't stick to this routine, there's a chance her dad will win full custody in two weeks. I know she doesn't want that, nor Mia. It's not that they don't love their dad. But they are closer to me, always have been, Scott often out painting and decorating or down the pub. I sigh and go to check on the girls. Ruby is sleeping soundly on her side of the room, strands of her black and purple hair curled on the pillow, cheeks red from sleep, remnants of eyeshadow still on her closed eyelids. I like watching her at this time, my only chance of 'illegal' entry into her room. There she lies, my beautiful grumpy little girl. I still remember the first time I laid eyes on her when she was flopped on to my belly sixteen years ago with that mop of black hair. Instant love. She'd been a surprise. Though Scott and I had been together for nearly a year by that point, we hadn't planned on having children until we married. Plus I was only just twenty.

I look at Mia who sleeps in a single bed on the other side of the room. She was very much planned. Scott and I had actually tried for two years to have her, a shock after falling pregnant with Ruby so quickly. But then she did eventually arrive, a little miniature version of Scott. I smile at her now. Surprise, surprise, she's fallen asleep with books open on her duvet, my little bookworm.

I close the door softly then pause at my mother's door. Strange to think she's not there. Sometimes, I'll press my ear against her door to check I can hear her rattling snores. Sometimes, too, I imagine what I would do if I couldn't hear her snores. Would I just walk away? Or would I rush straight in, screaming her name because, after all, she is my mother?

I rush downstairs and head outside. It's still dark, but as I cycle the thirty-minute route to the next town, Busby-on-Sea, the sun begins to rise. I prefer to cycle; it gets my exercise in and I'm closer to nature like this. I like seeing the hue the sky lets off at this time of the day, especially when it's a soft hazy yellow, signalling another nice, warm morning.

The large brand-new glass-fronted building of the sorting office looms ahead of me as I enter the town. I cycle up to it then jump off my bike, wheeling it to the bike shed before heading up the ramp towards the entrance. I slide my security card through the turnstiles and let myself in, nodding greetings at passing staff. I tend not to socialise much with the other posties; what's the point when my main focus are the people on my round? But it's always good to maintain pleasantries.

I walk through to the vast sorting area. It's lined with several rows of shelves, already a buzz in the air as posties sort through their patch's post, the low hum of the radio in the distance. All post for the county is sorted here, each area assigned a row letter and section number depending on the name of the location. Easthaven is located near the front, unsurprisingly under the Es. It's one of the smaller neighbourhoods so it doesn't cover as much space as some others.

I get a bit of ribbing for that from Craig, the postie who covers the large seaside town next to Easthaven. 'New girl's got the easy round,' he'd declared when I walked in that first day. But Craig soon learnt small doesn't mean easy when he had to take over the route after I took a day off six weeks ago to visit a solicitor. He finally had to admit what a challenge the Easthaven round was with its hills and 'higgledy-piggledy streets' as he called them.

'All right, Socks,' he says now as I walk by. They've all taken to calling me that because of the colourful hiking socks I wear under my walking boots.

'Morning, Craig,' I reply.

'Weather looking good again,' he says as I grab my bag and start sorting through the post. I nod. 'Talkative one today,' Craig remarks.

I peer up at him. 'Oh, sorry, my mother had a fall so I'm a bit worried, that's all.'

'Ah man. Sorry to hear that, mate.'

I frown. I really ought to visit my mother at the hospital sometime today. But then what's the point if she doesn't want to see me? Maybe a call to her nurse would be better?

As I think that, I notice a large jiffy bag addressed to Tamsin among the post. She did say she's expecting some post. There's a company stamp on it: *Faber*. Is that her publisher? I squeeze the bag to get a sense for what's inside. It feels like small hardback books. Maybe first copies of her next poetry collection? I saw it on her publisher's website when I did a little google last night. It's called *The Pause* and features the most amazing illustration of two women, looking out to sea. I recognise Tamsin's mother Dorothy as one of them. Clearly, the collection is about her. I pre-ordered it instantly and can't wait to get my hands on it. Well, I suppose I have my hands on copies right now! It still amazes me that she's achieved the very dream she set out to achieve. And yet here I am, a postie instead of the journalist I was so sure I'd become. That's not to say I didn't give it a good go, getting a job as an assistant reporter for a Manchester newspaper as soon as I left sixth form when I was eighteen. I wanted to get as far away from Easthaven as I could and Manchester seemed a good bet. But the pay and benefits couldn't justify my staying there after I had Ruby, so for a few years I was a stay-at-home mum. Then when a friend suggested I try being a postie, I went for it.

I quickly check for more post for Tamsin, finding a standard letter with a *Sable & Sons Funeral Directors* stamp on it and an ornate black rose illustration next to it. Must be to do with her mum. Poor Tamsin. I pack all the post then head out to my round.

Near the end, I briefly head into the patisserie, thanking Lester for having the girls and promising a proper cuppa tomorrow. I'm already running late. As I jog out, I bump straight into a suited chest. My notepad falls from my grasp, landing open on the ground below. I go to snatch it up but the person I've bumped into gets there first. I look up to see it's Douglas Gold, smiling down at me as he hands my notepad back. I quickly take it from him, shoving it into my pocket. The sun picks out the glint of his gold tooth and I wonder if he knows just how sinister it makes him look . . . or maybe that's the point?

'How's my house?' he asks. *My* house. I hate the way he says that.

'Everything's fine, thanks.' I try to manoeuvre around him, but he places a hand on the wall, stopping me.

'I heard your mother had a fall last night.' I frown. How did he find out so quickly? 'Must be difficult,' he continues without asking how she is, 'especially with a disabled mother and surly teenagers in that little house? No space to think. Not to mention how awful those NHS carers are. Would be nice to have the money to get some private carers, wouldn't it?'

What's he getting at? 'Lots of things would be nice but money doesn't grow on trees,' I say.

'Maybe I can make it grow on trees,' he says meaningfully, his brown eyes in mine. 'I like to help people in need. I'm not all business, business, business, you know.'

I bristle. 'We're not in need, thank you! We're doing perfectly fine as we are.'

'Oh I know, but it's always nice to have *more*.'

'We don't need more.'

Douglas nods knowingly, his longish brown hair feathering around his ears. 'Fine,' he says with a shrug. 'Just know I'm here if you need anything.' Then he turns on his heel and walks away. I shake my head. Such a strange one, he is.

I quickly make my way up the cliff-edge road, posting letters and packages. When I get to the manor's gates, I slow down when I see Carl pacing back and forth on the lawn, dark brow knitted in concentration. It's really uncanny how much he looks like Gabe. He adjusts his face into a smile when he sees me and strolls over. 'Hello, Liz. Do we have post already?'

'Yes,' I say, gesturing to the large package. 'I think it's Tamsin's books. Is she in?' I ask, straining to peer behind him. I see painters are inside and somebody is mowing the overgrown lawn at the back.

'Afraid not, Liz,' he replies. 'She's at an event.'

An event? Doesn't she say on her website she doesn't do events? Carl just continues smiling. 'I'll tell her you popped by.'

As he says that, I hear the crunch of car wheels behind me and turn to see a taxi draw up with someone with red hair in the back.

'Looks like she's back,' I say, smiling. I'm pleased, I would have been disappointed to have missed her. The back door of the taxi opens and Tamsin steps out, reaching in to grab several shopping bags from the floor well.

'You've been shopping!' I say, walking towards her, excited to see her again. She turns to me and I freeze.

My first thought is: *That isn't Tamsin.* She looks like Tamsin with her long wavy red hair – though maybe the shade is a little different, a little darker. She's the same height as Tamsin, too, but her face is thinner from what I can see beneath the huge sunglasses she's wearing. She's slimmer, wearing a long, slinky red summer dress.

'I was just telling Liz you were at a poetry event, Tamsin,' Carl says. I examine her face. Why does she look so different? Has she got different make-up on, dyed her hair since yesterday? Maybe she had some Botox done, that was why Carl lied about where she was? I just can't see Tamsin and Botox in the same sentence though. But then how would I know; the last time I saw her was twenty years ago!

She holds her hand out for the book package. 'I'll take my post, thank you.' I hug the package to my chest, suddenly feeling reluctant to let it go. 'Post please,' she says again in a hard voice. What choice do I have? I hand the package over. 'Ooooh, I wonder what's in here,' she says, lifting the box to her head and rattling it.

'They're your books,' I say. 'I thought you were expecting them?'

Disappointment spreads across her face. 'Oh.' She walks to Carl through the now open gate and discards the package on a nearby wall, giving him a lingering kiss.

'Tamsin?' I call out. She doesn't turn. 'Tamsin?'

Carl nudges her and she turns to me with a bored expression. 'Yes?'

'I forgot to say yesterday, I loved the fact *Remedies for a Black Tide* was included in your first poetry collection.'

'Oh, you're a fan, how lovely,' Tamsin says, yawning.

'Of course I am, I've always been. I still get the old black tide, by the way!'

Her brow creases. 'Black tide?'

I feel raindrops on my head.

'Oops, looks like it's going to pour down.' She turns away and jogs up the path with Carl as rain starts to pour. I notice she's left her beloved books behind. They're going to get soaked. I try to call out to her but the gates are closing and she can't hear me through the hammering rain. I stare at Carl's back and it strikes me again how similar he is to Gabe.

I look down at the tides below, memories of that first time I met Gabe rushing at me . . .

Chapter 6

20 YEARS AGO

I check my watch. Still another thirty minutes until I can head to the manor. Thursday is always therapy day. That's what that phone call was about the first day I met Tamsin. Her mother was making an appointment with a therapist whom Tamsin now sees every Thursday after her day of home learning. It means I can't head straight to hers after school, as I do most afternoons now. Frustrating because my paper round is on Friday evenings so that's two days in a row where I don't get to see her until *after* six. *Nightmare.*

I guess it *is* nice to sit in the cafe and have a hot chocolate while I wait though. It's only the cafe's cheap hot chocolate, not the one loaded with marshmallows and whipped cream. The envy when I see other people having the deluxe one is *real*. We joke that while Thursdays are Tamsin's 'therapy days', they're my 'thrifty hot-choc-olate days'. Dorothy overheard us talking about it the other week and in true Dorothy Lakewell fashion, the next day she arranged for Simone to make us both the most amazing, marshmallow-laden hot chocolate.

Dorothy is just the best. If I have any issues, like the time a girl in my class accused me of staring at her boyfriend (he was picking his nose, can you blame me for watching him in horror?) or when my mum refused to provide a signature for a university application, Dorothy would always be there to offer words of wisdom. 'Tell the girl the truth,' she'd say. 'She needs to know her boyfriend is an oaf.' Or 'Let me sign it. Your mother won't know.' She sometimes joins us for movie nights too, the three of us snuggling up on the sofa and gossiping. Truth is, sometimes I feel like *she's* my mum and Tamsin is my sister. It makes returning home to my mother even harder.

I look towards the manor. I wonder what Tamsin is talking to her therapist about. Probably her dad. It's been a tough year so far for Tamsin after her dad died in a car crash in January. I'd only met him a handful of times. He was usually away all week in London and then travelling here, there and everywhere most weekends. But from what I saw of the handsome Italian the times I did meet him, he was just as lovely as his wife, lavishing Tamsin with love and gifts whenever he was home. Tamsin and her mother were absolutely devastated when they learnt of his death. I feel bad saying this but since he died, Tamsin wants me around even more. Lester whom I do my paper round with reckons we're conjoined twins, joined at the hip. I wouldn't mind that.

I jog my leg up and down now. It's so hot and this thrifty hot chocolate is making me even warmer. I just want to sit with Tamsin by her pool with my bare feet dangling in the water.

As I think that, a boy walks into the cafe. A boy I *don't* recognise. I watch as he walks to the counter. I think he's around the same age as me – seventeen – with thick dark hair and vivid blue eyes against perfect pale skin. Emphasis on the word perfect because he really is and my heartbeat seems to notice too as it's battering my chest like a pair of happy little fists at the moment. He isn't wearing a school uniform nor the baggy jeans and t-shirts ensemble the other boys his age seem to always wear around here.

Instead, he's in smart chinos and a polo shirt with a pair of eccentric and distinctive red shoes. He orders a coffee, a black coffee. How *sophisticated*. Then he takes a seat in the corner and gets out a novel. He glances up at me briefly and smiles and my cheeks burn up like a furnace.

When he gets up to leave, I feel a sense of panic. I can't let him walk out of my life! So I discreetly follow him down Easthaven's promenade and on to the large green, so nervous I almost trip over a small toddler running along my path. In the kerfuffle, I lose sight of him. *Damn*. I scour the green but can't see him so I go to turn away. But then he suddenly jumps out at me from a nearby tree.

'Hello, stalker,' he says with a twinkle in his blue eyes. He called me a *stalker*. I want to die. I have *never* been so mortified. 'Your name's Liz, right?'

Shame is replaced by joy. He knows my *name*?

'That's right, and I wasn't following you,' I say as casually as I can. 'Anyway, how do you know my name?'

'Your name was called out in the cafe earlier.'

I blush even deeper then. 'Oh yeah, of course. What's your name?'

'Gabe. I bet you've lived here for centuries,' he says, leaning against the tree lazily and pulling a packet of cigarettes out, offering me one. I shake my head and he shrugs, plopping a cigarette between his plump lips and lighting it. Yeah, I admit it, the sight of him drawing the smoke in then breathing it out does all sorts of things to my body.

'I've been here all my life,' I say, leaning against the tree across from him, trying to appear cool. 'If that's what you mean by centuries, anyway. What about you?'

'Oh, my grandfather owns Easthaven Hotel so I've been *thrown* here for the summer to keep me out of trouble.' The Easthaven Hotel, a huge hotel at the other end of the promenade with views out to sea, used to be owned by a very rich French businessman. 'You live in the manor, don't you? I've seen you walking up there.'

'Oh no, that's not me, that's my friend, Tamsin. I *wish* I lived there.'

'Do you though? It can be pretty lonely living in big old places like that, trust me.'

'I suppose it must be. Still, I'd prefer that to living in the roughest estate in Easthaven.'

He shrugs. 'I don't know, I think it gives you grit.'

'Grit? I'm not sure how to take that.'

'In a good way,' he says with a laugh. 'It makes you interesting.' *Interesting*, he thinks I'm *interesting*. 'So are there any local pools around here?' he asks, looking around him.

'Apart from the sea?'

He laughs again. 'You're funny.' Now he thinks I'm funny. Funny *and* interesting. 'No, I mean like a lido or something? The one at the hotel is getting renovated; I miss it.'

'There's one at the manor. I'm sure Tamsin would be cool about you visiting.'

'Really? Are you sure?'

Am I sure? No, not really. Tamsin does after all struggle with having too many people around her. Is another person one too many, even if that one is as hot as this specimen standing before me?

'Sure,' I say, despite my doubts. 'I'll ask her later. Maybe you can come over next week?'

He pushes himself away from the tree, placing his hand on my shoulder and squeezing it. The point at which his hand meets my skin sends electricity through me. *So this is how it feels*, I think. None of the boys at sixth form do *anything* for me. Not that they pay me much attention, though I guess over the past few months, I may have noticed a couple in my media relations class giving me the once-over. But Gabe. There's something about him and that something is making it hard for me to breathe right now.

He frowns. 'Are you okay, Liz?'

I let out a breath. 'Sure, just hot.'

'What about tomorrow? We could meet in the cafe, same time?'

I inwardly flinch. Damn it, that's when I'm supposed to do my paper round! But I overheard Mother grumbling about it being rainy all next week. Gabe won't want to swim in the rain! I'll ask Lester to cover for me, I'll even pay him my money for that round. *It's worth it*, I think as I look up into Gabe's amazing blue eyes.

'As long as your friend is cool with it, that is,' Gabe quickly adds. 'If not, we can go in the sea, how's that? Is it a date?'

A date.

I shrug. 'Maybe.' Then I walk away, feeling like the coolest girl on the planet despite how excited I am inside.

I'm buzzing when I get up to the mansion. Even Dorothy notices, asking me what the big smile is for. I lie and tell her I'm just remembering something funny that happened at school. Before I head outside to see Tamsin, Dorothy stops me. 'Just so you know, Tamsin's feeling a bit out of sorts today.'

I nod, understanding. Tamsin can be like that sometimes after a particularly tough therapy session. Dorothy will often warn me beforehand so I can focus on trying to gently cheer my friend up.

'I have to confess, so am I,' she adds, peering towards the photo of her with her husband that stands in the hallway. 'It would have been our twentieth wedding anniversary today.'

Her eyes fill with tears so I give her a quick hug. 'I'm so sorry, Dorothy.'

She smiles and strokes my cheek. 'You're a good girl. Now go and cheer up your friend.'

As I head to the pool, I know exactly how I'm going to do that this time.

'There's a new boy in town,' I say when I get to her. 'You would *love* him. He looks like a mixture between Orlando Bloom and Zac Efron.'

Her eyes instantly light up and I continue to tell her about the whole thing, from start to end. 'Thing is,' I say as I finish, 'I kind of invited him to the manor as he said he wants to go swimming. I can *totally* say no to him though.'

I notice the flicker of worry in her eyes but she shrugs. 'Sure, why not? I'd like to meet him.'

So the next day, I find myself walking towards Lakewell Manor with Gabe.

'So are you and Tamsin at the local sixth form then?' he asks me.

'Just me. Tamsin homeschools.'

'Interesting.' I think he's going to ask why she homeschools but he doesn't. 'What are you studying?'

'A levels. Media studies, English and history. I want to be a journalist.'

He raises an eyebrow. 'Very impressive.'

We stop in front of the vast gates and I can see Gabe is as impressed as I was the first time I saw the place. I press the buzzer and Tamsin appears. I can tell instantly from the look on her face she's already bowled over by his looks, even from that distance. I sneakily watch his reaction to her. I mean, surely he'll be bowled over by her too? Though she hasn't made any particular effort like I have with my extra make-up and the new top I found in a charity shop, she still looks amazing in her usual flowy long skirt, her red hair plaited and trailing over one freckled shoulder. I inwardly sigh as I watch her. How can I compete with her? But Gabe actually doesn't seem as taken with her as I thought he would be. In fact, is it my imagination or does he keep sneaking glances at me?

The gates slide open and Gabe strolls in confidently, looking around him with interest.

'This place is stunning,' he says. 'Oh and nice to meet you, Tamsin. I really appreciate you letting me gatecrash.'

She giggles, actually giggles, her pretty face flushing. Yep, she sees what I see in this gorgeous boy.

'No problem at all,' she says. 'Come through, the pool's temperature is *perfect*.' We follow her through and sit at a bistro table with a jug of lemonade and three cups. I can see Dorothy keeping a watchful eye from the window above, but not coming out . . . yet. Over the next hour, the three of us talk about the usual stuff: school, music, desires for the future. As Tamsin shares her ambitions to be a famous poet, and I talk more about my plans to be a journalist, Gabe seems so interested and fascinated in what we have to say. I'm not used to boys listening as intently as him.

'What about you?' I ask.

'Oh, I want to be a novelist and photographer,' he replies. 'I've already written half my novel,' he adds, stretching his legs out as he directs his face up towards the sun. Tamsin takes the chance to look at me, biting her lip as if to say 'yes, he is as gorgeous as you said he was'. 'I want to be just like Ernest Hemingway,' Gabe continues.

'So you want to be an arrogant, racist and misogynist man then?' Tamsin asks him.

He looks at her with a faint smile on his face. 'No, I mean I want to write, make love and drink non-stop.'

We all laugh. 'Well, *this* is a good start,' I say, sipping the lemonade Simone made for us. 'To the drinking non-stop ambition,' I quickly add, worried he thinks I mean the making love part.

'I don't *think* he meant drinking lemonade, Liz,' Tamsin says. Do I sense some haughtiness in her voice?

'I know that, Tamsin,' I say, rolling my eyes.

Gabe stands up then and starts unbuttoning his shirt. Tamsin gives me a panicked look as my mouth drops open. He pauses then, looking down at us. 'Aren't we supposed to be swimming?'

'But . . . do you have trunks?' Tamsin asks.

'Of course!' He pulls his shirt off to reveal a pale, muscular chest before removing his trousers until he's standing in just a pair of light-blue swimming shorts. I can see Tamsin is blushing as much as I am. He gives us both a smile then dives into the pool as Tamsin and I look on, open-mouthed. Above, Dorothy continues to watch, a slight frown on her face.

'Are you coming in?' Gabe shouts as he emerges from the surface, his dark hair drenched and shining in the sun, his long, black eyelashes glistening.

Over the next couple of hours, after I change into one of Tamsin's swimsuits, we swim with Gabe, flicking each other with water and dive-bombing into the pool. Though it's very playful and innocent, inside I'm a bubbling wreck of desire.

After a while, Dorothy comes out, standing over us as we mess about in the pool. Gabe notices her first, going very still and shooting her a huge smile. 'You must be Tamsin's sister,' he says. 'I'm Gabe.'

She laughs. 'Nice try. As you well know, I'm her mother, Dorothy. I was just wondering if you'd like to stay for some food? It's just some nibbly bits, nothing special.'

Gabe peers at Tamsin and me. 'Is that okay with you both?'

'Absolutely,' we say at once then burst out giggling. 'Jinx!' we shout.

We get out and dry ourselves, sitting in the warm evening sun as Simone places an assortment of cold meats and cheeses with piles of bread on the large wooden table by the pool.

'So your grandfather owns the Easthaven Hotel, does he?' Dorothy asks Gabe.

Clearly Tamsin had told her mother all the details. It still surprises me, despite knowing them both this long, how much they tell one another. I wouldn't dream of telling my mother anything like that. Actually, I wouldn't dream of telling her anything. We rarely talk.

'That's right,' Gabe says, slathering some bread with butter.

'How long are you here for?' Dorothy asks him.

He shrugs. 'Just the summer.'

'You're not studying at all?'

'My grandfather has got me working at the hotel some of the time,' Gabe replies to Dorothy's question. 'I'm writing the rest of it.'

'You're a writer?' Dorothy asks, eyebrow quirking in interest.

'Gabe's a novelist,' I say. He smiles at me and holds my gaze.

'Why do you need to work at the hotel if your family has money?' Tamsin interjects.

Gabe doesn't seem to be able to answer that. Maybe he's embarrassed that his rich grandfather is making him work, as I am that my poor mother asks me for rent.

'It's good to work,' I quickly say for him. 'It's good to understand the merits of earning money, right?'

Tamsin laughs. 'Says the person who moans non-stop about her paper rounds.'

'But I have no choice, do I?'

Gabe looks between us with interest as Dorothy slides her hand over Tamsin's. 'Liz is right, darling. It is good to understand the value of work. Your father used to say the same. If you weren't so . . . nervous . . . I too would ask you to do a little something for my business.'

Tamsin crosses her arms. 'I can still do stuff for you, Mum.'

Dorothy frowns slightly. 'We can talk about it later.'

The dinner is a little strained after that. When it's time to go, Tamsin pulls me to the side while Gabe collects his stuff. 'Sorry I was a dork earlier,' she says. 'But he makes me *so* nervous.'

Tell me about it, I feel like saying. But weirdly, I don't want her to know how he makes me feel, so I give her a quick hug. 'It's fine.'

Gabe appears then and Tamsin lets us out of the gate. The sun is beginning to set as we walk down the cliff-edge road.

'It might be dark soon,' Gabe says. 'I can walk you home?'

'No, honestly, it's fine,' I say, horrified at the idea of him seeing my house after just coming from the manor.

'I really don't mind.'

'And I really don't mind walking home. I'm not a scared little girl.'

He smiles. 'You certainly aren't and that's why I like you.' He *likes* me. 'So Tamsin mentioned us coming over on Sunday, you cool with that?' I love the way he's always asking permission.

'Totally cool.' We reach the bottom of the road and stand on the promenade. 'See you at the manor at midday?'

Gabe holds my gaze then nods. 'Sure.'

As I walk away from him, I have to resist the urge to jump up and down squealing. But all that excitement dissolves when I arrive at my house to find my mother waiting for me. She's sitting in the living room, no TV on, not even a light, her brittle dyed blonde hair the only thing showing in the shadows.

'You didn't do your paper round today.' I go still. How the hell did she find out? 'I know you were at Lakewell Manor,' she spits. 'Veronica next door said she saw you walking up there with a boy.'

Oh no.

'So is this the way it's going to be now?' my mother continues. 'Sacrificing money and dignity for a boy?'

'It wasn't like that. I haven't missed one paper round in the two years I've been doing it, Mother, not even when I had tonsillitis.'

'I don't care!' she shouts, her voice echoing around the room. 'You don't pay rent, you're homeless, got it? See how your lover boy likes you then.'

I take in a calming breath. I'm so used to this. Mother always finds one excuse or another to batter me with her words. I've learnt it's best to remain calm. But it still hurts.

'It's not like that,' I say. 'I've arranged with Lester to do the entire round next month as it's his mum's birthday so I'll get the money back.'

She stands up and walks to me, dark eyes flaring with anger. 'I've told you before, I don't like you being at that manor, with *that* family.'

'They're a lovely family, Mother.'

'Lovely?' She lets out a bitter laugh. 'There is a great deal you don't know. How about next time you see your little Tamsin friend, you ask her why they had to quickly leave London and move to Easthaven?'

'Her mother has asthma! She needs the sea air.'

'You really believe that?' Then she smiles wickedly and walks out. 'I'm sure the truth will come out one way or another,' she calls over her shoulder.

I look towards the manor in the distance, frowning. What truth?

Chapter 7

Now

I sit at the kitchen table, dwelling on that odd encounter with Tamsin this morning, the tea I made now too cold to drink. There was just something *off* about her. But then it has been twenty years. And yet I also saw her yesterday and she was just like the old Tamsin I remembered. There's the sound of footsteps in the hallway, then Ruby walks into the kitchen as Mia calls a hello before running upstairs.

'You never told me you're friends with the poet who's moved back into Lakewell Manor,' Ruby says as she goes to the fridge to get her daily Diet Coke.

'Used to be friends,' I say, the *used to* feeling even more pronounced after my encounter with her earlier. How could she be like two different people from one day to the next? It goes to prove how little I know her now.

Ruby examines my face as she opens her can, the contents inside fizzing. 'Jeez, what's wrong with you?'

'Actually, it's Tamsin. Something was so off about her when I saw her earlier today.'

Ruby gives me an interested look. 'What do you mean?'

'I saw her yesterday and she was *just* like I remembered from when we were teens. But when I delivered her post today, I honestly could have sworn it wasn't her. It isn't just that she looked different from the Tamsin I saw the day before, but she didn't even seem to recognise me either. I mentioned a poem she wrote about our friendship and she was completely clueless about it.'

Ruby shrugs. 'Maybe she was high or something?'

I shake my head. 'Not Tamsin.'

'Not the Tamsin you *used* to know. When's the last time you saw her? Before yesterday, I mean?' Ruby asks, leaning against the kitchen counter.

'Twenty years ago.'

'That's a long time, Mum. People change. Don't overthink it, seriously.'

I chew on my lip. 'Something isn't right though, I can feel it in my bones.'

Ruby goes quiet for a moment, brow creased. Then she walks over to me, taking the seat across from me. 'Don't do this, Mum,' she says in a low voice.

'Do what?'

'You know what I mean. Do *not* go on some investigative mission over some gut instinct that you know will turn out to be wrong. After everything that happened last year, this is the *last* thing you need.'

I blink, looking away from her serious gaze. 'This has nothing to do with any of that.'

'Not yet, no,' she says, tone dark, 'but you know what you're like, Mum. It could spiral and you really do *not* need it to spiral. Just drop it, accept that people change.'

I look at her strained face. Maybe my wise, wonderful daughter is right?

I park my Royal Mail van in the usual spot the next day and sit in it for a while, looking out to sea. There's a faint mist over it, but beneath the calm of the fog, the waves fizz and twist. I feel that fizzing and twisting inside me. I couldn't sleep last night, thinking over and over about my encounter with Tamsin the day before. I have always had a gut instinct about situations, it's why I did so well when I worked as a journalist in Manchester. Like the time I was talking to a mum about her thirteen-year-old girl who'd been missing for a week. I could just *tell* she knew exactly where her daughter was. In the end, I managed to get it out of the woman with some gentle coaxing and a reminder that lying to the police was an arrestable offence: the kid was hiding in the mum's cellar, both of them desperate to avoid her having to go back to stay with the mum's abusive ex. I managed to convince them to tell the truth and in the process, get a great front-page story. But maybe, over the years, that gut instinct of mine has eroded. Ruby is right, I need to let it go. I'm tired and frazzled from my mother's fall. I must be simply imagining things.

I'm quiet as I do my round though and when the waitress that works in the patisserie informs me that Lester is on a delivery run, I'm actually relieved I don't have to talk to him, to *anyone*. I'm just not in the mood today. Annoyingly though, I have more post for Tamsin, some kind of poetry magazine and a letter from her publishers. I'd rather avoid her too today. As I make my way up to the manor, I feel nervous. But then I reason maybe it'll be a good thing to see her? Maybe she'll look like Monday's Tamsin again and I'll realise yesterday was just a blip due to her wearing new make-up and having had a few drinks.

As I approach the manor, an acrid smell fills the air. I see a swirl of black smoke is tangling up from the manor's gardens. I quicken my steps towards the manor's vast gates and peer through to see Tamsin standing on the lawn with a champagne flute in her hand. In front of her is a large metal bin with flames leaping from it. Nearby, Carl is rummaging around in some bin bags laid out on the lawn. He pulls out the peacock-blue maxi dress Tamsin was wearing that first day I saw her. The dress she told me was the last gift from her mother.

My mouth drops open in shock when Carl throws it into the fire. I duck out of the way, leaning shakily against the wall. Why on earth would she allow Carl to burn it?

Because it's not Tamsin, a voice inside whispers.

I push that voice away. What a ridiculous thought! Still, it doesn't seem right. I feel steel drive through me, the old journalist in me desperate for answers. That steel drives me back to the gates and I rattle them.

'Hey!' I call out.

But the sound of the crackling fire is too loud for them to hear me at first. I rattle the gates again, harder this time, and Tamsin looks up, noticing me. Carl follows her gaze and Tamsin tilts her head, watching me. Then she plants a smile on her face and strides over, piercing me with her gaze through the gate's bars. Without her sunglasses, I can see her eyes. But they look like a completely different shade of green from Tamsin's eyes. This close, I can see the foundation clogged in the lines of her face as well. Tamsin never did wear much make-up. She wasn't wearing much on Monday either when I saw her for the first time after twenty years.

'Hello there! Do you have any post for us?' she asks in a fake, sing-song voice.

I nod and hand the post to her through the bars. 'Why are you burning your clothes?' I ask as I do.

She shrugs, checking her long red nails. 'They're ugly. I've got a whole new wardrobe now.'

Ugly? 'But . . . that maxi dress was your last gift from your mother.'

'And?'

'I just thought it had some sentimental value, that's all.'

She waves her hand about absently. 'Best to get rid of all those sad reminders, only way to get over grief. I mean it has been, what, three months now?'

I frown. 'Six.' How can she not remember how many months have passed since her beloved mother died . . . and how can she talk so easily of leaving grief behind when she told me only the other day that it will never leave?

Because it's not Tamsin, that small voice says again.

No, that's impossible, irrational. Why would some random woman pretend to be Tamsin? As she walks back to the fire, I head back down the cliff, that small voice inside growing louder and louder.

◆ ◆ ◆

That evening, I can't sleep. I just keep going over and over the image of Carl burning the dress Tamsin's mother got her as she watched on with a glass of champagne in her hand, like she was at the theatre or something. And then our odd conversation earlier, dismissing her mother's death and the grief she felt when on Monday, it was so raw. I find myself turning on my light and looking at my notepad, reading over the details I've scribbled down of what happened earlier, almost to convince myself it really happened. But yes, there it is in black and white. What can I do about it though? Go marching up and demand proof she is, indeed, Tamsin Lakewell? It's ridiculous!

I groggily sort through the post the next morning, noticing a letter for Douglas Gold's son, Aubrey, among the pile of letters for the Golds. He goes to a local private school and I sometimes see him staring moodily out of a window during school holidays. With a father like Douglas, no wonder he's so miserable. A few hours later, before I head to the clifftop road, I pop into the patisserie. I *really* need a coffee before I risk the chance of bumping into Tamsin again. At least I don't have any post for her today.

'Everything okay?' Lester asks as I walk in and hand his post to him. 'Is your mum okay?'

'Oh, she's fine. Won't take my calls at the hospital so she must be her normal self.'

'Honestly, she's a strange one,' he says with a sigh. 'So the usual?'

'Actually, rather than tea, can I have a coffee? A *strong* one. I didn't sleep well.'

'Really? Why?'

'I'll tell you about it in a mo,' I say as I take my usual seat by the window. Lester's daughter Eva appears then from the back of the cafe, ready to head to sixth form. She goes to the same one as Ruby and studies fashion there. Ruby is jealous of the fact that Eva gets more free study hours than her, but Ruby's course – media production and technology – involves more time in the studio. She gives her dad a kiss on the cheek and waves at me before skipping off. When I see them together, it reminds me how much she looks like Lester: tall, perpetual smile on her face, unusual blue eyes. I sometimes wonder what her mother is like. Lester told me they split up seven years ago. 'Just one of those things,' he's said in the past. 'We fell out of love.'

'She's always so sunny,' I say as Eva disappears down the promenade. 'I wish Ruby would smile more often.'

'Ruby's the moon to Eva's sun,' Lester says as he brings my coffee over. 'Still lets off light but a different kind.'

'That must mean my mum's the black hole then.'

He laughs as he perches on the side of the table. 'What's up with you then?'

'Something's off about Tamsin.'

He frowns. 'Why'd you say that?' I tell him about the way she was on Monday compared to the way she is now. 'Ah, so you're saying the *real* Tamsin's been abducted by aliens and replaced by another woman?'

I roll my eyes. 'No, of course not. But something doesn't seem right, you know? Has anyone in the village seen her out and about?'

'Nope, not yet. She says on her website she's a bit of a recluse. Though there *is* something.'

'What?'

His brow creases. 'Eva did mention something Aubrey said to her last night. You know the kid's been suspended from his private school again for getting into a fight?'

I sigh. 'Isn't that the second time this term?' I lean forward. 'So, what did he see?'

'It's probably nothing.'

'*It's probably nothing* is journalist code for *it's definitely something*. Spill.'

'He told Eva he'd overheard an argument next door.'

I quirk an eyebrow. 'Interesting.'

'Don't read into it though, Liz. Couples argue. The ex and I would have them all the time. Surely you and your hubby had a few arguments?'

I think of the last argument I had with Scott and curl my hands into fists.

'No, this is different,' I say.

I peer out towards the manor, eyes travelling down to the Gold residence next door. So Aubrey overheard an argument, did he?

A thought occurs to me then as I think of the letter that's addressed to him in my bag. Maybe I can use it as an excuse to subtly grill Aubrey about the argument? Lester said he's been suspended from school again so chances are, he's home. Problem is, the letter's not important enough to entail me getting a signature nor too big to fit into their usual letterbox.

Unless I pretend it is? I look at my watch then drain my coffee, standing up. Lester looks disappointed. 'Leaving so soon?'

'I didn't realise the time. Have a good day!' I say. I walk out and away from the patisserie then pause, checking nobody's looking before I reach into my bag for a couple of blank special-delivery stickers I know are in there. Then I place one on Aubrey's letter.

'Just a little white lie,' I whisper to myself. 'No harm done.' A few minutes later, I'm in front of the Golds' villa. When I press the buzzer with a trembling finger, nobody answers at first, but then a bored-sounding male voice comes through. 'Yeah?'

He doesn't sound like Douglas. It *must* be Aubrey.

'Hi, it's Liz, the postie,' I say. 'Is Aubrey Gold in, I need him to sign for something.'

A sigh. 'Yeah, I'm Aubrey. I'll be down in a minute.'

I wait for a few moments before seeing a boy approach from the house. I haven't yet met the kid, just seen him around town. I know he sometimes hangs out with Ruby and Eva in the evenings when he's not boarding. His slim body is dressed in joggers and a t-shirt, his auburn hair wet. He's about Ruby's age but seems younger in a way. He walks towards the gates with the ease of a boy who's had a privileged life. But the dark circles beneath his brown eyes give away a wariness and sadness too. I imagine it can't be easy being the son of someone like Douglas Gold. He barely looks at me as he presses a code into a keypad nearby, yawning. The gates open and I step in, holding out the letter. Aubrey frowns. 'I need to sign for *this*? It's just a newsletter from the water polo club.'

I shrug as I hold my notepad out for him to sign. I usually use an electronic signature device but because what I'm doing isn't quite above board, I'm using a blank page in my notepad. A kid like Aubrey wouldn't know the difference. 'Don't blame the messenger,' I say. Aubrey sighs and scribbles his signature. He goes to walk away, but I call out to him. 'Aubrey!'

He pauses, turning back around. 'Yeah?'

'Strange what happened next door the other night, wasn't it?'

'You mean the argument on Monday night?'

The night after I first saw Tamsin. 'Yep, that's the one,' I say. 'Everyone's talking about it. What do you reckon happened?'

He shrugs. 'I guess it was just an argument. Though it *was* super-loud.'

'Yeah, I heard it was,' I lie, leaning casually against the bars of the gate. 'What time was it again?'

'I dunno, nearly midnight. It was the other woman who was the loudest.'

'What did she look like?'

He shrugs. 'Tall with dark hair.'

'Could you hear what was being said?'

'Nah. It didn't last long but it was, like, out in the open and stuff then they all went inside.' I'm about to ask him more questions, but then notice his mother watching from the door, a petite, curly-haired woman with a penchant for designer suits. He follows my gaze then quickly steps away, pressing a button to make the gates close again. 'I better go.'

I look towards the manor. So there was an argument and another woman was there.

The same woman who's now pretending to be Tamsin?

Arghhh, that damn inner voice! It's just so unlikely. I get my notepad out and quickly scribble down what Aubrey said. Then I take a deep breath and walk to the manor's gate, gasping in surprise when I see Tamsin's once pristine first-edition books of poetry have been left on the side, where she'd flung them the other morning, bird poo all over them.

'Any post?' a voice calls out. I look up to see Tamsin approach.

I'm unable to keep my eyes off the books. 'You left your poetry out all night.'

She looks over her shoulder at the books. 'Oh, silly me.'

'But they're first editions. Why would you leave them out overnight?'

'They're only books.'

I look at her in shock. 'They're your books. The first copies. You were so excited about them.' I shake my head. 'You've changed,' I can't help but say.

She clenches her jaw. 'It's been twenty years. I've changed, you've changed,' she says, looking me up and down. 'We were never suited as friends anyway, let's be honest.'

'We were best friends.'

She shoots me a cruel smile. '*If* you say so, Linda.'

My mouth drops open. 'It's *Liz*.' I shake my head. 'No, there's something off about all this.'

She laughs. 'Do you realise how crazy you sound?'

'Fine. If you really are Tamsin Lakewell, tell me something *nobody* else would know.'

She rolls her eyes. 'How would I remember *anything* about that time? It was years ago.'

'There are things you could never forget.'

Her eyes harden and she strides to the gate, grabbing the bars and rattling it. I jump back.

'You think you know everything,' she hisses. 'You think you're so bloody clever. Fine,' she says, shrugging. 'Prove I'm not Tamsin. Oh, wait a minute.' She pouts. 'How can you? I don't have any family left now my mother's dead. Not to mention I'm a reclusive poet with no photos of me *anywhere*. And the last time anyone saw me around *here* was twenty years ago. All they know is the redheaded Lakewell girl has returned,' she says, flicking her hair.

I look at her in shock. Is she brazenly confirming what deep down I've been suspecting the past couple of days: she isn't Tamsin? She leans in close, her breath acrid, her hair smelling of smoke.

'Plus who would listen to you anyway? A pathetic failed journalist and now divorced post lady fired from her last job. Imagine if the reasons for *that* got out.'

I stumble back, feeling as though she has slapped me.

'You haven't got a leg to stand on, little lady. Au revoir,' she says, blowing me a kiss.

I watch helplessly as she returns to the manor. I have no doubt in my mind now. She is not the real Tamsin. And if she isn't . . . where the hell is the real Tamsin and why is this woman pretending to be her?

I spend the afternoon chopping back the grass and weeds in the garden, mulling over what the hell's going on. I could call the police, tell them I suspect my old friend's identity has been stolen, but what evidence do I have other than gut instinct and a conversation I didn't record? Plus I *really* don't want to be chatting to the police again, after what happened last year. I just have to find ways to get evidence for what my heart and soul is telling me: my old friend is in danger.

But I don't have much time as my mother will be returning home this evening. She's brought back in an ambulance and promptly instructs me to go and get fish and chips as the hospital food was 'dire' (she's refusing to talk directly to me it seems, instead communicating via Ruby . . . what a relief!). So I head out to the local chippie with Ruby. As I wait in a quiet corner of the shop for our order, Ruby chats to Eva outside. Then I notice Aubrey approach the two girls and they all begin chatting and laughing. Aubrey seems particular enraptured by Ruby, watching her with fascination as she talks. I really don't like the idea of Ruby hanging out with Douglas Gold's son.

'My son said he saw you today,' a voice says. I jump in surprise and turn to see Douglas standing too close behind me. 'Sorry, did I shock you?' he says with a disconcerting smile.

'No. I'm fine.' I turn away. I'm not in the mood to talk to him. I never am.

'He said you were asking questions about next door,' Douglas continues, not taking the hint.

'Not really,' I lie. 'Just making conversation.'

'Can't blame you if you were,' he says. 'Strange couple.'

I pause. Do I take the bait? I don't feel I can trust Douglas at all and yet . . . he *does* seem to know everything that goes on in this village. I turn to look at him again, showing my interest. 'You and Tamsin Lakewell used to be best buddies, didn't you?' he continues. 'I remember seeing you walking up to the manor after school most days. And you went to a couple of the Lakewell Manor summer luncheons.'

Stalker much. 'Yes, we were close.'

'I met her a few times myself; our fathers moved in the same circles. Shy little thing. Very different from the Tamsin I met yesterday morning. I had to go over to complain about smoke fumes. Burning clothes, they were. Odd thing to do.'

So he noticed too. 'Yes, I saw that too. You say she seems different. How so?'

'Well, the Tamsin Lakewell I once knew wasn't what you'd call an extrovert. But the Tamsin I talked to yesterday.' He raises an eyebrow. '*She* seems to have well and truly come out of her shell.'

'I noticed the same,' I say, lowering my voice. 'I actually saw Tamsin on Monday and she was just like the Tamsin I used to know. But when I saw her again the next day, she was totally different. She didn't even seem to recognise me!'

'So what you're saying is, she's almost like a different person?'

'Exactly that! I know it sounds crazy, but it has crossed my mind.'

'Then where is the real Tamsin? And why would she be "disappeared"?' he says, using his fingers to make quotation marks.

'I don't know,' I say, sighing.

'I think I can help.' He pulls his phone from the pocket of his suit jacket and I wonder what he means. Does he know something? Maybe he's not so bad after all. 'I'll see if I can track down my restorer, so we can get her restored back to her original form.'

I roll my eyes. He's messing with me. 'Forget it,' I say, turning away again.

'I do apologise,' he says. 'My wife always tells me I take my jokes too far. I do see what you mean, this *new* Tamsin is very different. I can see it's bothering you. How about I rub your back if you rub mine?'

I look at him in disgust. What on earth is he suggesting? 'There's nothing I can do for you.'

'Don't be so sure,' he says in a quiet voice as he leans close to my ear. 'You do look after some of the village's most valuable assets, after all.'

'What do you mean?'

'The post of all the people here, of course,' he whispers, gesturing around him. 'All that information, those secrets, those titbits of knowledge right at the tips of your fingers. Such power!'

I shake my head. 'I only deliver the mail, I don't read it.'

'Of course,' Douglas replies with a mock-concerned look on his face. 'You would never *read* someone else's mail . . . would you?'

I blink. Does he know something? 'Never,' I lie.

'And so you shouldn't!' he exclaims. 'But maybe, accidentally, unwittingly, clumsily . . . you might lose a letter on your round?'

'What are you getting at?'

He steps even closer to me, his breath smelling of coffee and whisky. 'What I'm getting at, dearie,' he whispers in my ear, 'is all you need to do is lose one little letter, and I give you a bucketload of information on the couple next door. How does that sound?'

'Let me get this straight,' I say, folding my arms and feeling my heart thump against them. 'You're saying if I dispose of a letter on purpose for you, you will share information on your new neighbours?'

'Oh, it wouldn't have to be done on *purpose*. It'll just slip from your little red bag,' he says in a low voice. 'Fall into the sea or something, you know? Plenty of things fall into the sea.' I follow his gaze towards the waves in the distance. 'No big deal,' he says, flicking imaginary dust from his collar. 'Worth it for what you get in return.'

'And what would I get in return?' I ask, having no intention of taking him up on his immoral offer, but intrigued all the same. 'What sort of information do you have?'

He smiles. 'Ah the journalist in you is still alive and kicking. You would get information about the seemingly perfect couple,' he says, 'information which proves they might *not* be as perfect as they seem, *especially* Carl de Leon.' The name rolls bitterly off his tongue. 'So how about it? One little letter for some information?'

My pulse throbs in my ears. I know I should say no. I know this is wrong, so wrong. But what if Tamsin is in danger? What if I turn down his offer? Doesn't that mean I'm putting one letter before my old friend's safety? But then if I accept it, that's a step into murky waters, murky waters I've been trying to avoid the past year. So I shake my head. 'Nope.'

'Oh, come on. How about I throw you a little juicy morsel as a freebie?' He pauses for dramatic effect. 'Google Carl de Leon. You'll get some interesting results.' His name is called out to collect his order. But he stays where he is, waiting for my answer. 'So . . . ?' he says. 'Do we have a deal?'

I shake my head. 'Absolutely not.'

His face darkens. 'Well, if you change your mind, you know where I am,' he snaps. He goes off to collect his order as Ruby walks back in.

'What were you and that creep talking about?' she whispers.

'Nothing important. And what about you?' I whisper back, looking out of the window as Aubrey and Eva continue to talk. 'Would you say you and Aubrey are friends?'

She shrugs. 'Eva knows him. I've seen him around. He's cool I guess, for a rich kid.'

'His father isn't the nicest of men. I'd rather you didn't get too close to Aubrey.'

Her cheeks redden. 'God, Mum. You didn't seem to mind when you were just chatting to his creep of a dad. Speaking of which . . .' she says, voice trailing off as Douglas walks by. He looks like he's about to leave but then he pauses, turning to me.

'You know who Carl reminds me of?' he says. 'The boy who went missing. Remember him?'

I try to keep my face neutral as Ruby looks between us. 'I vaguely remember something,' I lie.

'Hmmm,' Douglas says, looking into my eyes. Then he turns on his heel and walks out. I release the deep, shuddery breath I was holding. Why did he say it like that?

'Who was Mr Gold talking about?' Ruby asks as we grab our order and quickly leave, her brown eyes filled with excitement. 'What boy went missing?'

'It was ages ago,' I say, quickening my step as we walk down the promenade. 'Come on, let's get this back before it gets cold.'

'Did you know him?' Ruby asks as she jogs to keep up with me. 'Were you friends with him?'

'Ruby, I told you already, it was ages ago. Just drop it.'

I realise I've raised my voice as a couple walking by turn to look at me. Ruby puts her hands up. 'Woah, I get the message, subject dropped.'

'Come on, let's head back.'

Ten minutes later, I sit with my mother and the girls in front of the TV in her room, eating our fish and chips. I'd even set Mother's bedroom up so we can all eat with her. I don't know why I bothered though, we barely talk, just watch some bland TV show. Ruby is clearly itching to get back to her room, her knee jogging up and down, and Mia is already reading a book that's open on her tray. As for Mother, I can see she's battling the desire to moan about something I've done but her continued silent treatment stops her.

I feel a wave of sadness and regret wash over me. *Family.* Is this what it is about, four people who barely exchange kind words let alone laughter, sitting in silence together? How many other families live like this? I peer out of the window towards the other houses. There are a few families on the street. The kids run around after school, giggling, mums chatting in the front gardens as they watch them. The elderly couples who occupy some of the houses seem happy enough, pottering about in their gardens, having family over for tea. I hear the tinkle of laughter over the garden fence most weekends, smell the barbecues. Sure, I know it's not all about barbecues and kids playing for my neighbours. I know they, too, must have many evenings sitting indoors like we are now, eating silently while watching the TV.

But at least their lives are interjected with the occasional fun and chat. I look at my mother's glum face and Ruby's bored expression. Surely it isn't as bad for our neighbours as it is for us? I think back to when Scott and I were together. It *had* been different then. We'd have more dinners around the table most nights, all together. Scott would insist. Ruby would talk more about her day at school, smile sometimes too. Mia would look up from her books more. Sure, there were lows, real lows. But it didn't feel like an endless stream of grey mirthless tedium. Truth is, it breaks my heart to watch us all sit so quietly and grumpy around the TV as we eat. What decent memories of family life will the girls be left with when they're older? I promised myself any children I had would have nothing like my childhood and yet here we are, sitting with the very poison ivy that tangled its limbs around my own childhood. Maybe if I'd forgiven Scott for what he did. Maybe if I hadn't done those stupid, stupid things after to lose my job. Maybe, maybe, maybe.

I think of what Tamsin's mother had once said to me. *We're all in charge of our destinies, Liz with an L. You need to take life by the horns and make it what you want.*

'So girls,' I say, turning to them. 'How was school today?'

'Shush!' Mother hisses, gesturing to the gameshow on TV. 'I missed the question.'

I feel a surge of irritation and lean over, grabbing the remote and turning the TV off. 'Let's talk, like a proper family.'

Mother laughs. 'A proper family, don't make me laugh.' She grabs the remote off me and turns the TV back on, turning the volume up.

I close my eyes, taking deep calming breaths. Fine, I'll just have to talk over the TV. I turn back to the girls. 'So? How was it?'

'The poet came into school and did a reading at the school assembly, didn't she, Ruby?' A reading . . . in front of a hall full of kids? Not a chance the Tamsin I know would do that. More and more evidence that this woman isn't the Tamsin I know.

Ruby nods. 'Yeah, did you know she's Mum's old friend?'

'Really?' Mia says, impressed.

'Who are you talking about?' Mother asks, suddenly interested.

'I thought you didn't want to talk,' I shoot back. My mother's nostrils flare.

'Mum's old friend is a poet!' Mia explains.

My mother looks at me, eyes cold. 'You mean Tamsin Lakewell is back?'

I nod. 'Her mother passed away.'

'No great loss,' my mother huffs.

'Mum!' I exclaim.

'Well, it's true,' she replies, 'I never liked her. I don't know why her mother encouraged her daughter's poetry, awful sentimental stuff.'

'Actually, Tamsin's poetry is beautiful,' I say.

'Not when she's reading it out,' Ruby says as she pops a vinegar-drenched chip in her mouth. 'I mean, the first poem she read was clearly about the death of her mother and she was reading it like some comedy piece! It was just bloody weird. It was supposed to be a poem about grief.'

'I doubt your mother would grieve for me,' my mother says to Ruby. 'Some people don't care about their mothers.'

I roll my eyes. 'Don't care for you? I feed you, care for you.'

'And break my leg!' my mother shoots back, gesturing to her plastered-up leg.

'That wasn't Mum's fault,' Mia says quietly.

'Thank you, darling,' I say, smiling at Mia.

'I'm done!' Ruby says, gesturing to her empty plate.

'Yeah, me too,' Mia says. I see her plate is half full.

'Oh come on, Mia, eat more won't you?' I say.

'Don't encourage her,' my mother snaps. 'She's already chubby as it is!'

I stare at my mother in shock. 'How dare you say that! She's absolutely perfect, both my girls are.' I turn to Mia. 'Your figure's just as a young girl's should be.'

My mother raises an eyebrow. 'Hardly.'

I go to open my mouth to protest but Ruby shakes her head. 'Ignore her, Mum, Mia knows she's fya. No words are going to change that.'

'Fire?' my mother asks, frowning.

'F-Y-A,' Ruby explains. 'It means lit. Amazing. Perfect.'

Mia leans over and high fives her sister. 'You are so right, sis.'

'Disgusting, the words you let these girls use,' my mother says.

'Oh shut up, Mother!' I shout. Everyone looks at me in shock and I stand up, grabbing the girls' plates. 'Come on, let's leave your grandmother alone to wallow in her spitefulness.'

The two girls exchange small smiles before following me as I march out.

'I'm not the spiteful one!' my mother shouts out after me. 'If only your daughters knew who the *real* spiteful one is here, hey?'

'Ignore her,' Ruby says.

'That's what I'm doing,' I reply. Mia gives my hand a squeeze and a sympathetic look then disappears into her room, Ruby doing the same. When I get to the kitchen and out of sight of the girls, I find all my bravado is gone, my hands shaking as tears rush to my eyes. I knew coming back to Easthaven would be difficult but I underestimated just *how* difficult. It brings back all those lonely years I spent with my mother before I met Tamsin. Why is she like this? I want to blame it on her own parents who were strict Christians, their beliefs so extreme it dominated their lives and sucked the love away, according to one rare moment of insight from my mother many years ago. But is that really an excuse? Plenty of people have difficult childhoods and turn out to be wonderful parents.

When I got pregnant with Ruby, I promised myself I'd be nothing like my mother. I'd be kind and loving, just like Tamsin's mother. It was difficult though. I didn't have any grounding in what it meant to be a decent mother. But I had my instincts, I'd always had my instincts, and you know what? I think I've done a decent job. Sure, Ruby can be dismissive sometimes but that's teenagers for you. And before Mia grew too embarrassed to show affection, she'd heap praise upon me, telling me I was the 'best, most cuddly, kindest Mummy'. Only the other week, she told me how horrible a friend's mother is. 'I'm lucky,' she'd said. 'I have you.' I used to think the opposite. In fact, I used to imagine Tamsin's mother being mine from the way I witnessed them together when I knew them. Lots of cuddles on the sofa. Big whoops of excitement when I got a good report from school. Tears wiped after bad falls and break ups. Gorgeous holidays, mother and daughter reading side by side, then laughing together in the evenings. Trips out to wildlife parks and shopping.

It hits me now just how devastated she'd be to know her daughter was in harm's way. Resolve rushes through me then. I may not be able to change my mother, but I *can* try to help my old friend. So when I'm finished with the dishes, I head out into the garden and sit on one of the two plastic chairs, getting my phone out and googling Carl de Leon, as Douglas suggested. A few pages into the search, I find something on *Carl de Leon CDL Finances*. It's a snazzy website for his company. I click on it and read the introductory text.

At CDL Finances, we help you take control of your finances by offering expert advice and guidance. Our service is a holistic one, tailored to your circumstances and ambitions. From start to finish, we offer a personalised, friendly approach which has led to wealth generation and security for hundreds of global clients. With offices in our founder's home town of Oxford, New York and Brisbane, we are here to meet your needs.

Quite the global company. I do a search on Google Earth for the offices of CDL Finances, expecting some glass-fronted homage to money. Instead, I find a small grimy-looking unit on an industrial estate on the outskirts of Oxford. 'Surely not?' I whisper. But yes, there it is, the name of his company inscribed across the top of the ugly-looking unit: *CDL Finances.*

Maybe Douglas is right and all is not as it seems with Carl de Leon? But how can I learn more? I lean back in my chair, chewing my lip. I think there might be someone who can help me. I go to my Facebook page and scroll through my friends list, finding the name I've been thinking of: Dean Best. We used to work together at the local rag in Manchester. Since then, he's moved on to work as a freelance journalist for the business and financial press. I quickly compose a message. *Hey Bestie, long long, no speak. How's little Noah? Anyway, reason I'm getting in touch is I wanted to ask about a company. If you have a few spare moments, could I give you a call?*

He doesn't answer right away but after twenty minutes, I hear my phone ping. I quickly pick it up to see a message from him. *Free now. Call me via Messenger.*

I smile and quickly make the call. He answers, a baby in his arms. 'Aw, Noah!' I say. 'Adorable. How's he been?'

'Exhausting. Why didn't you warn me, Liz?'

'I did, many times.'

'I really should have done it sooner, my forty-year-old knees can't take the constantly bending down to pick him up.'

I laugh. 'Get used to it, it only gets harder.'

'Great! So how can I help?'

'I'm trying to find out more about a company. Say someone is going around making out they're some kind of big-shot businessman but then you discover their offices are based in some grotty industrial site. Is there any way I can find out more about the company other than a Google search?'

He rolls his eyes. 'I was hoping for more of a challenge. Companies House, love.'

'Yeah but I have to apply for an account to get access to the records, don't I?'

'Nope, it's all online now. World's changed a bit since you were a hack.'

'I had no idea. So what do I do?'

'Just google the company name and Companies House. Do it while I'm here if you want.'

I grab my laptop from the side and do as he asks, instantly finding Carl's entry. I run my eyes down it. 'Interesting,' I murmur. 'There's something about *Accounts overdue* and *Confirmation statement overdue.*'

'Sounds like the company's in trouble. Check the bit that says filing history.'

I do as he asks. 'There's a file here called "First Gazette notice for compulsory strike off".'

He raises an eyebrow. 'Now that is interesting. It means the company will be struck off the register and dissolved if accounts aren't registered. Looks like the person you're looking into is about to lose their company. What's the date? It'll be at the top of the document somewhere.'

'Four weeks ago.' So Carl's business is clearly in a bit of trouble . . . and yet I saw a plush car parked in the manor's drive and what about those gorgeous suits he wears? 'Thanks, Dean. You're the best in more ways than name.'

He smiles. 'No worries. What's this all about, anything I can get my teeth into?'

'Just a personal thing.'

'Hmmm, not sure I believe you. I know how good your gut is. You ever thought about coming back into journalism? It's a shame you left, you're still one of the best journalists I know.'

I sigh. It's good to hear that but also so very sad. 'I'm happy being a postie,' I say. But am I? Sure, I enjoy being outdoors and chatting to people but it doesn't give me the same rush my old journalism days did.

'We should get a coffee sometime,' I say. 'Bring Noah.'

'Yeah, that'd be good. Right, better go, looks like the kraken is awaking. Take care.' I hang up and stare at my computer, diving deeper into the files. I see there's another director of the company. Someone called Imogen Grayson. I google her name and find there are actually quite a few results, mainly from social media platforms. I visit her Instagram account and am instantly met with a sophisticated grid of carefully posed photos of a beautiful raven-haired woman. Or should I say, *girl*. She seems to be only in her early twenties, yet she has over fifty thousand followers. She's clearly on her way to being an influencer of some kind. I check out her bio.

*Foodie * Fashion * Fitness * Felines*

As I scroll through her photos, I see why she's used those words in her bio. There are images of Imogen either at a plush restaurant, in the gym, posing in front of a huge ornate mirror or cuddling a beautiful grey cat. But the most recent post is different. It features a black and white close-up of Imogen's beautiful face, her eyes smiling into the camera. I click to read more:

From Imogen's family and friends

> *We are devastated to say that the brightest light of our lives, our darling Imogen, has been extinguished. After a short but ultimately intense battle with depression, Imogen took her own life on Friday. She is now with her dear Matteo where we are sure they will be enjoying many mojitos in heaven.*

> *We ask you, her wonderful followers whom she so dearly loved, to please use this chance to look after those in your lives who are silently suffering. If Imogen's death can do one thing, let it be to save even just one person's life, as we so wish we could have saved hers.*

I put my hand to my mouth, eyes filling with tears as I look at the beautiful photo. So young to have done that. I scroll back through Imogen's posts, trying to find any mention of Carl. But there are none. Then I notice a photo of Imogen sitting on an unmade bed half naked, looking out at a London skyline on New Year's Eve, over a year before she passed away. I zoom in, realising there's a reflection in the window of a man who could easily be Carl taking the photo. I can't be sure though.

I also notice there is one girl who comes up often, a girl with blunt cut peroxide hair, called Celia Pinks whom Imogen refers to as her 'dearest friend'. I click on Celia's profile. *Helping the best kinds of people get their voices heard,* reads her bio. What does that mean? She works in PR? As I scroll through her images, I realise she probably does, because most feature her at various parties, some even showing her with celebrities.

Celia's Instagram grid also includes photos from Imogen's funeral: the beautiful floral displays, the Order of Service. The caption of Celia's simply reads: *Still can't believe my best friend is gone.* My finger hovers over the 'Message' button. Should I? Would it be intruding too much? But then that didn't stop me when I was a journalist and this isn't a news item I'm researching: this is about a friend in danger. So I click the button and begin typing.

> *Hello, I hope you don't mind me getting in touch. I was so sorry to read of your friend Imogen's death. She seemed so wonderful. I hope you don't mind me asking, but did she know a man called Carl de Leon? I believe she was a director for his business? Sorry for having to ask over Instagram, I promise you I only have the best intentions. Thank you in advance.*

I sit back, heart thumping against my chest. Then I notice Ruby come into the kitchen, heading to the fridge. This is exactly what she'd not want me to do. I go to delete the message just as a reply pops up from Celia. *Cryptic message. Yeah, I know Carl. How do you know him?*

I ponder over what to write next, then begin typing. *He's been dating my friend, Tamsin. But now I think Tamsin is missing.*

Celia replies quickly. *Okay, this is crazy. You are feeding so many of my neuroses around Imogen's death. She was dating Carl! Was gorgeous but in a fake way, IYKWIM? I didn't like him. At all. Especially*

the way he just disappeared off the scene, breaking Imogen's friggin'
heart! You want to know why she took her life? HE'S why.

I lean forward in excitement. *Can we meet?* I type quickly. *Might be easier to chat in person?*

Celia replies: *Good idea. Can you come to London?*

I take a deep breath. 'It looks like I'm going to London,' I whisper to myself.

Chapter 8

20 Years Ago

I don't ask Tamsin about why they really moved away from London, as my mother had insisted I do two weeks ago. I don't want to dredge anything up that Tamsin and her mother would rather see left well alone. Anyway, I don't care. That's what I tell myself anyway, despite the incessant voice of curiosity inside being desperate to know. Not that I get much time alone with Tamsin to talk, because Gabe is at the manor with us most afternoons now, the three of us swimming, reading, talking. Not that I'm complaining, I love being around him. It's not the manor time I most look forward to though, it's the walks Gabe and I enjoy afterwards. Over the last two weeks, we've taken longer and longer detours back to the promenade, strolling along the beach too. He is just *so* attentive, always asking what books I'm reading, what films I've seen, what I think of this and that.

One day though, Gabe doesn't meet me as planned outside the manor. Tamsin and I wait for him, but after an hour, he still isn't there. So Tamsin and I agree I'll walk to the Easthaven Hotel to look for him. Maybe he's been stuck working late there? When I ask for him at reception, the woman behind the counter looks confused.

'Gabe, as in the owner's grandson?'

I nod. 'The very one.'

'No, he's not here.'

So he's not working . . . but he didn't come to the manor either. A terrible thought comes to me then. After two weeks of spending most afternoons and evenings with me, he's finally had enough. I walk away from the hotel feeling so dejected, I almost cry. But then I spot a figure sitting hunched on the beach. As I draw closer, I see it's Gabe dressed in the hotel uniform of navy-blue trousers and a burgundy shirt. Though he has his back to me, I can already tell from his posture and that gorgeous dark hair of his that it's him. I think about leaving him to it. I don't want to seem *desperate*. But I find my feet are walking towards him anyway. He turns as he hears the crunch of them on pebbles and I let out a gasp when I notice his face is bruised and bloody. I run to him and his head sinks low, his shoulders hunched.

'Gabe,' I say, crashing on to the sand beside him. 'What happened?'

'My grandfather is what happened,' he mumbles.

'Your *grandfather* did this to you?'

He shrugs. 'He gets like it sometimes.'

I gently put my finger on his chin and make him look at me, exploring all of his face. He has a massive bruise around his right eye and a cut on his cheekbone. There is also a graze on his neck. 'You need to go to the police.'

He laughs bitterly. 'Don't be so stupid, Lizbeth.' I blink, my fingers dropping from his chin. But he quickly grabs my hand and squeezes it. 'Sorry, I didn't mean to call you stupid, you're anything but. But I can't go to the police, okay? He's too powerful.'

'He can't get away with it.' I go to stand up. 'In fact, I'll go and talk to him.'

He laughs and yanks me back down. 'You're crazy. Just stay with me. Look how pretty the sky is.' I follow his gaze towards the pinkening skies. His hand is still softly grasping mine and our shoulders are pressed together. 'It's enough for you to be here with me, Lizbeth. No questions, no anger. I've had enough of that.'

'I *do* get it though,' I say softly. 'My mother, she—'

'She doesn't hit you, does she?' he asks, blue eyes fierce with anger. It makes me happy, to see him so passionately against the idea of someone hurting me.

'No! But she's – she's mean, really mean. If her words were fists . . . Well, put it this way, I'd be a lot bloodier and more bruised than you are right now.'

His face softens. 'I'm sorry to hear that.'

I shrug. 'We all have our issues, I guess.'

'It's not *your* issue, it's hers.'

My eyes fill with tears. 'Maybe.'

He doesn't say anything, just carries on looking at me until softly, slowly, he leans his head towards me, pressing his lips gently against mine. The world seems to tilt on its axis, the ripples of the sea before us seeming to still. It is all centred on that moment. That feel of his soft lips against mine. Of this hand clutched around mine.

When he pulls away, he looks worried. 'Sorry, I should have asked.'

I reply by pulling him towards me and kissing him back as he laughs against my lips. We stay like that for the next hour, kissing and talking. Even crying. Well, me crying anyway. I've not truly talked to anyone about my mother. Sure, Tamsin and Dorothy know what she's like. But I never really go into great detail with them.

When we stand to head back, I think of Tamsin. 'Tamsin will be wondering where we are,' I say, biting my lip. 'I'll call her when I get back home.' Gabe frowns. 'What's wrong?'

'It's probably best you don't tell her about us.'

'What is *us*?' I surprise myself by asking.

He smiles and give me another long, lingering kiss. 'This,' he whispers. Then he kisses my neck as I giggle. 'And this.'

'I feel bad not telling her,' I say.

'You know how she is though. She's fragile. I mean, she has all those therapy sessions.'

I shrug. 'Any of us would after one of our parents died.'

He shakes his head. 'But she started therapy way before her dad died.'

'She did? I didn't realise.'

'Yeah, I heard her mention having to see her therapist on the last birthday before her dad died. It must go farther back than that.'

I think of what my mother had hinted at and peer up towards Lakewell Manor which sits majestic against the darkening skies.

'Now come on,' he says. 'I insist on walking you home.' Before I protest, he puts his fingers to my lips. 'I couldn't give a damn where you live, Lizbeth. And I promise I will drop you off out of sight of your mother so she can't verbally abuse you. Deal?'

I smile. 'Deal.'

He holds my hand the whole way back and when we arrive at the end of my street, he really doesn't seem to care at all about the fact that it's not some grand manor or hotel. Instead, he pulls me into his arms, giving me a proper hug as he kisses my forehead. 'If you're worried about your mother, ignore, ignore, ignore,' he says. 'That's what I do when my father starts bleating. Well, I did before tonight anyway.'

'Don't you mean your grandfather?'

'Of course, Grandfather. Take care, Lizbeth.' Then he kisses me again and walks away. I don't need to remember his advice to ignore my mother when I walk in. My head is filled with Gabe's kisses and his words and his touch, so loud her usual criticisms as I walk in are blocked out. Now I understand the saying, walking on air, because I honestly feel like I am.

There's just one little puncture in my cloud of happiness though: Tamsin. I feel bad not telling her about kissing Gabe; she's my best friend after all. I feel even worse thinking about her waiting at the manor for us too. So I quickly call her number. But instead of Tamsin, her mother answers.

'Hello, Liz,' she says in a strained voice.

'Is Tamsin there?'

'I'm afraid she's gone to bed.'

'Already?'

'She's . . . been a bit emotional tonight. She got herself into a bit of a state after Gabe didn't turn up, then you didn't either.'

'I'm so sorry, I did find him and – and he was in a bit of a state himself. I couldn't leave him.'

'I understand. I'll let Tamsin know.'

'Please tell her I'm sorry and I'll see her tomorrow. Gabe too.'

There's a pause. 'Of course,' she eventually says.

But when Gabe and I turn up at the manor the next afternoon, Simone comes out. 'Tamsin is ill,' she says with a kind smile. 'Mrs Lakewell suggests you leave her for a few days but you are most welcome to come to the luncheon next weekend.'

I feel a thrill of excitement. I loved my first luncheon at Lakewell Manor the year before, sneaking food up to Tamsin's room and watching from her window as residents mingled down below. But still, that's a week away. Do I really believe Tamsin is ill?

In fact, I can see her at her window now, watching Gabe and me with an expressionless face. I ought to insist on seeing her. But the thought of being alone with Gabe again is too much of a draw. So I accept it and walk away with him.

Still, in the back of my mind I can't help but wonder: have I ruined things between me and Tamsin? I guess I'll find out at the luncheon next week.

Chapter 9

Now

I stand outside the bar where Imogen's friend, Celia, suggested we meet. It's called The Laundry Room and is in a trendy part of East London. I've been to London only twice in my life, once on a school trip when I was a teen, then again when the girls were young. I daren't drive here; I'm a nervous enough driver as it is without being subjected to London's busy roads. So after dropping the girls off at Scott's in Manchester (where he did his usual of not saying a word to me 'at the advice of his solicitor') I drove all the way back to Easthaven then got a train into London, telling my mother I was going to a Royal Mail conference, and arranging for extra carers.

I peer around me now. This part of London is different from the usual tourist spots I've visited. It feels strange getting off the Tube and walking past obscurely named bars and restaurants among people who look like they've stepped out of one of the godawful adverts I see in Ruby's gaming magazines. The Laundry Room is even more eccentric than the other bars around me too. There are proper laundry-style washing machines in the windows with people sitting on tacky-looking plastic chairs. I mean, really? I'll be honest; at first, I wondered if there was no bar after all and

Celia was just tricking me, that she wasn't going to turn up. But then I notice those same people are drinking and eating from tables made from tumble dryers.

So I step inside and see Celia instantly, sitting at the back of the room. She's wearing a high-necked silver top and a patterned skirt. She isn't as stunning as Imogen, but *is* striking in her way, with a long regal nose and sharp cheekbones. As I walk towards her, I feel even more out of place in my decidedly mainstream 'trip to London outfit': jeans, a logo t-shirt from M&S and trainers. But then I'm not here for a fashion show, am I? I'm here for Tamsin.

'Celia?' I say when I get to her. She's so busy looking at her phone, she hasn't noticed me. 'It's . . . The Jolly Postie,' I say, referring to my Instagram handle, the one I messaged her with.

Celia peers up, looking me up and down. 'Oh. Hello there,' she says in what I think is an American accent. 'I suppose you *do* look like a British postie.' Is that supposed to be a compliment . . . or an insult?

I take the seat across from her and smile. 'Thank you for coming.'

'Of course, anything for my Imogen.' Her blue, fake-lash-rimmed eyes fill with tears. 'Sorry, still hurts.'

'Grief never stops hurting,' I say. 'Grief is love.' I don't know why I say that. Meeting new people seems to make me want to recite the kinds of messages you see posted on people's Facebook timelines.

'Oh please,' Celia replies, rolling her eyes. 'Grief is a pile of stinking horse manure.' I can't help but smile. Now *that* is a message I'd like to see on Facebook!

'So, you were super-mysterious over our messages about why you're looking into all this,' she says. 'What's the deal?'

I explain all my suspicions including how Fake Tamsin – that's how I'm going to refer to her from now on – pretty much confirmed it after I saw her burning Real Tamsin's clothes.

'Wow,' Celia says. 'Pretty extreme thing to do. Have you gone to the police about it?'

'Not yet. I don't have any evidence and what with her whole poet brand being so reclusive, I can't find any recent photos to prove the two women are different.'

'Why do you think this woman's pretending to be her then?'

'After what I saw about Carl de Leon's failing business, I was wondering if it's some con to get their hands on Tamsin's money?'

Celia nods. 'Yeah, that wouldn't surprise me. And then where do you think the real Tamsin is?'

I sigh. 'I don't know, I've kind of been avoiding thinking about that.'

She frowns. 'Interesting, isn't it, how this guy's girlfriends seem to either die or disappear?'

I feel a shudder run through my body. 'I very much hope Tamsin doesn't end up dead too. Are you – are you *sure* Imogen's death was suicide?'

Celia quickly shakes her head. 'She wasn't murdered, if that's what you're thinking. She'd tried to take her life a few times before, so I'm pretty sure it was suicide.'

'Oh, I'm so sorry.'

'Yeah, it was tough,' Celia says, taking in a deep, shaky breath. 'Especially as her brother, Matteo, died a few months before.'

I remember Matteo was mentioned in the post announcing Imogen's death. 'So Matteo was her brother?' I ask. 'That must have been difficult, to lose both of them in such a short space of time?'

Celia nods. 'Darling, darling Matteo. Such a gentle lovely man. He'd just sold his tech company for a million. To celebrate, he bought the car of his dreams, an electric Porsche. First time he goes out in it? He crashes it.' She shakes her head. 'So tragic.'

'Oh no, how awful. Imogen must have been devastated.'

'Yes, they were so close. *Anyway*,' she says, 'I wanted to check it's definitely the same Carl so I did a call out to our friends to see if anyone had any photos of him, and someone *just* sent me something a moment ago.' She holds up her phone, revealing a photo of a group of people. It appears to have been taken at a rooftop garden, the Shard visible in the background. Imogen is standing with a group of similarly gorgeous people and next to her is a man with closely shaved hair. It's only a side profile, but I know instantly it's Carl. That Disney prince jawline is unmistakable.

'Yes, it's him!' I say. 'Can you send it to me?'

'Already done. It's from a party we went to last year, the one and *only* time we all met Carl. Imogen had been seeing him for three months and there was always some excuse or another for us not to meet him. In the end, I was like, "Girl, if you don't bring him to Shay's party, I am marching over and insisting."'

A casually dressed waiter comes over then to take our order. 'Mojitos, two,' Celia says.

'Oh I don't want an alcoholic drink,' I say.

'Oh you will,' Celia insists.

I raise an eyebrow. This girl is clearly used to getting her way. When the drinks are brought over in two tumblers with mint leaves sticking out of them, Celia takes a long hard sip of hers. But I hesitate for a moment. I need a clear mind for this and yet actually, I do quite fancy a drink. It's been too long and it's not like I'm driving anywhere. So I take a discreet sip and you know what, it's rather lovely: minty, sweet and refreshing, just what I need in this stuffy bar.

'How did Carl and Imogen meet?' I ask.

'New Year's Eve. I woke on New Year's Day to an excited text from Imogen. Just three words. *Met The One*. I'd heard it all before from her, her favourite hobby was falling in love.' She shrugs, taking another sip of her drink. 'So I didn't think much of it. Anyway, she met him at this organised New Year's Eve party thing in Knightsbridge that she'd been invited to. Apparently, he was at the party on his own – I know right, red flags already? I mean, who goes to a New Year's Eve party on their own?'

I nod in agreement, but the truth is I went to a New Year's Eve party alone last year. I was temporarily renting a room in a horrible little flat in Manchester while I waited to get a job and one of my flatmates invited me to her friend's house. Admittedly, she was drunk at the time of the invite, but sitting alone at home that night while the girls were with Scott, all the fears for a future alone sitting heavy on my shoulders, I'd impulsively gone. I left after ten minutes, the sight of two people snorting some substance off a coffee table showing me what a mistake I'd made. And then someone recognised me and started shouting at me, 'That's the dodgy postwoman!' so I made a sharp exit.

'Anyway,' Celia continues, 'he just goes right up to her, bold as brass, and tells her she's the most interesting-looking woman in the room. I mean, this was a room full of models and celebrities, so obviously Imogen was totally *into* a compliment like that. Plus, as she said herself, he's totally hot. Like, really hot, even I can't deny it. Charming too.' Celia sighs. 'So he takes her back to his epically expensive hotel suite and that was that; she was head over heels.' I think of what Tamsin said about her first meeting with Carl at the grief meeting. Sure, it was no New Year's Eve party in Knightsbridge, but there was a similar vibe: a self-assuredness on Carl's part, an 'eyes meet across the room' flash of excitement. That's his thing, it seems: sweeping women off their feet.

'I listened to Imogen gushing about him over brunch a few days later,' Celia continues. 'Honestly? I thought he sounded like a dick, but hey, if he made my girl smile, that was cool with me. I presumed it'd be over a month later. But then the next thing I know, Imogen tells me he's moving into her apartment. I was like . . . wow.'

'How long after they met did he move in?'

'Two weeks?'

'Wow indeed. How long before you met him?'

'It didn't happen until Shay's party three months later, the one from the photo. There'd always be some excuse. And whenever I went over to Imogen's for drinks or whatever with a bunch of other friends, Carl wouldn't be there, just that godawful aftershave of his lingering in the air. It was like he was actively avoiding meeting her closest friends. Always rings alarm bells for me.' Celia frowns slightly as she looks down into her drink. 'She seemed happy enough though. Genuinely in love, actually. I can't fault that. I mean, they had arguments, but it wasn't like she *changed* when she was with him or anything.'

I nod. 'Same with Tamsin. From the brief moments I saw them together on Monday, anyway. What did you think of him when you finally met him?'

'Didn't like him,' Celia says firmly. 'He reminded me of Pinocchio! All shiny and perfect-looking, but something missing.' I smile. She really has a way with words. 'Except turns out he wasn't the puppet,' she adds, her face darkening. 'He was the puppet master.'

'How did it all end, then?' I ask. 'You said they only lasted six months.'

'Nothing dramatic. He just said he didn't love her any more.' Celia frowns. 'That can hurt more than a big fallout, can't it?'

'I imagine it can.'

'Imogen was devastated. *That's* when she changed. She really loved the guy, you know?' Celia looks away, but not before I see her quickly wipe a tear from her cheek. 'She hid away, kept herself to herself. I tried to get through to her, but she'd had dark moments in the past. We all knew to give her time and space. She'd always come out in the end, but this time—' Her voice breaks. 'This time, she didn't. Our friend Umar found her in her room. He had a key to feed the cat when she went away and he hadn't heard from her, so . . .' Celia shudders. 'I still remember his call. I mean, he called me first, before an ambulance or anything. "She's hanged herself" was all he said, over and over.' She shakes her head. 'Worst call of my life.'

'I'm so sorry.'

Celia swallows, visibly trying to pull herself together. Then she straightens her shoulders and looks me in the eye. 'A few weeks after Imogen's death, I learned something interesting.'

'What's that?'

'A couple of months before she met Carl, she put an offer in on a gorgeous apartment overlooking the Thames. She was so excited when it was accepted.' The smile disappears from her face. 'But a few months down the line, whenever I asked her about it, she said the sellers were dragging their feet. After she passed away, I asked our real-estate friend, who'd been helping her with the purchase, what had happened. He told me Imogen's credit checks had failed. She barely had enough to even cover the rent on her place in Chelsea!'

My mouth drops open and Celia leans across the table, blue eyes filled with anger. 'The weird thing is, there is *no* way she wouldn't even be able to afford her rent. Not only did she have sponsorship money from her social media stuff, she'd also inherited some money from her older brother Matteo.' She takes another slug of her drink and slams it on the table. 'So suspect, no? And then your message comes in saying she's named as a director in Carl's company. I mean, what the hell? I had no idea! It got me thinking: did he convince her to plough a bunch of money into his shitty little company?'

I lean back in my chair, taking a sip of my drink and thinking about what Celia just told me. 'So he conned her then?'

Celia nods. 'I actually went to the police about it.'

'And?

'Nothing came of it. I mean, sure, the detective did his due diligence, I'll give him that, but he didn't have much to play with plus ultimately, a girl took her own life.'

'But maybe you'll have more now we know where Carl is?' I say.

'Sure! Why don't you give the detective a call?' Celia rummages around in her bag. 'I have his card somewhere.'

'Actually,' I say quickly. 'I'd rather you talk to him. I mean, he *knows* you.'

'*Exactly*. He knows I'm a pain in his ass,' Celia admits. 'If a new person hounds him about the same thing, he'll really see I'm not crazy.'

I swallow nervously. I really don't want to attract the attention of the police again. Especially because I have absolutely nothing to back up my theories about Tamsin, apart from my own instincts. 'I'd really rather not,' I say again. 'If that's okay?'

Celia regards me with interested eyes, then shrugs. 'Sure, if you insist.' She is quiet for a moment then tilts her head. 'Why are you doing this, Liz? I mean, you haven't seen Tamsin for twenty years.'

'Tamsin and I were best friends once,' I say with a sigh. 'She meant a lot to me. It's my duty to help her.'

She smiles. 'You're actually a good person, aren't you? I tell ya, that's rare.' She lifts her empty glass. 'So, another mojito?' I hesitate. 'Come on, you've come all this way,' Celia pushes, 'and Imogen would want me to buy you a few drinks for doing this for her.

Anyway, I'm intrigued about what it's like to be a postwoman! I'm so *bored* of meeting the same old people. PR, marketing, influencers, blah blah blah,' she says, waving her hand around. 'It's all I've done since I moved here from the States five years ago. It's about time I socialised with proper salt-of-the-earth British people.'

Again, I don't know whether that's meant to be a compliment or not.

I look at my watch. I've been here only for half an hour. I don't need to get back until six to feed my mother. I smile at Celia. 'Sure, why not?'

On the train back later that night, I'm still buzzing from the mojitos I've drunk and how *fascinated* Celia seemed with little old me. In fact, I found myself confiding in her about how awful my mother is. Turns out she has a toxic father. By the end of our drinks, Celia and I promised to keep in touch, maybe meet up again too. I smile at my reflection in the window. I like that idea. In the same way Celia finds me fascinating because I'm not like all the other creatives and marketing types she hangs out with, I find her fascinating because she isn't part of the 'salt-of-the-earth British' set I've grown up knowing.

Tamsin held that same fascination for me and yes, Gabe too. They'd opened up a whole new world for me. I stare back down at the photo Celia sent me of Carl at her friend's party now. How very similar he is to Gabe in his looks, blessed with the kind of face people turn to look at as he walks down the street. Does that handsome face hide a deceitful heart? The fact that his last girlfriend lost most of her money in his business and was driven to suicide suggests it does. And what of Tamsin? What are the consequences for her being with this man, her identity stolen by a stranger? I suddenly feel the wave of exhaustion that comes from afternoon drinking sweep over me. It's not *just* the drinking, it's everything to do with Tamsin, so much to take on, but take it on I must.

◆　◆　◆

When I wake, I'm surprised to see the train is at a complete standstill. I look at one of the other passengers, an elderly woman who's knitting. 'How long has the train been like this?' I ask her.

'An hour,' she says with an eye-roll. 'It's still another hour from Easthaven.'

I look at my watch. Seven already. Bugger, I'm already an hour later than I said. I quickly call the hotline for her carers but it goes straight to voicemail. 'Bugger, bugger, bugger,' I hiss.

I'll try Lester's number. I'm sure he wouldn't mind popping by. But then I realise, *how* can he pop by? He doesn't have a key and my mother can't answer the door, can she? I take a deep breath. I need to calm myself. I'll be back by eight. She'll just have to wait. She won't bloody starve to death, will she? I call our home phone, bracing myself for the earful I'm bound to get from my mother when I tell her I'll be late. I'm pleased when it's engaged so I leave a message.

Finally, the train begins to move and the next hour is agony as I prepare myself for the wrath of my mother. At least the girls won't be there to witness it as they're an hour and a half away in Manchester. When the train eventually pulls into Easthaven station, clouds have gathered during the journey and now they're producing the kind of rain that guarantees a complete drenching as soon as you step into it . . . and I don't have an umbrella. I get off the train and hurry out of the station, taking shelter in the doorway of a shop nearby as I try to figure out what to do. There isn't a taxi rank here, the station is so small. Buses are unreliable.

Looks like I'm just going to have to walk and endure the rain . . . and the dark. Though the sun hasn't properly set yet, it feels like it has. I consider calling Lester for a lift. But on Saturday evening, the patisserie hosts music evenings. He needs to be there. It hits me then, I really don't have many people I can call on in my hour of need. If the real Tamsin was here though, I have a feeling she'd come get me. Oh well, I just need to get on with it. I step out on to the street, straight into a puddle.

'Great,' I snap. I bow my head and start heading in the direction of my street. The rain is so heavy, I can hardly see where I'm going, rain driving into my face like bullets. A clap of thunder makes me jump and lightning cuts a silver streak in the sky above. The storm must be right on top of me! Tyres splash in water nearby and a car draws up: an ugly but clearly expensive dark-green Bentley. The window winds down and Douglas smiles out from the darkness of his car, white teeth flashing.

'Lovely evening for a walk,' he says sarcastically. I can see from the wry smile on his face that he's enjoying watching me get soaked.

'I've walked in worse,' I say, wrapping my arms around myself and trying to stop my teeth from chattering as I continue walking.

'Jump in,' he says, kerb-crawling alongside me.

'No thanks, I'm fine.' As I say that, there's another clap of thunder. I can't help it, I jump.

Douglas raises an eyebrow as he peers behind me. 'That lightning nearly got that tree,' he says. 'Sure you want to deprive your daughters of a mother? Oh come on, why are you being so stubborn?' he says.

I bite my lip. I really rather wouldn't get a lift with him. But if he's right, if the lightning was that close . . . I sigh. 'Fine,' I say. *It's just a quick lift*, I tell myself. *No big deal.* I walk around the car and get in the passenger side. The car smells of his sweat mixed in with a strong stench of aftershave. I move as far away from Douglas as I can, crunching up against the passenger door.

His eyes slide towards me as he speeds up down the rain-drenched road. 'So, do we have a deal?'

'Deal? What deal?'

'You rub my back and I rub yours. Especially now I'm giving you a lift.'

I shake my head. 'I told you, no.'

'Fine! If you want to choose a measly little letter over your friend.'

'You do realise how unethical this is of you, withholding information about a woman who might be in danger?'

'Unethical? That's rich coming from you,' he shoots back, lip curling, 'someone who manipulated a letter just so they could talk to my teenage son.' I freeze. *He knows.* 'Oh come on,' he says with a laugh. 'Not a chance his little water polo club would send something important enough to require a signature. Though clearly what my son had to say about the couple next door was important enough for you to do a little tweaking.' I swallow, unsure what to say. 'And that's all it would take,' he says. 'A little tweak. No big deal. A small white lie. One teeny tiny accidental drop from you and you get some quality intel to help a friend in need.'

'*Do* you think Tamsin's in need? I mean, from the information you have?' I ask, feeling panicked.

He tilts his head. 'Maybe.'

He clearly knows something to suggest Tamsin is in trouble. 'What do you need me to do then?' I ask, almost regretting the words before they erupt from my mouth. Damn those mojitos!

'It's like I said. Just accidentally lose a letter.'

'Whose letter?'

Douglas smiles. 'Lester Dufau.'

My shoulders slump. It had to be Lester of all people, didn't it? 'No,' I say, shaking my head. 'He's my friend.'

He raises an eyebrow. 'I'd be careful who you're friends with. He isn't the man you think he is.'

'What do you mean?'

He shrugs. 'Not my place to say. Now, about that letter?'

I shake my head. 'Not a chance.'

'Fine,' he says as he drives us past the promenade, 'if you don't want to choose a teeny tiny letter over a friend in need, then that's on your head.'

I frown. 'This letter. Is it important?' I ask. Because that's all I'm doing, simply asking.

'Why do you think I want it lost?'

I sigh, chewing at my lip. It's not like I'll have to give the letter to Douglas. It won't be a breach of privacy. Letters get lost all the time, if the public only knew just how much. But it's Lester! He's my friend! *So is Tamsin,* a small voice inside says. *Imagine her alone, scared . . .*

'Fine,' I say to Douglas, mind made up, tummy squirming. 'Tell me what to look out for.'

'Excellent,' he declares in a triumphant voice that makes me instantly regret it. 'It'll be a simple white letter, should be arriving this week via special delivery. Easy to remember, no?' I nod, jaw clenching. 'And I wouldn't think about *pretending* to lose it, but delivering it anyway,' Douglas says, dark eyes glinting. 'I *will* know.'

'Don't worry, I won't. So, the information?'

'Turns out Mr de Leon's previous girlfriend is dead.'

I feel a burst of frustration. 'I *know* that already.'

He looks at me in surprise. 'Well, well, you're more astute than I thought.'

'I used to be a journalist, remember? Honestly, if this is the kind of information you're promising then you can forget our deal.'

I turn away, but he grabs my elbow, fingers digging into my skin. 'How's this instead? Carl has been to prison.'

I look at Douglas in surprise. 'Really?'

He nods. 'Fraud by false representation, the naughty boy. He worked for his uncle's firm and helped him falsify records. Ended up being imprisoned for five years.'

'Interesting. When was this?'

'He was released ten years ago,' Douglas says as he drives up the road towards my street. 'Almost feel sorry for him. He was trained by his uncle and took the fall for most of it. Unlucky boy.' His dark eyes slide over to me. 'Not like you, though. You managed to avoid any prison time, didn't you?'

My pulse throbs in my ears and the air feels heavy, unbreathable. 'Stop the car!' I shout out. 'I'm getting out.'

'Don't be childish. We're nearly there.'

'You're evil.'

He raises an eyebrow. 'Now now, The Jolly Postie, no need to get personal. If I were truly evil, I wouldn't have offered you a lift, would I? Lord knows what can happen to a woman in the dark.'

I squeeze myself tighter into the corner of my seat. How have I managed to get involved with this man? I keep quiet until he draws up outside my house. Then I notice a familiar car. My heart sinks. It's Scott's car.

What the hell is he doing here?

When Douglas stops, I jump out of the car without even saying thanks and run down the path to the house, Douglas speeding off in his car behind me. I walk inside to find Scott sitting in the living room with the girls and my mother, a tray of food on her lap. He must have carried her down. It feels strange to see Scott. I still find myself attracted to him, I can't help it. It's like the first time I met him when I was nineteen. I'd just got a job at the Manchester news-paper a few months before and had saved up enough of a deposit to rent my first flat, a small one-bed on the outskirts of the city. The landlord had agreed I could redecorate the living room as long as I used a painter-decorator he recommended. That turned out to be his nephew, Scott of Scotty M's Decorators. It wasn't quite the Mills & Boon story of Tamsin and Carl's. But I'd had an inkling when I saw the blond-haired and muscular man standing at my door that Saturday morning that I was on the precipice of something.

He'd been quiet, respectful, getting on with his work while I read on the small balcony. I'd notice him watching me occasionally though. I was slimmer back then, legs tanned and toned. My hair was longer too, to my shoulders with a sweeping fringe. Looking back at photos from then, I was more attractive than I gave myself credit for. Scott told me after we got together that it was my long tanned legs that did it.

I couldn't help sneaking glances at him either. How could I not? He *was* attractive, in that typical blond working-man way, especially when he took his flannel shirt off to reveal his muscled biceps. Maybe a bit too short for my liking but still, he was undeniably hot and, even better, as different from Gabe as I could get. A blond working-class northerner to Gabe's dark-haired, smooth-talking southerner.

Scott finished the work by the end of the week. He was doing the job in his spare time, he'd told me during the brief moments we'd engaged in conversation. His usual job was fixing cars at a local garage, but this was his passion. When he spoke of his decorating business and the care he took in his painting, that was almost more of a turn-on than those muscles. I was sad to see him leave at the end of the week, making promises to use him in the future. But as he was about to turn away to leave, he'd paused. 'I hope this doesn't sound unprofessional,' he'd said in his polite northern tones, 'but I was wondering, do you fancy getting a drink sometime?'

I was elated. My last boyfriend had been an advertising exec at the paper, a dull handsy man called Colin who still lived at home with his parents. But here was a good-looking *normal* man, asking me out on a date. Of course, I said yes instantly. What followed was a strangely formal courtship, with us meeting each Saturday night for a cheap pub meal and a chat. Each date would progress us through the 'stages' of intimacy, a first kiss on the first date and so forth. A year later, I discovered I was pregnant. In fact, Scott proposed during the dinner we'd arranged with my mother to break the news of the pregnancy. It was the first time he'd met her. The last thing I'd wanted to do was put him off in those early days with a meeting with my mother. And anyway, I rarely saw her after I moved to Manchester. But I couldn't avoid this dinner, the one where we'd be telling her I was pregnant.

Annoyingly, she and Scott got on well. Even when I broke the news about my pregnancy, my mother reacted in a way I'd never dreamed she would: with a smile (albeit forced), even a 'congratulations' thrown in. She was clearly so enamoured with the handsome blond man sitting at her table, and so shocked he'd chosen me as his girlfriend, she managed to suppress her usual bitter self. The whole thing was a weird experience, with my mother pretending she was some kind of fifties housewife, preparing the kind of meal I'd always dreamed of her preparing for me. I'd found it so unsettling, I just wanted to get out of there. But then Scott proposed, right there, the last place on Earth where I'd dreamed of being proposed to.

'What are you doing here?' I ask him now as I give the girls a hug, a bonus to see them so unexpectedly.

'I called him,' my mother snaps. 'I was starving!'

'I'm only two hours late,' I reply, 'the train was delayed. You did not have to drive all this way from Manchester, Scott.'

'I didn't. We were visiting my cousin Steve an hour away,' he says. 'Anyway, I would have come even if I was in Manchester. How could I not when your mother called? What were you doing in London anyway?'

'Seeing a friend for drinks.'

'I thought you were at a Royal Mail conference?' my mother says.

'It was cancelled,' I quickly lie, 'so I called a friend to meet for drinks.'

'Drinks.' Scott sniffs the air, nostrils wide. 'Yes, I can smell it on you.' I inwardly kick myself. He'll use this in court. 'I hope this hasn't become a habit, the drinking,' Scott says. 'It might explain the strange theories Mia told me she overheard you spouting about an old friend being replaced?' Mia blushes. She's only a kid, how dare he use her like this? And anyway, when did she overhear me?

I grit my teeth. 'That's not for you to worry about.'

'Isn't it? You're the mother of my children, Liz. Combined with the way you flew off the handle last year—'

'Because *you* cheated,' I say, hating the fact that I have to bring it up in front of the kids but I can't help it.

Ruby takes Mia's arm. 'Come on, let's go and get a snack and let our parents do what they do best, *argue*.' She shoots us daggers then walks out.

'Let's not do this here,' I say. 'You're upsetting the girls.'

'I'm just worried about you, Liz, that's all,' he says in a fake, consolatory tone.

'Why, thank you, Scott. How kind,' I reply sarcastically, aware of my mother watching us with a glint in her eye. 'This plays very neatly into your attempts to get full custody, doesn't it?' As I say that, my stomach drops. In just ten days' time, I could lose primary custody of my girls.

His jaw twitches. He looks around him. 'Can you blame me? Look at this place. Sorry to say this, Ruth,' he says to my mother, 'but there's damp on the walls, you know. I can smell it. It's not suitable for kids to be here.'

'Liz said she'd get it sorted,' my mother huffs.

'I will do, when I save enough money! You can go now, Scott, I'll take it from here,' I say, not wanting to get into a discussion. 'In fact, you may as well leave the girls here, no point dragging them back to Manchester when I'll be picking them up tomorrow afternoon anyway.'

'I don't think so,' he says, 'they're coming back with me. It's not their fault you got so drunk you were unable to feed your mother.'

'Yes, imagine that,' my mother says, 'swanning off to London to get drunk with her new man.'

I roll my eyes. 'New man? I don't think so. I've been put off men for life,' I add pointedly, giving Scott a hard look. 'It was a female friend actually.'

'You don't have *friends*,' my mother says.

Scott's lips twitch up into a smile. I feel anger bristle inside me. 'Oh and you do?' I snap at my mother.

'No, I don't,' she replies. 'Like mother, like daughter.'

'We are nothing alike!'

'That's right, I don't make up friends!'

I pull my phone from my pocket with shaky hands, finding the selfie Celia had taken of us on her Instagram page. *Drinks with a real-life British post lady!* the caption declares. I show it to Mother and she snatches the phone from my hands. 'See?' I say.

'Oh I *do* see,' she says wickedly. 'You're a lesbian. My daughter, a lesbo. Oh it just gets worse.' She holds my phone up to Scott and I grab it off her to see she's scrolled down to a photo of Celia kissing a woman, the caption reading: *Living That Gay Life. #lgbtq #bornperfect #equalitymatters #accelerateacceptance*

I feel my cheeks burn with colour. 'So what if she's a lesbian? Straight people *can* be friends with gay people, you know!'

But my mother isn't listening, she's just shaking her head in disgust. 'It explains a lot, why you were so close with that Tamsin girl, going over after school every day, coming back all flushed and mussy-haired. Add in that Gabe boy and who knows what happened in that manor? No wonder it all ended like it did.'

'Mother!' I shout. 'You are awful!'

'Only telling the truth!' she shouts back.

'Wow,' Scott says, shaking his head, 'great environment you have here for the kids, Liz.' Then he storms down the hallway, gesturing for the girls to come with him. I take in a breath, forcing myself to stop the tears I feel coming.

'Well done, Mother,' I hiss at her. I take some quick deep breaths, then calmly walk down the hall after Scott and give the girls a hug goodbye. As I do, I notice Ruby examining my face with curiosity. That's two mentions of Gabe that she's overheard lately. I know my daughter, I know her curiosity will be piqued.

As they both hug me, Ruby says loud enough for her grandmother to hear: 'I don't mind if you're a lesbian.'

Mia nods. 'Me neither. Actually, it's pretty cool.'

I can't help but smile. My girls always make things better. 'I'm not a lesbian, girls. But I appreciate the support anyway. See you tomorrow, all right?'

They both nod and leave the house. I lean against the closed door and feel tears spring to my eyes. My mother and Scott together are a lethal combination. It took me a while to realise that. In fact, it took me a while to see just how much like my mother Scott is, except he had charm mixed in, which ultimately, was more dangerous. It began as little undermining digs. About my weight, about my accent . . . even about the way I chewed. Negativity seeping into everyday conversations. It made me uncomfortable, but as soon as he'd say something, the charm would be switched back on and I told myself it was okay, maybe he was right anyway.

When Ruby was born, it got worse. Occasional sharp digs became more regular. When I asked him to stop, he'd accuse me of being oversensitive and not being able to take a joke. He would start arguments over nothing if he'd had a stressful day at work, then accuse *me* of starting those arguments. At the beginning, when I tried to defend myself, he'd turn my words around, try to make out *I* was the one being abusive. He'd tell me I was lucky he didn't hit me, the way I wound him up.

When we visited my mother, the two of them would become a tag team, conspirators in the 'anti-Liz' campaign. No wonder Mother loved him so much, he was her enabler and she his. I fought back, don't get me wrong. But there's only so many times woodworms nibble at a piece of furniture before it begins to weaken. I revisited a technique I used to adopt as a child around my mother: I went into myself. As their words rang out, I let them pass through without thought or recognition. I suppose it came across as me simply not caring. I wasn't like it with Ruby and Mia. They were my light and joy. But I became almost robotic with Scott. He said it drove him to other women. But the truth is, he was just a little boy who didn't like not getting the attention he thought he deserved.

Still, part of me sometimes wonders if he's right. Part of me wonders if my mother's biting words are right too. When you're told enough times you're a piece of dirt, you begin to believe it.

When I get into work on Monday, I feel a sense of determination to prove I'm not. There are so many things I can't control in my life. My mother. Scott. My past. But I can try to help Tamsin. But how? Though I know more about Carl, I don't know anything about the woman who I suspect has taken Tamsin's identity. I mull it all over as I sort through the post the next morning. Then I freeze. There's a letter for Lester, a letter that looks just as Douglas described: a white A4 special-delivery letter. It feels heavy in my hands and official-looking too, like there are several documents within. A stamp is on the front: *Copley Solicitors.*

Solicitors. That means it's important. What is Douglas so desperate to keep from Lester? And why did he imply Lester wasn't as genuine as he seems? I take out my phone, googling the solicitors. Turns out they specialise in property law. Can I really do as Douglas asks? But what if I don't? That means I rescinded on my agreement with Douglas. What would the consequences of *that* be? He seems so powerful. He's our landlord after all. What if he kicks us out? Plus he knows about the little tweak I did to his son's water polo letter. Sure, it's a small thing but combined with the other little misdemeanours I've carried out lately, it could cost me my job! I really couldn't cope with losing my job. And then there's the fact that he can dig up more information to help Tamsin.

But Lester is my friend!

I stuff the letter in my bag. I'll think about it as I do my round.

When I get closer to the patisserie around lunchtime, I see a crowd is gathered outside. I draw closer then realise with a sigh that they're gathered around Fake Tamsin. She's wearing a black floppy straw hat and an emerald-green maxi dress with a plunging neckline, a book of poetry in her hand . . . *Tamsin's* latest book. I look around at the crowd. How many of these people would have met her twenty years ago? I know she hasn't returned since she and her mother moved back to London twenty years ago after what happened, so they won't have seen her since. Still, I recognised Tamsin instantly when I saw her last Monday. But this Tamsin, she looks so different, despite her hair.

'This one is called "The Pause",' she calls out. 'It's from my latest collection which is also called *The Pause*.' She begins reading:

She's the pause in my sentence,
The memory that seeps,
Through the branches of conversation,
Through the cracks in my sleep.
The 'oh, she's gone' raindrop,
The 'no more' refrain,
That stutters my words,
And conjures my pain.
But a pause is just a moment.
A brief time to grasp,
The wonder of her,

A wonder that lasts. She finishes with a flourish, taking a bow as people clap. But I don't clap. Ruby's right; the way she recited the poem is completely *off,* like it was a fun nursery rhyme rather than a verse about grief. I notice Carl nearby, a slight furrow in his brow as he watches the performance. He catches my eye briefly, then quickly turns away.

I see you.

'I see you,' a voice from behind me says.

I jump, letting out a yelp. It's Douglas again. Why does he seem to be everywhere I am?

'Seems strange, doesn't it?' he says. 'How someone who says she's a recluse chooses to stand in the middle of a busy promenade and do a reading to over fifty people?'

'Hmmmm,' I say.

'So, any sign of Mr Dufau's letter this morning?'

It feels heavy like lead in my bag. 'Not yet,' I lie.

'Look out for it, it shouldn't be long before it arrives and you know what to do when it does,' he says, peering towards the patisserie. 'And don't feel guilty, remember what I said about Lester. He's not the man you think he is.'

'Why don't you just tell me what you mean by that.'

'Not my place to say.' Then he strolls off towards the crowd.

My phone beeps and I see it's a message from Celia asking how I am. I can't resist; I lift my phone up to take a photo of Fake Tamsin as she reads out another poem. Celia will love this!

'No photos please!' Damn it, Fake Tamsin has noticed. I quickly lower my phone as people turn to look at me. 'As I announced *before* this exclusive reading,' she says haughtily, 'I prefer *not* to have my face plastered all over the internet. In fact, you should know better, as the local postie,' she says, her eyes drilling into me. 'Isn't discretion one of your remits?'

'Hardly discreet,' I hear someone say nearby. I turn to see it's Tilda Beashell whispering very loudly to her friend. 'She was poking about in our front garden the other day. She's always been so nosy, like at school, when she'd just sit and watch us all, making notes.'

I feel my cheeks flush and quickly walk away from everyone's watchful eyes. As I pass the patisserie, I see Lester gesturing for me to come inside. I actually *could* do with a cuppa but I feel so guilty about his letter. I still have no idea what to do. As I approach the counter, the letter feels even heavier in my bag now, like a huge, solid rock. I hand him the other letters I sorted for him, but *not* the letter.

'Made your tea already,' he says as he hands me a cup. 'Even saved you a couple of Danishes, aren't you a lucky lady?' He seems so chipper and happy, it makes me feel even worse about his letter. But then I think of what Douglas said about him: that I don't know everything about him. I examine Lester's face. What secrets is he keeping?

'She's a confident one, isn't she?' he says, gesturing to Fake Tamsin outside.

'Never used to be,' I murmur.

'Yeah, I remember her being all mysterious and reclusive . . . apart from with you. People change though, don't they? She popped in earlier actually and asked if I wouldn't mind hosting a poetry night or two.'

I raise an eyebrow. 'What do you think about her? You met her a few times when we did our rounds and I became friends with her. Do you think she's different?'

'Nah, not really. Same red hair. Same green eyes. Though I guess she does seem more confident, holds herself differently, now you mention it. But people change, Liz. It's been years since we all saw her.'

'Seems she's enjoying the attention, something the *real* Tamsin never did.'

'The *real* Tamsin?'

I pause. Do I want to tell him more about my suspicions? I decide not to. 'I mean the pre-fame Tamsin,' I quickly say. 'The Tamsin I knew wasn't OTT like that.'

'Well, like I said, people change, sadly.' He looks at my post bag. 'Sure there's no more post for me? I was supposed to get something today.'

Guilt shreds through me. To make things worse, I can see Douglas hovering outside, peering in the window. The letter within my bag seems to throb with menace through the thick material.

'Nope,' I quickly say, aware of Douglas's eyes on us. 'Not today.'

He frowns. 'That's annoying.'

I try to keep my face as neutral as possible, telling myself I haven't thrown it away yet. I just can't give the letter to Lester while Douglas is watching.

'While you're all here,' Fake Tamsin suddenly shouts out from outside. Lester and I go quiet, turning to look at her. 'I'd like to invite you all to our luncheon tomorrow afternoon in the manor's grounds to celebrate the launch of my new collection,' she says, gesturing towards the manor. A little excited murmur runs through the crowd but I shake my head in disbelief. This would be the *last* thing Tamsin would want. And surely this fake woman too? Won't it bring more scrutiny? But clearly she's unhinged and grown confident at how easily she is getting away with her deception. 'My parents used to open up the grounds once a year for residents and that has no doubt been sorely missed over the past twenty years. So I thought you'd all be intrigued to see it again before I finally sell it to my favourite Easthaven man, Douglas Gold, who will be using the land to build more of his beautiful villas.'

My mouth drops open as I watch Douglas sidle up to Fake Tamsin with a big smile on his face. Since when have they become best buddies . . . and can I *really* trust the man if he's cosying up to her like this?

When could you ever trust him? a small voice asks.

'All residents of Easthaven are invited tomorrow from twelve noon onwards,' Fake Tamsin continues. 'Apologies if it's a little messy. Its charm still holds though. Oh and prosecco and nibbles on us.' She lets out a peal of laugher. 'Well, not literally *on* us, though who knows what the day will bring? Be there or be square!' Then she walks off, her arm linked through Douglas's.

I feel anger swell inside. That's made my mind up. I reach into my bag. 'Look what I just found as she was talking?' I pull Lester's letter out, heart thumping ten to the dozen. 'It managed to squirm into the bottom of my bag,' I say, handing the letter to Lester.

He takes it, smiling. 'Great, been waiting for this.'

I feel a sense of relief. It was the right thing to do. But a warning bell still rings inside. You don't cross Douglas Gold . . . and that's what I've just done.

'Will you go to the drinks then?' Lester asks me.

I look towards the manor. Maybe it *would* be good to go and have a little snoop around, find clues to the real Tamsin's whereabouts. 'I might do,' I say.

'Maybe we could go together?'

I look at Lester. He seems nervous. Has he developed a thing for me? Does that sound presumptuous? Look, I know I'm no Kim Kardashian, but the fact is, we're both single parents, both in our late thirties and we have 'good banter' as Ruby would say. I suppose he is quite easy on the eye. So no, I'm not upset at the prospect of him liking me a little. But I promised myself no men after Scott. And anyway, if I want to snoop around, I can't have him with me. 'I'll be working, remember? So I can't guarantee it.'

He shrugs, but I can see he's trying to hide his disappointment. 'No worries, I think Eva has an exam tomorrow morning anyway so has the rest of the day off after; she can come with me.'

I look out towards the manor. Tomorrow I'll do some digging.

Chapter 10

Twenty Years Ago

I walk towards the cafe to meet Gabe before the luncheon, feeling nervous as hell. I'm wearing a black dress with yellow sunflowers all over it. My mother declared that I looked like a 'floozy' as soon as she saw me, just because the hem doesn't quite reach below the knees. But the neck is high and I saw a lot of shorter dresses at the charity shop when I went there yesterday. So I tried to ignore her remark. But now, as I approach the cafe, her words dig their heels into me. Maybe I do look like a floozy? Maybe I'm wearing too much make-up? I couldn't decide whether to go with the red lipstick or the pink, but decided on the red in the end. Now I'm wondering if it's too bright? And should I have worn tights instead of leaving my legs bare? But my legs are tanned and I went to all that trouble of shaving them this morning.

I honestly consider turning away to head back home and change. But then I spot Gabe waiting for me outside the cafe with a huge smile on his face and all my worries disappear. He looks more handsome than he ever has with a white shirt and navy-blue chinos, plus those crazy red shoes of his of course which he told me his mother gave him. There's still remnants of a bruise around his eyes but it somehow makes him look even more handsome, and his dark hair is tousled and cute. When I approach him, he lets out a low whistle.

'Lizbeth, you look divine.'

That's all I need to hear. Divine. Not floozy. Divine. *Take that, Mother.*

We don't hold hands as we approach the manor. Tamsin still knows nothing. We've actually been meeting up loads this week, walking a little further out of town and sitting on the beach, holding hands, kissing, talking. It feels really odd now not being able to touch him. As we draw closer to the manor, I feel nervous about seeing Tamsin. Was she really ill? Or was she jealous that Gabe and I didn't head straight to the manor a week ago when I found him on the beach? Can I blame her? I'd surely feel the same way if she was kissing Gabe on the beach.

As we flood into Lakewell Manor's grounds with the other residents, Dorothy spots us and walks over, looking amazing in a flowing tropical-patterned dress, her strawberry-blonde hair piled up. 'Oh Liz, look at you, so sophisticated in that dress.'

Sophisticated. Divine. And there my mother was, calling me a floozy.

'And look at you, dear Gabe,' Dorothy says as she turns to him, 'such a handsome young man.'

'Why, thank you, Mrs Lakewell, you are looking rather stunning yourself.'

She smiles and bows at him. Then she points to the manor's entrance. 'Tamsin's over there, sulking until she sees her two favourite people. Enjoy!' Then she turns on her heels and walks off, greeting people.

Gabe and I head towards Tamsin. As we do, I can see she is as nervous as me. She looks utterly beautiful too. She has her red hair up and is wearing a long, floaty peach-coloured summer dress. My dress feels gaudy and cheap next to hers, my make-up over the top.

For the first time, I notice Gabe take a pause as he looks at Tamsin. In fact, when we eventually get to her and they're standing together, it strikes me how much more suited to each other they are with their wealth and beauty. But just as I'm thinking that, Gabe quickly brushes his hand against my back while Tamsin isn't looking. Gabe and I are perfect.

'You look so pretty, Liz,' Tamsin says, grabbing my hands. 'Doesn't she look pretty, Gabe?'

'Very,' Gabe says with a nod. 'Both of you do.'

'I'm so sorry I haven't seen you the past week,' Tamsin says. 'Truth is, I've had the most awful hay fever.'

I frown. Tamsin has never had hay fever in the year I've known her. But what does it matter? If she needed time, then so be it. She comes between us and links both her arms through ours.

'I'm so pleased my two bestest friends are here,' she says. I see what she's doing, trying to signal there are no hard feelings. 'So, shall we steal a bottle of champagne and hide away somewhere?'

Gabe's eyes sparkle mischievously. 'Finally I get to live the Ernest Hemingway life.'

'*Without* the making love, I hope,' Tamsin says with a wink. I feel my face flush as Gabe catches my eye. We've only shared kisses so far. But still, I can't help reacting. Tamsin leads us towards a table filled with champagne bottles and shoves one into my hand. 'Quick,' she says. 'My bedroom, now.'

'What about the cellar instead?' Gabe suggests, pointing towards the door in the hallway that leads down into the cellar. 'You said your father's wine collection is there. We can grab more drinks easily if we're down there, plus it's soundproof, right? No one will hear us.'

'You mean the *dungeon*?' Tamsin replies dramatically. 'Sure, why not?'

We check nobody's looking, then head down to the cellar. It's a vast space, some of the walls made from the cliffs themselves with pillars dotted here and there. As well as a whole area at the back with shelves and shelves of wine, there are also lots of ornate furniture and other expensive-looking items such as grand clocks and beautiful vases all over the place.

'Wow, this place is something,' Gabe says in awe as he looks around him. 'What is all this stuff?'

'A lot of it is my dad's,' Tamsin says. 'You know, family heirlooms and stuff that came here after he . . .' Her face trails off and I squeeze her arm. I know how hard it is for her to say that word: *died*. 'Anyway, check *this* out.' She goes to a safe and presses a number into the pad. It clicks open and she gently reaches in, pulling out an absolutely stunning ring with a huge purple jewel on it. 'It was my grandmother's. It's worth *hundreds* of thousands of pounds. It'll be mine when I get engaged.'

Gabe and I walk over, looking down at it in amazement.

'It's like the blue carbuncle,' Gabe whispers, 'except it's purple.'

'The blue what?' I ask.

'It's a precious jewel from a Sherlock Holmes tale,' Gabe explains.

Tamsin carefully places the ring back in the safe. 'Do *not* tell my mum I showed it to you. So, where do you want to sit? There are, like, three antique sofas in here.'

We help Gabe pull out an old sofa from a dusty corner to create a den of sorts and over the next couple of hours, we neck champagne directly from the bottle, getting *incredibly* drunk.

'Let's play truth or dare!' Tamsin announces after a while.

I feel my tummy turn over. Doesn't truth or dare usually end up with kissing? What if Gabe and I have to kiss, it'll be obvious we've done it many, many times before. Or even worse, Gabe and Tamsin?

'I'll start,' Tamsin says, cutting through my thoughts. She turns to Gabe. 'Gabe, truth or dare?'

'Dare, *obviously*,' Gabe says.

'Fine,' Tamsin says. 'I dare you to tell me it's true you're working at the Easthaven Hotel for your grandfather, like you said you are?'

Gabe blinks, suddenly looking very nervous. Why's she asking a stupid question like that?

'I *know* Gabe works at the hotel,' I quickly say. 'I've seen him in his uniform. Anyway, that's not a dare, Tamsin, it's a truth!'

'It *is* a dare!' Tamsin protests, staring at Gabe with her arms crossed. 'So Gabe? I dare you to tell me, are you working at the hotel, like you said you are?'

Gabe suddenly stands up and puts his hand to his mouth. 'I drank too much champagne, I'm gonna puke.' Then he runs from the cellar.

I go to run after him, but Tamsin grabs my hand, yanking me down. 'Leave him.'

'Why are you being so mean to him?' I ask her. 'He's our friend.'

'I don't trust him.'

'Why?'

'He doesn't work at the hotel,' Tamsin whispers. 'I was chatting to one of the waitresses serving drinks before you came. She works at the hotel too, she started last week. She's adamant the hotel owner's grandson would no way be working at the hotel.'

'But I don't understand, I honestly saw him wearing the hotel outfit last Friday.' I pause a moment. Should I tell Tamsin about his grandfather beating him? But I promised Gabe I wouldn't. 'Let me go and talk to him.'

'Do what you want,' Tamsin says with a shrug as she sinks back into the sofa and crosses her arms. 'I just don't trust him, that's all.'

I head out to find Gabe, eventually locating him by the steps leading down to the beach. When he sees me approach, he looks pained.

'I don't know what's got into Tamsin,' I say, joining him.

'It's not her fault. She's right, I don't work at the hotel any more.'

'What do you mean?'

'My grandfather kicked me out after I saw you last Friday.'

I look at him in surprise. 'But why didn't you tell me? We've seen each other loads since then.'

He hangs his head. 'I was ashamed. I've – I've been sleeping on the beach.'

I put my hand to my mouth, eyes watering. 'Gabe! That's awful. Why didn't you say?'

'I was embarrassed?'

'Embarrassed? Are you kidding? You've seen where I live. You *need* to tell Tamsin. She told me she doesn't trust you. If she knew the truth, she would trust you.'

He looks at me in alarm. 'She doesn't trust me?'

'But if she knew all this, she'd understand. Let's go and talk to her.'

He thinks about it then shakes his head. 'Not you, just me. I think it'll be good for Tamsin and me to talk, you know?' I suddenly feel very, very jealous. I try to hide it but it must be obvious from my face because Gabe laughs and kisses my cheek. 'Don't worry, you're the one for me, Lizbeth. I'll come back after I've talked to her.' Then he strolls off towards the mansion.

I wait for over half an hour, all sorts of things going through my mind. I mean, the first time Gabe and I spent some proper time alone, we kissed. And we *have* all had a bit to drink; dumb crazy things happen when drunk.

When he does eventually come back, he's with Tamsin. They're both smiling and it seems they've resolved their issues.

'Oh Liz,' Tamsin says when she gets to me, 'I was *so* wrong about Gabe. I wish you'd both just told me the truth. I now get why you guys talked for so long last Friday. Anyway, good news!' she says with excitement as she smiles at Gabe. 'Gabe told me he's homeless and I just asked Mum if Gabe can stay here, we have *loads* of rooms. And she said yes!'

My mouth drops open with shock. He's going to be living with Tamsin?

'Only temporarily, of course,' Gabe quickly says.

Gabe gives me a weak smile and I try to look happy for him. But I can't help but feel terrible about the idea of the two of them staying under the same roof. As I leave Lakewell Manor alone after that luncheon, I can't help this terrible feeling of doom spreading over me. Have I just lost the love of my life in one afternoon?

Chapter 11

Now

The next afternoon there's a real buzz in the air in Easthaven, residents dressed in pretty summer dresses and smart trousers as they head to the manor. It really is a lovely day, the sky bright blue and the sea below calm. I look at my watch. Just the villas to deliver post to then I can slip in too. I'd woken up with my tummy full of nerves this morning. It isn't just this luncheon but the fact that it's exactly a week until the family court hearing with Scott. I try to remove it from my mind. I've prepared all I can. I need to focus on Tamsin right now. I quickly head towards the villas then pause: I recognise someone among the crowds going into the manor. Specifically a platinum-haired someone with a long gold pleated skirt and a white crop top revealing a taut tummy. It's Celia! I'd told her about the luncheon in a text last night but never dreamed she'd come along. I stride through the gates towards her, touching her arm. 'What are you doing here?' I say under my breath.

'Oh come on, you think I'd pass up the opportunity of seeing this fool?'

'No, no, you *can't* go in there,' I say.

'Why? I won't say anything. Well, *maybe* not,' she adds, eyes sparkling mischievously as she continues walking past me, her long gold skirt swishing in the sun.

I jog after her. 'Please, Celia, please don't cause a scene. We need to be clever about this.'

'Do I look like someone who'd cause a scene?' she asks, her huge globe earrings bouncing with each step she takes.

'Actually, yes, yes you do.'

Celia laughs. 'I do, don't I? An ex always said that about me. She said, "Celia, why do you always look like you're up to something?"'

'Honestly, Celia, I don't want you to get hurt. God knows what they're all capable of. Carl will recognise you and then . . .'

'And then what? He'll kidnap me and have me replaced by another woman in front of all the guests? He can't do anything to me here. I'm going, Liz.' We hold each other's gaze. She looks very determined. 'And even better, we can go in together. It'll show him we're on to him. The two of us together, marching in. It'll scare him senseless, right? Give him a taste of his own medicine?'

I watch the crowds entering the manor. Celia *is* right. It would send a message to him and Fake Tamsin. A message I'm not to be messed with. Celia looks down at my red Royal Mail polo top and black shorts. 'Though I'm not entirely sure you're dressed for the occasion.'

'I'm meant to be working still.'

'Well, forget I said that then. It's charming, so *on brand*.' She links her arm through mine and I remember what my mother had said a week before about me being a lesbian. Who cares what my mother thinks?

'Fine,' I say. 'Let's do this. But only if you promise to behave.'

Celia salutes. 'I solemnly swear to be a good little square.'

I sigh. Somehow I don't believe her. As we walk towards the manor, my stomach is a knot of nerves. I didn't allow myself to think hard about the fact that I'd be returning to the place that has filled my nightmares for the past few years. But I need to do this, for Tamsin. Ahead of us, familiar faces flock inside, others milling around the front gardens, where black tables have been set up among the trees. Though the manor is clearly a crumbling mess, they've managed to make it look half decent with a tidy-up. I'm disappointed to see all the beautiful wind chimes are now gone. Even if they were rusting, they were still pretty.

I catch a glimpse of the large metal bin tucked away behind a bush and get a flashback to watching Tamsin's clothes being set on fire. I shudder when something occurs to me. Was the reason they were burning them because there was blood on them?

A waiter passes by with a tray of drinks.

'Fancy,' Celia says, grabbing two glasses of Prosecco and handing one to me.

'Oh, I can't,' I say, placing mine back on the tray. 'I'm officially working, remember?'

'You have to look the part!' She grabs the drink again and makes me hold it, the waiter disappearing before I have a chance to return it. I sigh. She is *so* forceful!

'Well, your girl certainly has money,' Celia remarks as she looks around. 'Not sure about the taste though.' She curls her lip at the nearby sculpture of a white dolphin.

'Not *my girl*,' I say.

We walk through the flung-open doors of the manor. I look around me in amazement. How does it look the same? Surely the march of time would have changed it? It certainly seemed that way when I would look up from Easthaven and see tumbling walls and out of control ivy. But in just a week, it has been cleaned up and polished. Yes, the disrepair shows in the cracks and discolouration of the walls and the broken tiles beneath the soles of my shoes. But it could be as though I'm back here twenty years ago. In fact, as I look at the table filled with Prosecco bottles in the kitchen, I can almost still see Tamsin stealing one of them.

'That is some pool.'

I draw my eyes away from the cellar door now and follow Celia's gaze to the back garden. The doors are flung open, people drinking and eating canapés by the infinity pool outside which looks like it's been returned to some of its former glory. I have to take a moment to adjust myself, so many memories accosting me as I stare at it.

'This must have cost a fortune to set up,' Celia says as she sips her drink, watching the jazz band playing music from a wooden decked stage in the middle of the garden as more waiters walk around, serving drinks and canapés.

'Whose fortune though?' I ask. 'Tamsin's? The *real* Tamsin's?'

'Quite.' Celia narrows her eyes as she searches the crowds. 'Now where *are* Mr and Mrs Flashy-Pants?'

'Liz?' a familiar voice says. Lester is standing nearby with his daughter, Eva.

He looks awkward in beige chinos and a white shirt, clearly feeling out of place. But still, I have to admit he looks handsome. Eva looks beautiful in a long silk patterned jumpsuit and I feel bad the girls aren't here. But Mia is at school and Ruby doesn't have the luxury of having the rest of the day off. 'I thought you couldn't come?' Lester asks me now, clearly surprised to see me after I said I wouldn't go with him.

'I'm not here officially, just popping in,' I quickly say. 'So you closed the patisserie then?'

'Just for an hour,' he says. 'Will reopen to make the most of passing trade.'

'Oh, this is my friend, Celia,' I say, conscious of what an unlikely pair we might seem, me in my postal outfit, Celia all dressed up to the nines and unusual-looking.

'Nice to meet you, Celia.'

Celia barely notices him, eyes still searching the crowds for Carl. 'Yeah, hi,' she says dismissively.

Lester raises an eyebrow. 'Well, have a nice time.' He gives me one last look, then walks off with Eva.

I notice Fake Tamsin by the pool then. She's wearing a long slinky dark-green dress, her fake red hair sleek and brushed to the side so it drapes over the pale skin of her shoulder. 'There's Fake Tamsin,' I whisper to Celia.

Celia follows my gaze, arching an eyebrow. 'Hot.'

'A fraud, more like.'

'So where is that bastard, Carl?' Celia asks, hungrily scanning the group around Fake Tamsin.

'Remember,' I warn, 'don't do anything dramatic.'

'I won't. I just need to *see* him.' She downs her drink and marches off, weaving between the guests as I jog to keep up with her. Some people greet me and I give them a quick wave. So many locals are here now, it seems, but then who would turn down free food, drink and the chance to see the village's most famous resident in action in its largest property? I wonder what they would think if they knew she was an imposter?

Another waiter passes and Celia grabs another glass of Prosecco from his tray, replacing it with her empty one. I take the chance to add my untouched drink to his tray and quicken my step to catch up with Celia.

'Don't get too drunk,' I say to her, noticing she's already had half her new glass.

'Drunk, on two glasses of Prosecco? Hardly.' Her eyes widen as she peers towards a group of people standing by a veranda looking out to sea. 'Is that *him*?'

I follow her gaze to see Carl standing with the Beashells. Tilda Beashell notices me watching and narrows her eyes at me.

Ridiculous, how angry she still is about me daring to step into her pristine front garden.

'Look at him,' Celia spits as she glares at Carl. 'Even more smug with his hair longer.'

He's wearing white trousers and a blue suit jacket, his white shirt unbuttoned to his chest. Oh God, it makes him look even more like Gabe. 'It's definitely him, then?' I ask.

'Oh yes, absolutely. Same laugh, too,' she adds as we watch him throw his head back and laugh at something Tilda says. Celia shakes her head in disgust. 'How dare he live the life of Riley while Imogen is in her grave. Does he even *care*?'

Her eyes fill with tears and I put my hand on her arm. 'He'll get his comeuppance,' I whisper. 'He *has* to.'

We watch silently as Fake Tamsin strolls over to Carl. He smiles tightly at her and scans the crowds. Then his face goes white. He's spotted Celia. She lifts her hand and waves at him. He blinks in shock, then turns away, smoothing his hand over his dark hair, clearly rattled.

Celia drains her glass and slams it on a nearby table. 'He's not going to get away with this.'

'No!' I say, but it's too late, she's striding over to Carl. He notices her approaching and panic fills his eyes. He looks around him, clearly searching for an exit. For a moment, I wonder if he might jump into the pool to escape the fireball that is Celia heading towards him. But instead, he takes a deep breath to compose himself and then fixes a smile on his face as Celia stands before him. I move closer, so I can hear. Half of me is filled with dread – I knew this would happen the moment I spotted Celia strolling towards the manor. But the other half is rather enjoying this.

'Hello Carl,' Celia says as she crosses her arms, and looks him up and down.

Fake Tamsin glares at Celia. 'Who's this?' she asks Carl.

'I have no idea,' Carl replies in a surprisingly calm voice. 'Do I know you?' he asks Celia. God, how easily he can lie.

'You know who I am,' Celia hisses. 'I'm your ex's best friend, Celia?'

Carl smiles, charm personified. 'I think you have me mistaken for someone else.'

'It's obvious Carl doesn't know who you are,' Fake Tamsin says, giving Celia a glacial look. Then she notices me watching, her face growing even colder.

'It's obvious he absolutely does,' Celia replies, matching Fake Tamsin's look with one as cold as ice. 'I wouldn't forget the face of the man who caused my best friend's death, would I?' She holds up her phone, showing him the photo from the party with Imogen. 'I mean, this is you right?'

Toby and Tilda raise their eyebrows as they look at the photo, and I smile to myself. What balls Celia has! I prefer a more discreet approach.

'That isn't Carl,' Fake Tamsin says, rolling her eyes. 'This is ludicrous! Who are you anyway? I don't recognise you. Are you from Easthaven? Only Easthaven people are invited.'

'I came with Liz,' Celia says, gesturing to me. *Oh no.* Guests turn to look at me and now I completely understand what people mean when they say they wish the ground could swallow them up whole. I wish the ground, the sea and the sky could swallow me up!

Why did Celia have to bring me into it?

Fake Tamsin tilts her head at me. 'Naughty post lady, I only invited Easthaven residents. This isn't a plus one, you know. And this certainly isn't a "plus one of your crazy friends"!' She laughs and Tilda laughs too, clearly delighting in this public humiliation of her garden invader. I feel my face turning to fire. 'In fact,' Fake Tamsin continues, taking in my uniform, 'are you *really* supposed to be attending parties while working?'

'She shouldn't really,' Tilda says. Toby frowns at his wife. I notice Carl is quiet all this time, deep in his own troubled thoughts judging from the look on his face.

'I just popped by in between delivering your post,' I say.

'And ended up stumbling into a party with free drink and food?' Fake Tamsin says. 'How convenient.'

Tilda smiles, moving closer to Fake Tamsin, two horrible women in cahoots. Toby shoots me a sympathetic look, but Tilda is still revelling in it all. I look around me. People are whispering as they stare at me, others laughing. Okay, she's being a bully now. All my anger at what she's done to my friend, the real Tamsin, builds up. I look at her, emboldened by that anger. 'And how convenient someone who purports to be an introvert is holding a party like this?' I gesture around me. 'Tamsin is an introvert, someone who shies away from gatherings, according to her website. And actually,' I say, putting my finger on my chin as I look at her, 'your hair, it's got a lot darker since I saw you a week ago, not to mention your dress sense has changed. In fact, you seem like a *whole* different person.' Everyone else looks confused by what I'm saying, but not Fake Tamsin, not Carl either.

Fake Tamsin sighs. 'Oh dear, our local post lady has clearly lost it.' She turns back to Tilda and Toby. 'Now, as I was saying . . .' And with that, she continues talking to them as though I'm not there.

'Wow, she really is some piece of work,' Celia says. 'Let's get out of here. Clearly those two scumbags aren't going to admit to anything.'

We walk into the manor. When we get to the hallway, it's empty. I peer towards the doors leading upstairs.

'What are you thinking?' Celia says, following my gaze. 'A little detective work?' I nod and she grins, linking her arm through mine. 'Let's do this!'

I hesitate. Do I really want to be doing this with Celia? She's not the most discreet of investigative companions. But then she *is* fun and she can keep a lookout. 'Come on then,' I say.

She grabs a bottle of Prosecco from a table as we pass and I think of that night when we did the same, twenty years ago. I shake the memories away and lead Celia up the stairs. As I walk up them, I imagine Tamsin doing the same at night, a chamomile tea in her hands to help her sleep. Where is she sleeping now? Is she even *sleeping*? I shudder as I reach the top of the stairs. There's a hallway here with a large arched window that looks out over the pool. I can see Douglas down there now, chatting up a busty blonde I don't recognise. We quickly duck out of the way of the crowds below and head to the first of six doors as I check behind me.

Still alone.

I peer towards the room where I know the library once was. I guess that would be the place to keep anything interesting as it was also used as a study. I'm not quite sure what I'm looking for though. Maybe some kind of proof the fake couple are transferring money from Real Tamsin's accounts because this is surely their motive, scamming Tamsin for her money?

Maybe I can find some clue to Tamsin's whereabouts too? I go into the library. It's huge, with shelves lining three of the walls and a large desk in the middle. All the same pieces of furniture that used to be here remain. I imagine they were once draped with the dust sheets that have been discarded to the side.

I quietly close the door behind me and watch as Celia walks around the room, drinking from the Prosecco bottle as she does. I wander around too, taking in the familiar antique mahogany desk and patterned chaise longue which sit by a window looking out to sea. Tamsin used to love sitting there, writing poetry as I read.

I pause as I notice there are two books of Tamsin's poetry strewn on the floor, the spines and pages bent. I shake my head and pick them up, smoothing the pages and placing them back on the shelves. Tamsin would never treat her books this way. I go to her desk. There's a small MacBook sitting closed on it and a framed photo of Tamsin with her mother from twenty years ago.

'If only it were a recent photo, I'd have proof this isn't Tamsin,' I say.

'You need to try to find out where she lived before,' Celia replies.

'All I know is she lives an hour from London; that really could be anywhere.'

Celia sighs. 'Very true. Did she mention any friends, other family?'

I shake my head as I pick the photo up. Tamsin's mother looks just as I remember her with short strawberry-blonde hair and a wide smile on her face. They're sitting at a table by the sea with a cake stand between them filled with sandwiches and pastries. I feel tears fill my eyes.

'I'll make sure I find her for you, Dorothy,' I whisper to the photo. I sigh and place the photo back down, searching the desk's drawers. But there's nothing there, just Tamsin's pretty notepads and pens. As I go to move away from the desk, my foot catches on a waste-paper basket and it topples over, its contents spilling to the floor. 'Bugger,' I say.

Celia walks over and we crouch down, picking up discarded receipts and wrappers and placing them back in the bin.

Then I pause. There's a photo among the rubbish and I realise with horror it's an old one Tamsin took with Gabe's camera of me and Gabe together in the cellar, right here at the manor at that party all those years ago. I lift it with trembling fingers. We're both holding champagne bottles. I look tanned, my eyes sparkling, my long dark hair to my shoulders. Gabe is so handsome next to me, peering down at me with a smile. I remember the photo being taken, Tamsin all excited about using a professional camera. But we never saw the photographic results because it was Gabe's camera.

I turn it around. On the back, in Gabe's distinctive flourish, are our initials. *G&L July 2002*. Had he given the photo to Tamsin and she'd kept it all these years?

'Who are they?' Celia asks, not recognising the young me. I find I don't want to answer. 'Liz?' Then she notices something else. 'Look.' She holds up a small envelope. 'Looks like it's addressed to Tamsin.'

'We should read it. It might be useful.'

She raises an eyebrow. 'Naughty postie.'

'I was a journalist once, remember?' I take the envelope from her and pull out the card that's inside. There's a local florist's name on it with a date – last Monday, the very day I last saw the real Tamsin – along with a small handwritten note.

Hi Tamsin, so good to talk on the phone last week. Hope today goes well, thought I'd send some flowers to brighten up the place. Lester. X

I think of what Douglas said about Lester having secrets. He didn't mention anything to me about chatting to Tamsin. In fact, he made out her arrival was a complete surprise! Is Lester involved somehow? Surely not!

'What the hell are you doing in here?' a voice booms from the hallway. We look up to see Fake Tamsin watching us from the doorway. I stuff the photo and note in my pocket then quickly stand up with Celia. 'Are you snooping?' Fake Tamsin asks, crossing her arms as she glares at us. 'I knew you wouldn't be able to resist coming here and looking around,' she says to me.

'We were trying to find the loo,' Celia lies as she hides the bottle of Prosecco behind her back. 'Come on, let's get out of here.' She grabs my arm and pulls me from the room, shoving past Fake Tamsin.

But before we reach the stairs, Fake Tamsin grabs my wrist, stopping me. 'You realise we're at war now, don't you?' she hisses.

'Wow, so dramatic,' Celia says. A waiter passes then with more Prosecco, so Celia walks off to grab some.

I hold Fake Tamsin's gaze. 'I know what you've done,' I hiss back. 'Where's Tamsin Lakewell, the *real* Tamsin? That's all I want, to find my friend.'

Fake Tamsin's laughter echoes around the landing. '*I'm* Tamsin, you idiot.'

'You're not,' I say. 'I know you're not.'

Fake Tamsin shakes her head. 'You are *pathetic*.'

'No, *you* are if you think you can get away with this.'

Fake Tamsin leans close to me, so close I can see the grains of loose powder on her skin. 'Watch your back, Lizbeth.' My legs go weak and I have to clutch on to the table.

Lizbeth. That's what Gabe used to call me. How can she possibly know? Surely it's no coincidence? I rush downstairs, desperate to get away, desperate to avoid the memories clashing against me like violent waves. The photo I found. And now this.

Lizbeth.

My pulse thumps painfully in my temples. Does she somehow know? Then it hits me: what if Tamsin told Carl everything? She implied he was her soulmate after all. And then Carl told his fellow con artist. Oh God. I look around me, the walls of the vast hallway pushing into me. I need to get out of here. But as I go to turn towards the front door, I notice people gathered by the edge of the cliff beyond the infinity pool, peering down at something below as gasps ring out among them.

A feeling of horror fills me and I find my feet moving towards the edge of the cliff as though hypnotised, heart pounding in fear. I push my way through the crowds and look down at the small curve of beach below, then stifle a cry. There's a body down there!

As I look down at the body, I realise with relief it's a man. I couldn't help but fear the worst until I saw it. That finally, horribly, the mystery of Tamsin's whereabouts had been solved, down there on the beach. But that relief is soon replaced by new terror as I realise the body is wearing very distinctive shoes: the red patent leather shoes Gabe used to wear. The body is dressed just like he usually did too, in tan chinos and a white shirt, the exact outfit he was wearing the last time I saw him all those years ago. And his hair, dark and thick.

I back away, putting my hand to my mouth to muffle a scream.

Chapter 12

As I look down at the body lying on the sand below, I rationalise with myself that of *course* it can't be Gabe's body down there! It's been twenty years. It horrifies me to think of it, but there would be nothing of him left, surely? I have to get away from here! As I leave the crowd, I bump into someone. I turn and see it's Fake Tamsin again, her eyes sparking with malice. 'Don't worry,' she whispers. 'It's just a mannequin. I bet it looks familiar though?' she asks me. I blink, unable to gather my thoughts to even know what to say. A mannequin? Why would a mannequin be down there? I look at Fake Tamsin. Did she orchestrate this? She leans close to me, her lips by my ear. 'I know what happened to Gabe, Lizbeth, and you're not going to get away with it, just as Tamsin hasn't.'

I look at her in horror. This isn't about money . . . it's about revenge!

◆　◆　◆

When I arrive at the sorting office half an hour later, I can only just about hold myself together. Does Fake Tamsin know Gabe somehow . . . and know what happened to him? Is that why Carl hooked up with Tamsin?

But what is it they have planned? If this is really about revenge, then what does it mean for Tamsin . . . and for me? Maybe I should call the police. But with what evidence? And I'd have to tell them what happened twenty years ago. The thought terrifies me, especially with the kids' custody hearing next week. It's the last thing I need. I need to just get home and think, really think. Tamsin is clearly in danger. I just need to hope she is, well yes, *alive* and being held somewhere so I have a chance of helping her.

When I step into the main sorting area, my manager Greg is waiting for me with a disappointed look on his face. I really don't need this. 'So sorry I'm late,' I say, trying to keep the tremble from my voice as I hurry towards my section. 'Just one of those rounds. I'll make sure I get out of your hair asap.'

'Will you come into my office?' he asks, face serious.

'Sure.' I follow Greg into his small office, watching as he closes the door and goes behind his desk.

'So, it was one of those rounds, was it?' he asks.

'Y-yep,' I reply hesitantly. What is he about to say?

'Do you mean the type of round where you get to sip Prosecco at a party?'

I go very still as he turns his monitor around so it's facing me. On the screen is a photo of me at the party earlier, a glass of Prosecco in my hand. I close my eyes. *Bugger.*

'I didn't drink the Prosecco,' I say. 'And I wasn't there long. I was delivering post and got invited in.' Another white lie. They're mounting up lately.

'Do you realise how bad this looks?' Greg says. 'In your uniform, holding a glass of Prosecco?'

'Who sent it to you?' I ask.

'It was sent to the whole management team, Liz, not just me.'

'Oh God,' I whisper. 'Who was it that sent it?' I ask again.

'You know I can't tell you that.'

I curl my fists. It's Fake Tamsin, it has to be! Is this what she has planned for me, destroying my life bit by bit? 'So what happens now?' I ask, pushing the anger down. It won't do me any good right now.

'I convinced them a verbal warning was all that's needed.'

I breathe a sigh of relief. 'Thank you, thank you *so* much.'

'I can't do this next time, though. So keep your nose clean, okay?'

'I promise.'

He lowers his voice, leaning close. 'You know how much heat I got for hiring you in the first place. I don't want what happened back in Manchester to happen here.'

I blink. 'Of course.'

As I walk out, dread fills me. If I lose my job, then I have no chance of keeping custody of the girls. I need to keep out of this.

When I get back home, I run over everything in my mind, writing everything I know down in my notepad. By the time the girls are back from school, I realise my best course of action might be to talk to Carl. Though he's charming and handsome as hell, he strikes me as a little weak. I noticed he seemed hesitant when Fake Tamsin was doing her reading the other day and something tells me he's in over his head. I make a plan to talk to Carl the next day, when I'm on my round . . . *carefully*. As I think that, my phone rings. I look down to see it's Scott. I take in a deep calming breath and answer it. He doesn't usually call so maybe it's important?

'I'm not happy about Ruby's latest TikTok video,' he says as soon as I answer. 'Have you seen it?'

I think back to her last video. 'The one about the teen girl in Chichester?'

'No, the one about the teen boy from Easthaven twenty years ago,' he says.

Gabe. Did she do a video about Gabe? 'I haven't seen it, no,' I say.

'I don't like the fact it's set in Easthaven. It makes her clearly findable.'

'I'll chat to her about it. Tell her to remove it.'

'You do that. Otherwise it's just another thing to add to my list of concerns.'

I shake my head. 'It's not just up to me to monitor her TikTok, Scott. Jesus.' I slam the phone down then quickly check Ruby's TikTok, watching the video Scott is referring to which was posted this morning. Ruby is standing against the backdrop of the sea, the manor above. I can see it's evening, the sun setting behind her. She did meet up with Eva last night so she must have done it then. It's filmed in her usual greyscale with only her vibrant hair coloured in.

'It's time to go back in time,' she says mysteriously, turning to look up at the manor. 'Twenty years ago to be exact, to this small seaside village where a novel-writing hottie known as Gabe Artaud went missing. No big deal, some might say. He was a summer visitor to the popular beachside location, like many others. But on the very night he was last seen, a fisherman saw a man of his description – tall, dark and handsome – standing right up there,' she says, pointing to the manor, 'at the edge of the cliff. A few moments later, a body was seen by the same fisherman, floating in the sea and never to be seen again. Was it Gabe's body? Certainly, no trace of this teen has been discovered since, dead nor alive. And the body in the ocean was never found. What happened to Gabe Artaud?'

She turns to the camera, eyes filled with drama. 'Twist alert! The real mystery though is who *is* the man claiming to be Gabe Artaud? I say *claiming* because while he told those who asked that he was the grandson of a local hotel owner, after this mystery teen's disappearance, the real grandson came forward to confirm the handsome, dark-haired stranger who had been seen around the village over that summer had been *pretending* to be the real Gabe Artaud. And when looking at photos of the *real* Gabe Artaud, you can see why: they can't be any more different.' A photo flashes up of the real Gabe, a spotty blond-haired young teen. 'Not exactly dark-haired and handsome, is he? In fact, this handsome mystery man was called Gavin Abraham. Not quite as posh a name, right? And he worked at the hotel as a porter for the summer until he was eventually caught stealing from guests' rooms and fired. Mystery deepens too: a search for Gavin Abraham shows there is no such person on official record and the references he gave the hotel were faked. So who even knows what this dude's real name is? And why did this missing teen pretend to be Gabe Artaud? Even more importantly, why did he suddenly go missing after being seen on a cliff? Did someone uncover his deceit and make sure he was gone . . . for good? But what makes this case even more interesting,' she says as the camera zooms in on the cliff edge, 'is that at a party earlier today, a mannequin was found on the beach below that cliff wearing the very same distinctive red shoes it was reported Gabe always wore. Is he coming back to haunt the village? Follow me if you don't already as I spend the next few weeks uncovering this mystery.'

I sit back, my hand on my mouth. Gabe – the Gabe I knew – wasn't the hotel owner's grandson, like he claimed to be? No wonder there wasn't a big drama after he went missing. I shake my head. Scott is right, this is *way* too close to home.

I run upstairs and knock on the door to the girls' room. 'Yeah?' Mia calls out.

'Can I come in?'

'Yep.'

I walk in to see Ruby on her bed with her headphones on, her computer on her lap. Mia is curled up on her side, reading a book.

'Mia, darling, can you go and get all the knives and forks and stuff ready for dinner,' I say. 'I want a quick chat with Ruby.'

Mia sighs and swings her legs off the bed, heading outside.

I go to Ruby, who hasn't even noticed me yet, and wave in front of her face. She removes one side of her headphones. 'Yeah?'

'Can we have a chat?'

She frowns. 'Sure.'

'Your dad just called about your latest video. We've both agreed we want you to take it down. It's too close to home.'

'You're kidding, right? It's already super-popular.'

'It outs where you live, Ruby.'

'No it doesn't. As far as people are concerned, I've just visited at the weekend.'

'No arguments, Ruby, it's coming down.'

She examines my face. 'What is it about you and this Gabe guy?'

I clench and unclench my fists. 'I'm serious, Ruby, do not get involved with this case. It's nothing. He just left town, no big deal.'

She raises an eyebrow. 'Nothing, hey? Then why are you reacting like this?'

I take in some deep, low breaths. 'You know I don't interfere with your TikTok stuff. But this time, I'm asking – no, *begging*. Do not *cover* this case.'

Ruby is quiet then she nods. 'Sure, Mum.'

I breathe a sigh of relief. 'Good.'

Then I walk from the room, aware of Ruby's eyes on me. I just hope she listens to me. If she's anything like I was at her age when I got my teeth into a story, she won't.

◆ ◆ ◆

As I sort the post the next day, I notice there are three letters for Carl including one that requires a signature. Good, it'll give me an excuse to go to the manor and talk to him. I finish my round quickly, passing people talking about that damn mannequin. It seems Ruby's TikTok is compounding the gossip even more, despite it being taken down. It was up long enough for local teens to see it and it feels like all I hear as I do my round is his name: *Gabe, Gabe, Gabe.* When I get to the manor, my stomach is fizzing with nerves. I see Carl instantly, sitting on a bench in the garden, peering through to the hallway inside. He looks exhausted, dark circles under his eyes, more stubble on his cheeks. I even think he's dressed in the same suit from the luncheon yesterday: a more wrinkled, dirty version. *That's strange.* He looks up, noticing me.

'I have a letter for you to sign for,' I call through the bars of the gate.

He stands up and approaches, face still clouded over. 'Interesting friends you have,' he says as I pass him the signature device.

'You mean Celia?'

'Was that her name?' he says casually. 'I really have no idea what she was talking about, you know.'

I sigh. 'Carl, drop the act. I know you know her . . . and I know you were with Imogen. I've seen photos of you with her at a party. There's no mistaking it's you.'

He doesn't look at me, instead pretends to focus on the device he's holding. But I see from the way his jaw tenses that he's struggling to figure out what to say next. Finally, he regards me, his deep blue eyes sad. 'Actually, could you spare a few minutes? Maybe you can come in and we can talk?'

I look around me. Is it really a good idea to go into the manor with this man? I cross my arms, shaking my head. 'I'd rather stay out here in the open, thanks.'

He sighs, raking his fingers through his dark hair. 'Fine. Look, I know you and Tamsin were great friends all those years ago. But she isn't the same girl you know.'

'*That's* an understatement,' I say with a bitter laugh. 'I know that woman you're with isn't the real Tamsin Lakewell, she's pretty much admitted that herself.' His eyes widen. I can see this is a surprise to him. Clearly he doesn't realise how overt she's been with me. 'She's playing a game, Carl, clearly not just with me either. Didn't you think that mannequin was odd?'

He keeps his gaze steady and I can't tell if he knows why it's so important.

'Maybe it's some kind of scam you're both up to,' I continue, 'I don't know. What I do know is the real Tamsin is in danger.'

He blinks, then readjusts his face, shaking his head. 'The *real* Tamsin. Can you hear yourself?'

'Can *you* hear yourself?' I say, grabbing the gate's bars. 'Please, Carl. I know you know more than you're letting on. What was it you wanted to talk to me about?'

His face hardens. 'If you continue to harass us like this, I will need to call the police.'

'Go ahead, I'm sure they'll be very interested in your past.'

He glares at me and thrusts the device into my hands. 'And your past too from what I've heard.' Then he walks down the garden and into the manor, slamming the door behind him.

Well, that went well. I sigh and walk away. Clearly I'm not going to get anything out of him. When I'm halfway down the road, I realise I only delivered the letter to Carl that needed signing. I still have two undelivered letters for him in my bag. I take them out then pause. It only takes a moment to decide: I place the letters back in the bag and walk away.

Time to get even more serious.

◆ ◆ ◆

As I walk up the path to my house with those two letters in my bag, I remember how I'd reacted to Douglas when he asked me to hide Lester's letters: I have a moral compass.

Have I? I know what I'm about to do is wrong. In fact, it could be against the law. But then, according to the Postal Services Act 2000, it would only be an offence to open someone else's mail 'without reasonable excuse' or if I 'intend to act to another's detriment'. Nobody could deny I absolutely *do* have a reasonable excuse, a woman's in danger. I'm doing the opposite of acting to another's detriment, I'm acting to help someone! I quickly start heating up my mother's soup, then switch the kettle on, tapping my fingers against the counter impatiently as I stare at the two letters for Carl. As the kettle's steaming, I hold the small letter over the vapour, quickly opening it. I know how to do this; after all, I've done it before.

The first looks like a flyer from the grief group counselling the real Tamsin mentioned, run by Sable & Sons Funeral Directors, the directors I think Tamsin used for her mother's funeral. I sigh. Not exactly evidence. I put it aside and pick the other one up and steam that open. Though it's not exactly evidence either, it *is* interesting. It's an invoice from a groundworks company for the bulldozing of the manor in two days' time. I frown. It's what I've wanted for the past twenty years but now the time has come, I don't know how I feel. Yes, there were awful memories within those walls but there were so many wonderful ones too. And is this what the real Tamsin would want?

The sooner I find her, the better.

I take a quick photo of the letters with my phone in case I need to refer back to them. Then I carefully seal them shut again. There, it's as though nothing ever happened to them.

When I take my mother's tray up, she looks even angrier than usual.

'We got a letter today,' she huffs.

'What letter? I deliver our post, there isn't anything for us today.'

She gestures towards an open letter on the side. 'Carer brought it up, was posted through the letterbox this morning.'

I go to it, frowning. The envelope is addressed to The Residents. I unfold the letter and read it.

This Notice is to inform you that beginning on July 5th the monthly rent for the house you currently occupy, No 8, Regal Gardens, Easthaven will be increased to £1,200 per month. This rental payment is due on or before the 5th day of each month.

If you wish to continue your tenancy, the new monthly rental payment of £1,200 is required by July 5th. Please be advised that all other terms of your original rental agreement remain in effect.

Please sign the Notice below, indicating your agreement and continued tenancy or indicating your disagreement and subsequent termination of tenancy.

Thank you. We appreciate your continued tenancy.

Sincerely,

Douglas Gold

'That's a £400 increase,' I say in disbelief. 'He can't do this!'

'Well, he is doing it, isn't he?' my mother snaps.

'No,' I say, shaking my head. 'I'm sure this is illegal. You'll – you'll have to get a lawyer to write a letter.'

My mother laughs bitterly. 'Which will cost money we don't have.'

I peer out of the window towards the Golds' villa. Douglas is doing this on purpose. He must have discovered I delivered Lester's letter to him. I shove the letter into my pocket and march out of the house. He can't get away with this!

When I get to the promenade, I notice four local women gathered at the small noticeboard by the patisserie, shaking their heads as they look at something. One of them is Tilda Beashell. As I rush past, she looks up, a cruel smile spreading over her face. 'Well, speak of the devil,' she says loudly.

I pause and look over. 'Excuse me?'

'Come and look,' she says, gesturing to the noticeboard.

I walk over with trepidation, aware of the cold looks being directed my way. I wouldn't expect anything less of Tilda, but the other three women she's with, they're usually so friendly with me on my round. 'What's going on?' I ask, noticing Lester is peering out with curiosity from the patisserie too.

Tilda steps out of the way so I can have a look. I sigh as I take in what looks like several letters pinned to the noticeboard with a photo in the middle: the same photo I took from Tamsin's bin of me and Gabe in her cellar. I'd placed it in my notepad. Then my stomach plummets when I realise what the notes really are.

Pages ripped from my notepad.

Chapter 13

My knees weaken. How the hell did they get there?

'21st April, 9.45 a.m.,' Tilda reads out in a loud voice. 'Anya & Keir Throwley arguing in garden.' I follow her gaze towards Anya who is among the four women, looking at me in disgust. 'There's one about you here, Lester!' Tilda calls through to him. '18th May. 12.05 p.m. Lester seems interested in me. Asked me to luncheon. Not sure what to think,' she reads out.

I feel heat work its way all over my face as Lester frowns in the distance. I'm silent. What can I say? I never dreamed people would see these. And now I read them in black and white, see the looks on people's faces, I realise how bad it must seem. But the intention was always good! And then there's the photo of me and Gabe, right there for all to see. I'd slipped the photo into the notepad. How had it gone missing, I was only using it this morning? I must have dropped it during my round.

'Did you do this?' I ask Tilda.

'Of course not!' she huffs back. 'I just found them up here. There are dozens of them, one of top of the other.' She lifts the notes up to show that she's right, there *are* even more. 'Have you been *stalking* us, Liz?' she asks, her expression hard.

This can't be happening. Who would do this? Who would go to these lengths?

What a stupid question! Of course it's Fake Tamsin! Or Douglas Gold. Surely they're in cahoots with one another now? And if it is her, that means she has all the thoughts I scribbled down about her little deception too.

'Suddenly gone very quiet, hasn't she?' Tilda says.

Anger starts to take over the humiliation as I reach for the notes, yanking them all down from the noticeboard and shoving them into my bag. From what I can see, there's nothing about my investigations into Tamsin. Then I reach for the photo of Gabe but Tilda stops me.

'Wait, let me see this properly,' she says, snatching it from my hand. 'That's the poor boy that went missing all those years back. The one who *pretended* to be Gabe Artaud, according to your daughter's TikTok?'

Lester comes out of the patisserie then. 'Fancy a cuppa?' he asks.

I think about saying no. But I really need a friend right now. 'Yes, please.'

I follow him into the patisserie. 'You can hold the fort for a bit, right?' he asks Eva. She nods, watching me with worried eyes as Lester takes me upstairs to their flat. It's larger than I thought, with huge windows looking out to the sea. I take a seat on a large comfy sofa and promptly burst into tears. Lester looks shocked and sits beside me, pulling me into his arms, his dreadlocks brushing against my shoulder. 'Liz, what's wrong?'

'I'm so humiliated, all my notes for everyone to see. Plus that note I wrote about you . . .'

'Hey, hey, it's fine, really.' He tilts my chin up so I can look at him through my tear-drenched eyelashes. 'No harm done.'

'There is. Of course there is. *Everything* is going wrong!'

'What's going on, Liz? You haven't been yourself lately.'

I look up into his blue eyes and realise I so desperately want to tell him. But how can I trust him? I wipe away my tears. 'It's nothing.'

'Clearly it isn't.'

'I just – I don't know if I can trust you, Lester.'

He looks at me in surprise. 'How can you say that?'

'You spoke with Tamsin on the phone the week before she moved here and yet you acted like you were surprised she was back when I saw you last Monday.'

He blinks, clearly surprised I know this. 'It's no big deal.'

'Really?' I ask, scrutinising his face.

He sighs. 'Fine. You know her family used to own this building?' he says, gesturing around him.

'I didn't know.'

'Well, they did. Then Douglas's dad took it over when I was a kid. My mum used to say his father won it during a poker game with Tamsin's father. Now we rent the unit off Douglas; he's been threatening to sell it. So I wanted to check with Tamsin's mother if she thought the way her husband passed over the deeds was legit. Maybe if it could return to the Lakewell estate, we would be able to keep the place.' He sighs. 'Desperate measures. Anyway, when I managed to track Mrs Lakewell down, I learnt she'd passed away. Tamsin called me to explain and we agreed we'd meet up to chat about it all once she found any documents.'

'And yet you didn't tell me all this?'

He shrugs. 'I didn't think I needed to. It's no big deal. I did try to talk to Tamsin about it the other day actually but she didn't seem to have a clue what I was going on about.' He looks into my eyes. 'Do you trust me now?'

Can I? I realise then I simply have to. Things feel more and more slippery and I need as many people on my side as I can get. 'Yes,' I say.

'So tell me, what the hell is going on with you? I know it's just more than the custody hearing.' I take a deep breath, then tell him as much as I can . . . apart from the bit about Gabe. After, he sits back on the sofa beside me. 'Wow. So you think Carl and Fake Tamsin are trying to con the real Tamsin out of money?'

'Yeah.'

'And you haven't called the police yet?' I shake my head. 'Liz, you really need to.'

'But I don't have any evidence!'

'You have to, Liz. She's your friend. I remember how close you both were, I used to watch you during my paper round, you know, through the bars of the gate as you read to each other.'

I look at him in surprise. 'Really?'

He laughs. 'Sorry, that makes me sound like a stalker. I mean, I only caught glimpses of you both.' His face darkens. 'And the guy you used to hang out with. The missing dude, the one who called himself Gabe, right? It worried me, you hanging out with him. Guys like that, you can tell a mile away they're fakes.'

'I wish you'd told me and Tamsin; it would have saved us a whole load of heartache.'

His face darkens even more. 'What did he do to you?'

I look down at my hands. 'It was a long time ago. Best to leave it in the past.' But as I say that, my heart clenches. The past is *impossible* to leave behind.

Chapter 14

20 Years Ago

The first time I see Tamsin and Gabe after he moves into the manor is the Monday afternoon after the luncheon. I worry they will be different with one another. But the truth is, nothing is different. In fact, Gabe messages me to meet up the next day, just us two, and it's like normal, the two of us talking and kissing on the beach. I still sometimes can't believe he prefers me to Tamsin. But then are Gabe and I really so different? Sure, he might be heir to a hotel empire but the way his grandfather treats him, he might as well be as poor as me. In fact, *I'm* better off. At least I have a roof over my head.

As we meet up more often over the next two weeks, he begins to open up to me, telling me about his family back in London. Turns out he has four younger brothers and a sister.

'My little sister Gwen is awesome, seriously,' he says. 'You'd get on. She's strong and plucky like you. In fact, she got told off for impersonating a teacher the other month.'

'*I* wouldn't do that!'

'Yeah, you're like a tame version of her.'

'Why aren't they here with you?'

'I'm the only one old enough to get involved in the family business, according to my father.'

'What's your father like?'

'A mini version of my grandfather.'

I grimace. 'Sorry about that.' I lean back against his chest. I like doing that as I can hear his heartbeat as he plays with my hair. 'So what are you planning to do after the summer?' I ask carefully. I'm conscious it's August now and soon the summer will be over.

He shrugs. 'Maybe I'll stay here.'

I'm pleased he can't hear my heartbeat as it goes wild at the thought of him staying. 'Do you think Dorothy will let you stay at the manor?'

'I wouldn't want to. I'd rather get a job, find a small place. I've always wanted to live by the sea. Plus I get to see you,' he adds, kissing the top of my head. I feel like crying tears of joy when I hear him say that.

But I manage to control myself. 'I'd like that,' I say, tracing my finger down a vein in his hand. 'You can write your novel too, it's so inspiring by the sea.'

'Yeah, imagine us with a little flat overlooking the sea, both writing away.'

I can't help it, I'm too excited to contain myself as I kneel and look at him, my hands on his shoulders. 'Are you serious? You'd want to live with me someday?'

'Of course I am.'

'Oh my God, I love you!' It just pops out. It's ridiculous really, I've only known him a month. But it's what I feel, truly, madly, deeply.

He doesn't say anything at first and I want to bury my head in the sand. But then he tilts my chin up and looks into my eyes. 'I love you too, Lizbeth.'

The next two weeks are bliss. We talk more about the little flat we'll own one day, even go to visit a few that are up for sale, posing as a young couple interested in buying them. We tell each other we love one another more and more. Then one warm night beneath the cover of darkness, tucked away beneath a craggy remote rock, I lose my virginity to Gabe, sealing our love and our future. As I lie with him after on the blanket he's laid out for us, I broach the subject of telling Tamsin about us.

'She'll find out eventually,' I say.

He frowns. 'I don't know. I feel like it'll jinx things.'

I can't help but wonder why he's so reluctant to tell Tamsin. Maybe he's right, maybe telling her would jinx things? It all feels so precious and, because of that, maybe fragile too. We're in our own little world when we're together, not a soul but us knowing about our love. Telling Tamsin would change that. But she does have to know. She's my friend! It's bad enough I've kept it from her this long.

I laugh. 'Come on, Gabe. She has to find out eventually!'

'Fine. But let's not do it when we see her tomorrow as Dorothy's staying at a friend's house and Tamsin might want to chat to her mum after. Let's wait until the weekend when Dorothy is there.'

'Okay, that makes sense.'

The next afternoon, while Tamsin and I are swimming, Gabe says he's too hot so heads inside to cool down. But when he still hasn't returned after half an hour, I go to look for him. As I walk across the hallway, I notice the cellar door is slightly ajar. That's where he must be! I decide to go down there, my tummy shivering in anticipation. It is *so* difficult being with him and not being able to kiss him, to touch him. I sneak through the door, quietly walking downstairs in the hope of surprising him. As I approach the bottom of the stairs, I see him standing at the side of the room with his back to me. I go to step in, then pause as I realise the safe is open . . . and Gabe is placing Tamsin's grandmother's amazing ring into his rucksack.

Is he stealing it? I quickly hide in the darkness of the stairwell, heart thumping as I continue watching him in horror as he pulls another ring that looks exactly the same as Tamsin's grandmother's from his rucksack and places it in the velvet box within the safe. My heartbeat hammers. This is all planned, he even got a replica made. My head begins to spin and I suddenly feel sick. I put my hand to my mouth and quietly tiptoe back upstairs, rushing to the downstairs bathroom to throw up in the toilet.

What the hell did I just see? Gabe, stealing a ring worth hundreds of thousands of pounds from my friend.

He's desperate, a small voice inside says. *He's been abandoned by his grandfather, made homeless!* But no, this isn't him stealing an old heirloom clock to pawn at a local shop to pay for food. This is huge. This is hundreds of thousands of pounds! My head pounds with a quickly evolving headache and my heart seems to pulse in time with it. I gulp in deep breaths, trying to calm myself. Maybe this is to do with the flat we talked about? It could cost hundreds of thousands of pounds to buy one outright in Easthaven.

Still, even if he was doing it for us, it's *wrong*. He has deceived my best friend, taken her future engagement ring away, an important heirloom she clearly adores judging from the way she showed it to us with pride. Even worse, it's something passed down the generations that her late father hoped she would one day wear. The Gabe I know surely wouldn't be so cruel. But just how well do I know him? Not really.

I put my head in my hands and sob. I have to tell Tamsin. I have to. I take a deep breath and check my face in the mirror. Yep, I look like I've just had my heart ripped out and torn to pieces. I let myself out of the bathroom and pause by the cellar door. Yep, I can still hear Gabe down there, probably trying to steal a few more heirlooms while he has the chance. I purse my lips and shake my head, before quietly making my way back outside to find Tamsin reading by the pool.

When she sees me, she knows instantly something is wrong. 'My God, what's wrong?' she asks me.

I open my mouth to tell her, then pause. Though I know in my heart I have to tell her, it still feels like such a betrayal of trust towards the boy I've fallen for. But not telling my best friend I just caught someone stealing something so precious to her is surely a worse betrayal of trust?

'*Tell* me, Liz, what on earth is wrong?' Tamsin asks.

'I – I just caught Gabe stealing the purple carbuncle ring,' I stammer, still reeling from the awfulness of it.

Tamsin sits up with a start, her book falling from her grasp. 'No, surely not.'

'Yes, honestly Tamsin, he's doing it right now.'

She follows my gaze inside towards the cellar door, eyes filling with tears. 'Are you *sure* that's what you saw?'

I nod. 'I saw it with my own eyes. He took your grandmother's ring from the safe then replaced it with a replica. He – he must have memorised the code when you showed us the ring at the luncheon the other week.'

Tamsin swings her legs off the sun lounger and stands up, pacing back and forth by the pool as she shakes her head. 'He's been using me all along.'

'I'm so sorry, Tamsin. I know he's your friend.'

'Friend?' She stops walking and looks at me, tears falling down her cheeks. 'He's more than a friend. He told me he loves me!'

The whole world seems to stop turning then. I stagger backwards, as though Tamsin has actually hit me. 'He – he told you he loves you?'

Tamsin rushes forward and grasps my hands. 'I'm so sorry, Liz, we've been seeing each ever since we had that chat at the luncheon.

I swear I was going to tell you! In fact, Gabe and I agreed we would tell you this weekend.'

My legs fail me and I collapse to the ground. Tamsin looks alarmed, kneeling with me as she pulls me into her arms. 'Liz, oh my God, Liz, I'm so sorry. I didn't realise it would hurt you this much. I know you like him, I can see that, but the attraction between Gabe and me—'

'You don't get it!' I scream at her. 'I've been seeing him too. I – I *love* him too.'

All the colour drains from her face. 'What?'

'That night his grandfather beat him up, we – we kissed. We've been seeing each other ever since.'

Tamsin's green eyes fill with hate. 'The bastard! He's been using us *both* just to steal from me.'

I hang my head. The pain is unbearable. 'I – I can't believe it. I just *can't* believe it.'

'Believe it. Men are bastards. Mum always says it, even Dad cheated on her but she forgave him. We *have* to confront him. Both of us.' She stands up, fists clenching and unclenching. I look up at her, at the way the setting sun turns her hair to fire. She looks like Boudicca or a warrior Viking woman about to go to battle. And yet I feel like one of the poor villages they have raided and pulled apart. 'Get *up*, Liz!'

I allow her to pull me up. I allow her to wipe my tears away. But all the time, I just want to wade into the sea below and never come back. *Anything* but feel this pain I'm feeling. Gabe has been lying to me this whole time. Playing us off against each other.

I follow Tamsin inside, my whole body trembling. Tamsin is trembling too, I can see it as she opens the cellar door, her pale hand shaking on the doorknob. But the look on her face shows me it isn't heartbreak that makes her tremble so. It's anger. Pure unadulterated anger. If anger is her first reaction, then surely she doesn't love him like I do? And what about him? Does he genuinely love her? As he kissed her neck and whispered in her ear, were his words genuine? The thought makes me feel sick again and it takes all my strength not to throw up right there and then.

We walk quietly down the stairs, like two little mice. When we get to the room, Gabe is zipping up his rucksack. As I look at him, it feels like my insides are collapsing and I need to lean against the wall to stop myself from falling again.

So this is what heartbreak feels like, a little voice whispers inside.

And now we're going to confront the boy who has broken my heart.

Chapter 15

Now

'So, what did the Gabe Artaud impersonator do?' Lester asks me.

'We caught him stealing Tamsin's family heirlooms.'

'No way! What a bastard,' Lester says, shaking his head. 'I knew he was a slimy so-and-so the first time I saw him at the luncheon.'

I look at my watch, not wanting to talk of the boy who broke my heart. 'I really must go,' I say as I stand. 'I have to talk to Douglas Gold. You know he's put up my mother's rent?'

'You're kidding? That man.'

'Yep. I better go. But it's been good to talk.'

'Any time.'

As I walk to the Golds' villa, I try to ignore the dark looks I get. When I get there, I see Aubrey taking out the rubbish, his face bruised and pale. 'Aren't you back at school yet?' I say through the gate.

'Went back for a day. Got into a fight. Got suspended again.'

'Oh. You're okay though, right?' I ask, taking in his bruises. He nods, avoiding my gaze. 'Is your dad in?' I ask.

'Yeah.'

'Can you get him for me?'

He frowns. 'Why?'

'I just need to talk to him.' I lean closer, examining the bruises on his face. They look fresh. 'Are you *sure* you're okay? You know if you need to chat . . .'

He swallows and for a moment I think he might confide in me. But then he sighs, raking his fingers through his auburn hair. 'I'm fine, really. But . . . it's nice of you to ask. Ruby says you're kind like that.' I feel a sense of pride at my daughter telling him that. 'I better get my dad,' he says. I watch as he strolls inside. He doesn't seem like a happy kid. Interesting how you can have one of the biggest houses in town but still be unhappy. My girls might live in a house with damp, as Scott pointed out, but they're happy.

When Aubrey comes out, Douglas is with him, a huge smile on his smug face. Aubrey goes to sit on a swing chair nearby, watching us.

'Liz, what a lovely surprise!' Douglas says as he walks down his drive towards me.

I hold his letter through the gate's bars. 'Hardly a surprise considering you've increased our rent.'

Aubrey's brow creases.

'Ah, yes, of course,' Douglas says. 'Rents have to go up, my dear. How else am I supposed to survive?'

I laugh as I look at his villa. 'Survive? Yes, you're clearly struggling, aren't you? You can't do this, you know. I have rights. Four hundred pounds extra is excessive.'

'Your mother agreed to a month-by-month contract when we renegotiated it a while back,' he says. 'I've given her over a month's notice. If she can't afford it, then I'm sure there are plenty of other houses out there for you all. Maybe not in Easthaven though, not after all those *notes* you wrote about the residents,' he adds in a loud booming voice, 'there's a lot of anger directed towards you right now; I doubt anyone will want to rent out a place to you.'

I clench my fists. 'I thought I dropped my notepad but maybe it was stolen? Maybe *you* were the one who stole it? I saw how cosy you were with the couple next door.'

Douglas's face hardens and he moves closer to the gates. 'I am not a petty thief. I told you there would be consequences if you reneged on our agreement.'

'You're not just punishing me,' I hiss, 'you're punishing my family.'

Aubrey looks even more upset as he glares at his dad.

'No, *you* are with your disobedience and your nosiness,' Douglas hisses back at me. 'In fact, your daughter takes after you, doesn't she? We've all seen her TikTok video she put up before it was taken down. How do you feel about her digging into the case of that missing boy twenty years ago?' he asks knowingly. He gives me a smug look then turns on his heel, going back inside his villa. I go to walk away but then hear Aubrey calling my name. I turn back to see him walking quickly towards me. His eyes are flashing with anger. He clearly despises the way his dad is.

'There's something I forgot to mention about that argument I overheard next door,' he whispers, peering over his shoulder to make sure his dad is back inside.

'What is it, Aubrey?'

'There was screaming. Like, really feral kind of screaming.' I put my hand to my mouth. 'I heard things breaking too,' he continues, 'like things were being thrown around.'

'Why didn't you call the police?'

He drops his gaze. 'Dad always says you shouldn't get involved in people's business. He would have bollocked me.'

'You know what?' I say, clutching on to the gate as I look at him. 'My mother says the same. But we don't always have to listen to them, do we?' He shakes his head. 'You still have the chance to talk to the police now,' I say. 'Tell them what you heard.'

His fingers flicker over the bruise beneath his eye. 'No, I – I can't. Dad would . . . he wouldn't be happy. I just wanted you to know, that's all.' He peers behind him again, seeing his dad watching us. 'I better get back.'

'Okay Aubrey, thank you. And remember, I'm here if you need me.'

He nods and quickly strides inside. I take a moment to think about what he said. This argument wasn't just about raised voices. Something awful happened that night. I wrap my arms around myself as I look towards the manor.

'Where are you, Tamsin?' I whisper.

As I do, my phone rings. I pull it from my pocket to see it's a withheld number. I put the phone to my ear as I start walking back down the road. 'Hello?

'Hello, is this Elizabeth Barrowman?' a deep baritone male voice asks.

'Yes, it is. How can I help?'

'It's Detective Colin Clarke from Belgravia Police Station in London. Have you got a moment to chat?'

I stop walking, heart pounding. The last time I spoke to a detective was last year, after all the drama. I feel the same sense of panic I'd endured then. 'Of course,' I say. 'What's it about?'

'Imogen Grayson.'

I feel a sense of relief. This must be the detective Celia's been talking to. She must have given him my number; I know she's been updating him. But then I *had* asked her not to get me involved. Still, it saves me having the nerve-wracking job of going to the police myself now they've come to me instead. I quickly hurry down the road and sit on one of the benches overlooking the sea.

A hard wind whips my short hair around my face, and I jog my foot up and down, wishing I hadn't given up smoking all those years back.

'I'm calling because we've had a couple of calls from the friends of a woman I believe you know, Tamsin Lakewell?' he says. 'Celia Pinks mentioned her name to me and it's taken a couple of days to do a search and discover the calls her friends made.'

'Why have they called?' I ask, feeling a sense of dread.

'They are concerned as she didn't turn up for a memorial that was arranged in her mother's name at the weekend. They're aware she is staying in Easthaven at her mother's old property but they mentioned she hasn't been in touch with them since the second day of her arrival. Apparently, it's highly unusual as they have a WhatsApp group she contributes to daily. When they try to call her mobile phone as well, it seems to have been switched off. Celia mentioned you have concerns too?'

'That's right. In fact, I was going to call you guys about it today. I'm really concerned about her.'

'Yes, Celia explained you have an interesting theory, that Tamsin Lakewell has been replaced by a new woman pretending to be her?'

I sigh. 'I realise how outlandish it must seem, but the woman who's impersonating her has pretty much admitted it.'

'She has?'

I tell him about our conversations, missing out the part about Gabe.

'Interesting,' he says afterwards. 'So where do you think your friend is now?'

'Honestly? I'm worried they're holding her somewhere against her will.'

There's a pause. 'Do you have any evidence of this?'

'Not really. The son of a neighbour said he overheard an argument. He said it sounded violent, things being broken and screams. He saw another woman there too.'

'Which neighbour is this, then?'

I hesitate. Do I really want Aubrey dragged into this? But how will it look to the detective if I refuse to say who he is?

'Aubrey Gold,' I say reluctantly. 'He's the son of the Golds who live in the villa next to Lakewell Manor.'

'Hmmmmm. And this is a large manor that sits at the top of the cliff, am I right?'

'That's right.'

The detective is quiet for a few moments. 'I looked it up. Quite the history that place has, with rumours of a young man's body being seen in the waves below twenty years ago?'

I clutch the phone tight against my ear. Why would he bring that up? Then a thought occurs to me. I've never met this detective. I just had a call from him, out of the blue. Then something else occurs to me.

'How do I even know you're a police officer?' I ask.

'I can assure you I am.'

'Really?

He laughs. 'What are you talking about?'

'You could be pretending to be a police officer to get information from me.'

There's a sigh. 'Call Belgravia Police Station, the number's readily available online. Ask to be put through to me.'

I frown. Maybe he is a police officer. God, this is going to make me look even more crazy, but what if my instincts are correct? 'Fine, I'll do it now.'

I put the phone down and google the number, feeling less and less sure about my suspicions as I do. When I call it, I ask to speak to Detective Clarke. His phone rings and he answers quickly.

'Believe me now?' he asks.

'Yes, sorry.' This isn't going to look good. 'So what's next? I am really worried about Tamsin. Will you come and question Carl and the other woman now?'

'That's the plan. I just have a caseload from hell at the moment.'

I go to protest, but then bite my lip. He's right. His hands are tied. Plus I've already embarrassed myself with him. 'Fine, thank you,' I say reluctantly.

I end the call and sigh. At least this detective is on it. But it doesn't sound like a huge priority.

Benches are dotted at intervals down the beach, painted in matching pastel colours of the cottages above. It's quiet at this time of day, kids at school, most people at work. Young mothers walk by with pre-school children and babies though, and the odd elderly couple. Hazy grey clouds hover above, reflecting my mood.

What am I going to do?

I look at the sea, hoping it might be able to give me some answers. But the waves seem choppy and all I can imagine is Tamsin's body being turned over among them. That's the image that haunts my dreams that night.

When I do my round the next morning, I feel like a zombie, having barely got any sleep. Most of the people on my round seem to have heard about my notes too, giving me filthy looks. But that doesn't seem important any more. *Tamsin* is important. I wish the detective had shown a little more urgency. It feels like every second counts now. What if Tamsin got hurt during the argument Aubrey overheard? Somebody must have got hurt with that 'feral screaming' and all that banging and crashing. What if she's being held somewhere, badly hurt, hovering at the edge of death? I shake my head. I have to trust the police will deal with this. I've done all I can! I need to focus on the custody hearing next week. That's what's really important.

When I reach the promenade, I see Tilda at the noticeboard again. My stomach drops. Surely there aren't more pages from my notepad? I walk over and am relieved to see it's not notes, it's just some poster. But as I draw closer, I realise it's a poster with Gabe's picture on it.

Chapter 16

I stare at the poster. The photo on it is a close-up, taken from the one I'd found in Tamsin's office and pinned up here. Tilda must have taken a photo with her phone before I yanked it off the notice-board. Printed on the top in red capital letters is JUSTICE FOR MISSING TEEN. Then below his photo, more words:

As seen on TikTok!

This young man was one of the many young people to visit Easthaven for the summer twenty years ago, hoping to be inspired by the views to write the novel he was always dreaming of finishing. But then one day, he went missing, the body of a young man of exactly his description seen falling from the cliff by Lakewell Manor, never to be sighted again. All enquiries by the police ran cold due to the fact the very same boy lied about his identity. Does that mean he deserved to go missing without a trace though? Now we, the residents of Easthaven, want justice for this young man. Were you a resident of Easthaven in the summer of 2002? Did you witness anything unusual? Call this number or email the address below to report your information.

'Why are you doing this?' I ask in a trembling voice. 'Did Fake – I mean, *Tamsin* put you up to this?'

'Tamsin and I are working on this together,' Tilda says. 'We just feel it's so very sad the mystery was never solved.'

'What's this to you, Tilda?'

'What's in this for me?' She gives me a look of disapproval. 'I have two teenage sons, Liz, as you well know. This strikes a chord.'

'Twenty years later?'

'Why are you interrogating poor Tilda?' a voice says. I turn to see Fake Tamsin approaching. '*You* should be the one being interrogated, Liz. You're the one who knew this poor, darling young man.'

I open my mouth and close it. What the hell am I supposed to say?

'Yes, you mentioned that, Tamsin,' Tilda says, crossing her arms as she glares at me.

'Did *Tamsin* also mention she knew this young man?' I say. If this woman wants to take on Tamsin's identity, then she needs to take on her past too.

'Tamsin did mention that, yes,' Tilda said. 'She also said you were rather jealous of her and the young man's closeness.'

My face flushes as I glare at Fake Tamsin. I can see what she's doing, trying to pin this solely on me.

A couple walk over, reading the poster. As Tilda explains the case to them, I go up to Fake Tamsin.

'I can see what you're doing. You knew Gabe, didn't you? Or the man who called himself Gabe, anyway.'

She doesn't answer, just keeps her cold stare on me. If she does know him, how? Tamsin and I barely knew anything of Gabe, his lies and deceit meaning everything we thought we knew about him was wrong, not least his name. All the people of Easthaven knew was that he was the handsome boy who frequented the cafe all summer, pretending to be the son of a local hotelier. Then he mysteriously disappeared.

'Is that what this is about, revenge?' I ask in a trembling voice.

'Revenge for what exactly, Liz?'

I step closer, getting right in her face. 'I know what you're doing. The police know too, they'll be coming to question you and Carl any time now.' The look on her face falters and I feel a sense of triumph. 'Where is Tamsin? Tell me!'

She's quiet for a moment, then she looks away, smiling. 'Oh, just reliving her nightmares. When I get bored of that, I may just have to put her to sleep for good, just like *Gabe* was.'

Chills run down my spine. She knows. How the hell does she know? Then she turns on her heel and walks away, her words echoing in my mind. *Put her to sleep for good.* Is she threatening to *kill* Tamsin?

◆ ◆ ◆

When I get home from my round, I'm surprised to see Aubrey on our doorstep, talking to Ruby who's back early after a mock exam. They haven't noticed me yet and seem deep in conversation. Behind me, a car comes to a stop in front of our house. I see with irritation it's Douglas's car. He winds his window down.

'Aubrey,' he says in an ice-cold voice. 'What on earth are you doing in this part of town?'

Aubrey stares at his father in fear. Yes, *fear.* He really is scared of him.

Douglas looks Ruby up and down. His nostrils flare and he closes his eyes briefly, pinching the bridge of his nose. I know what he must be thinking: what the hell is my son doing with a girl like her? If only he knew Ruby deserved ten times his son, a *hundred* times!

'Get in,' Douglas snaps at Aubrey. Aubrey quickly looks at Ruby, then back at his father. 'Now!' Douglas shouts.

Aubrey quickly scurries down the path, brushing past me to get through the gate and then jumps in the car, Douglas driving them off.

'Jesus,' Ruby says when I get to the front door, 'who does Mr Gold think he is, the Godfather?'

'What was Aubrey doing here?'

'He was just dropping off some PS5 games.'

'You know how I feel about that family.'

'Aubrey's different from his parents. You're the one who got a lift with his dad the other day anyway. You do realise he's a *complete* pervert, don't you?'

'What do you mean?' I ask as we walk down the hallway to the kitchen.

'Eva told me. He got arrested for stalking a woman when he was a teenager. He even got done for beating her boyfriend up.'

'My God!' This man is even worse than I thought.

'He's really bad news, Mum, the things Aubrey tells me about him.'

'You think I don't know that?'

'Anyway,' Ruby says, 'much more interesting, Aubrey was saying Tilda Beashell has been putting posters up about the missing teenager. She even mentions it's on TikTok. It's not fair I had to take the video down, Mum, especially now everybody is talking about it!'

I rub my temple as a headache spreads across my forehead. To make matters worse, I can now hear my mother calling out to me. 'It's just the way it is, Ruby.'

'But why?' she asks, following me inside and into the kitchen as I make her grandmother's soup. 'I've got some really good new info on him!'

I pause. 'What kind of info?'

'Apparently, pages from the novel he was writing were found. It was about this steamy love affair a stranger has with two teenage girls.'

I feel my face flush. 'You shouldn't be talking about stuff like that.'

'God Mum, I'm sixteen.'

'Who told you all this?' I ask as casually as I can.

'Some person who commented on my TikTok video. Not that I'll be able to see it any more considering you asked me to delete the video from my account,' she says with an eye-roll.

'So they said some of his novel was found. When and where?'

'Oh, *now* you're curious all of a sudden,' she teases. She shrugs. 'I don't know, it's just what they said.' She leans against the counter as I butter some bread. 'So just how well did you know this dude who pretended to be Gabe Artaud?'

'I told you, I really don't want to talk about it, it was years ago.'

'You might not want to talk about it, Mum, but plenty of people around Easthaven are. There are even rumours you were one of the girls from the novel.'

I shake my head. 'This is getting ridiculous.'

'Is it? I had some idiot at school today saying he'd heard you pushed the missing boy from the cliff as you were jealous of the other girl.'

My mouth drops open, the knife I'm using clattering to the floor. Fake Tamsin is doing this.

'Are you okay, Mum?' Ruby asks.

I recover myself, quickly picking up the knife. 'I'm fine. You have to try to ignore it all; they're just silly rumours.'

'As long as that's what they are, rumours,' she says, eyes drilling into mine. 'We can't have stuff like this being said with the custody thing happening soon.'

I feel tears spring to my eyes. This is spiralling out of control. 'I know, sweetie. That's why you need to ignore the rumours.' I plonk the bowl of soup and bread on to a tray and hand it to Ruby. 'Do me a favour. I have a headache. Can you take this to your grandmother?'

Ruby grimaces. 'God, do I have to?'

'Yes, you do.'

She sighs and carries it upstairs. When she's gone, I slump against the wall. Things really do feel like they're spinning out of control. But what the hell can I do about it?

◆ ◆ ◆

When I arrive at the sorting office the next morning, Craig is waiting for me. He looks upset. Just what I need.

'Everything okay?' I ask him.

'Greg wants to talk to you. I think it's pretty serious.'

My stomach sinks. 'What now?'

'You better go and find him.'

Has Greg found out about the notepad? Surely he'll understand when I tell him why I take notes? I go to my boss's office, knocking on the door. He gestures for me to come in so I do, my head pounding in dread. 'Well, I've not been to any other Prosecco parties since we last spoke,' I say with a nervous laugh.

But he doesn't laugh back. 'A resident on your round has complained about missing post.'

'I see,' I say, trying to keep my voice as calm as possible. 'Which resident?'

'Carl de Leon.'

Bugger bugger bugger. 'Maybe it's arrived today,' I say, aware of those very letters in my bag as I speak, ready to be delivered later. 'You know how some letters can take longer than normal.'

'I've checked. It hasn't.' He gives me a look and I know in that instance there's more to this. The four walls close in around me. 'I've been sent video footage from outside Lakewell Manor,' he continues, voice drawn. 'It shows you holding the missing letters in front of the property, but then you put them in your bag. It's clear to see, Liz.'

I feel sick. I dig around in my bag. 'They're here!' I say, pulling them out. 'I – I wasn't thinking straight. I thought they were – they were my letters, I put them in my pocket and—'

'And then there's the notes you wrote about residents.' I close my eyes, pinching the bridge of my nose. 'Yes, I know all about those too, Liz. You do realise how unethical all this is?'

'But taking notes was a way to help them. There was this woman back in Manchester, a Mrs—'

'You mean Diana Beale?' he asks sadly.

I flinch. 'I wasn't talking about her.'

'But she is part of the problem, proof there's a pattern emerging here of you opening post when you shouldn't.'

I feel my legs go weak. I sit on a chair and put my head in my hands. Diana Beale was a divorcee Scott had an affair with. She was beautiful with black hair to her waist and green eyes. Older than Scott, which probably made her even more alluring to a little boy like him. When I first talked to her, before she embarked on an affair with my husband, I thought she was lovely. So friendly, vivacious, kind. She even invited me to have a cuppa in her garden. It became a regular thing, once or twice a week, I'd end my round with tea and cakes in her lovely garden. But then the rumours of an affair started. I was devastated. But she had no idea I was Scott's wife. I'd continue to smile and chat with her like I usually did. But in the background, I watched her. I'd walk around the side of her house and peer in the garden. And soon that progressed to steaming open her letters. It was only a few times. Then I took it a step too far, my anger boiling over. When I found important letters addressed to her, I made sure they went 'missing'. Of course, it was going to be discovered eventually. It was hardly a coincidence that the woman complaining about lost post was having an affair with the postman's husband. I got hauled in and suspended; she even called the police when she discovered what I'd done, which resulted in a humiliating interview with a detective at my house, neighbours' curtains twitching at the sight of a police car outside. Scott found out and that's what really made him decide to leave.

It looks like history is repeating itself now. But at least I have a truly legitimate reason. 'I'm so sorry, Greg,' I quickly say now. 'If you can just give me one last chance—'

He puts his hand up. 'I'm sorry Liz, but pending further investigation, I have no choice but to suspend you.'

Chapter 17

I have no choice but to suspend you. I have no choice but to suspend you. I have no choice but to suspend you. Those words rotate round and round my head as I lie in bed later. I've lied to my mother and told her I was ill. I even call her carers, telling them to do some extra hours and do her snacks and dinner. Of course, they're happy to. More money for them.

The truth is, I've lost all my fight. What the hell was I thinking, taking home those letters? Have I lost my bloody mind? I curl my hands into fists, smashing them into my stomach. 'Stupid, stupid, stupid!' I don't know how long I lie there. I hear the kids come in from school but I've left them a note to say I need to sleep as I'm feeling ill. I ought to be coming up with a plan of action, a way to get my job back. I know I ought to be thinking of Tamsin too. That horrible thing Fake Tamsin said echoes in my mind: *When I get bored of that, I may just have to put her to sleep for good.*

Every minute counts. But what use have I been so far? All I've ended up doing is risking the roof over my family's head and custody of my children too. This isn't going to look good at my hearing if Scott gets wind of it. It's just five days away. I'll lose the girls! I'm tired, tired of it all. So I curl up in bed and sleep, just as I did in the days after Scott left and I lost my job the last time. And surely I will lose my job this time too? There's nothing worse than taking a customer's post home with you. Not to mention steaming it open to have a look. Greg will be able to see that's what I've done when he has a closer look. He'll know the telltale signs.

Not to mention that little notepad of mine. There are only so many chances the Royal Mail will give me. I don't know what else there is for me if I can't be a postie. The thought of being unemployed sinks in like poison. As it does, I hear my mother stirring in the room next door when the carers arrive to make her mid-afternoon snack and help her to the toilet. I can hear her asking why I'm not doing it.

'Your daughter's ill, remember?' the carer explains.

'Where is she?' my mother snaps, her usual charming self.

'I'm here,' I shout out.

'You sound all right to me,' my mother shouts back, reminding me when she used to do the same when I was too ill to go to school.

'Well I'm not!' I say, adding a little cough.

She says something back, but I don't hear it because I've buried my head under the duvet. A little while later, there's a knock on my door. 'Mum?' Ruby calls out. 'Mum, are you feeling okay?'

'Just in bed darling,' I croak back. 'Not feeling well.'

'Can I come in?'

I sigh. 'Sure.'

She lets herself in and sits quietly on the edge of my bed. 'Are you okay, Mum?' she asks softly. 'I know you're not ill, by the way. I can tell. What happened?'

I want to lie. I want to tell her I really am ill. I don't want her to endure this burden with me. But the only sure thing I can do now is to tell the truth. So I admit it: 'I got suspended from my job.'

She looks at me with shock and disappointment. 'Again?'

'Yeah, again.'

'But the custody hearing is so soon!'

I reach out and clutch her hand. 'I know, darling, I'm sorry.'

'What happened?'

I tell her about opening Carl's letters, feeling awful shame as I do. I also tell her about everything else I've discovered: Imogen's death, Carl's duplicity, Fake Tamsin pretty much admitting it all and the terrible danger that Real Tamsin is in. I even tell her about Gabe minus that last evening. All the time, she listens quietly. It's a lot for her to take in. The past *year* has been a lot for her to take in. But I'm done with the lies.

'You're going to tell me you told me so, aren't you?' I say. 'You told me not to get involved with the Tamsin thing.'

'I'm not going to say that, Mum. I like the fact you're trying to help someone.' She squeezes my hand. 'That's all you do, try to help people. But it just gets thrown back in your face. I'm proud of you though.'

'Oh darling,' I say, stroking her cheek. 'I wish I had as much faith in myself as you do.'

'Have you eaten?'

I shake my head. 'I'm not hungry.'

'I'm making you something.' She squeezes my hand again then walks out of the room. I really am lucky to have her, and Mia too. But with the custody hearing looming and me losing my job, how much longer will I have them?

I spend the weekend moping about, the looming threat of the custody case and the awfulness of being fired making it hard for me to want to wake up, full stop. But I do wake with resolve on Monday, making the kids their breakfast and giving them big hugs before they go off to school, something I usually miss out on when I'm working. I try not to think too hard about the fact that this might be my last chance to wave them off to school. It hurts too much.

Before she leaves, Ruby gives me a quick hug. 'It'll all be okay, Mum,' she whispers in my ear.

After they've left, I sit in the kitchen, sipping some tea as I go through my notes for the court case tomorrow. I've made a little speech, listing all my qualities. My solicitor suggested I highlight any of Scott's bad points, but I don't want to stoop so low. The fact is, he's a good dad, despite the cheating. After a while, the words blur in front of me, so I look at my camera reel instead. I need to get rid of the photos I took of Carl's letters. I don't need any more evidence mounting against me. I sigh and go to delete them, then pause as I look at the black rose symbol on Carl's group therapy letter. There's something familiar about it. I mean, I remember seeing that symbol on the letter Tamsin received from the same funeral directors. But I'm sure I've seen it elsewhere too. It suddenly hits me then. I quickly open Celia's Instagram feed and find her photos from Imogen's funeral. Something catches my eye among the flowers. I zoom in. It's a placard, *Sable & Sons Funeral Directors* written on it, a black rose symbol above.

The same funeral home Tamsin used for her mother! I sit up straight, heart thumping. So two of Carl's girlfriends – Imogen and Tamsin – used the same funeral home. Surely it can't be a coincidence? I google the Sable & Sons funeral home, finding its website:

> *When a loved one passes away, you need the reassurance that the funeral director you have chosen will deal with you and your loved one's wishes professionally, sympathetically and with respect. This is where Sable & Sons comes in. A family-run business, we have been serving London and its surrounding home counties for twenty-five years. As an independent, family-owned funeral directors, we pride ourselves on our dedicated and experienced team,*

as well as our well-appointed premises including offices,
chapels of rest, gardens and storage facilities.

Is this what connects Imogen and Tamsin? Is this how they were chosen to be Carl and Fake Tamsin's 'victims'? I click around the website, but don't find anything notable. When I get to the 'Call Us' button, I hesitate for a moment. Do I really want to be doing this? What have I got to lose?

I dial the number and it's answered quickly by a sombre-sounding man. 'Hello, Sable & Sons Funeral Directors, how may we be of service?'

'Hi. I, erm, I saw you offer a service where you put together plans for people who wish to arrange their service before they pass away?'

'That's right, we offer the choice of four simple plans to ensure all your wishes are covered. Would you like me to send you more information?'

'Yes, my mother. She's . . . terminal.' I feel a bit guilty saying that, but it would feel so weird planning my *own* funeral.

'I'm sorry to hear that. We can either send you a pack with all the details or make an appointment for a face-to-face visit? We find face-to-face is better as you get the chance to meet the team and see our facilities. In fact,' he says over the sound of rustling, 'we actually have a cancellation for tomorrow at eleven a.m. Would that suit you?'

I bite my lip. Am I really doing this? 'Sure,' I say.

Chapter 18

Sable & Sons Funeral Directors is situated in a quiet, upmarket part of Chelsea in West London. Clearly, it's aimed at higher-end clientele. Once again, I feel out of place here in London, strolling along these pristine streets in my supermarket-bought navy suit, the very same suit I'll be wearing to the custody hearing tomorrow.

My stomach sinks. *Tomorrow.* How has it come around so soon?

I stop outside their townhouse premises, staring at the huge black rose symbols that dominate the bay windows at the front. I take a deep breath and walk in, hit instantly by the scent of roses. Around me are displays featuring brochures and leaflets, the same black rose symbol on all of them. The walls are panelled with dark-brown mahogany and gentle low music tinkles out from some speakers. I walk to the front desk where a slender young man with neatly combed dark-brown hair sits. Will he notice I'm not their usual type of customer?

'Hi, I have an appointment at eleven?' I say.

'Ah yes,' he says in a voice that seems too old for him. 'Let me take you through.'

I follow him to the back of the room. He knocks gently at one of three doors there.

'Come in,' a gruff voice commands. He opens the door to reveal a large room with windows overlooking gardens at the back. Two men sit at a large mahogany desk, one in his thirties, the other much older, maybe late sixties. They look like the man at the front desk with their brown hair and slim, tall frames. I suppose it *is* a family business.

I walk past a large opulent white coffin that dominates one side of the room. It's open and for a moment, I almost expect a body to be in there. But as I walk by, I see its plush black velvet interior is empty. The young man from the desk bows slightly, peering at who I presume is his father, then backs out of the room, closing the door behind him. It all feels a bit much, but then I suppose that's the way with places like this. I take one of the leather seats across from the two men and they both smile.

'I'm Thomas Sable,' the older man says in a confident, booming voice. 'Founder of Sable & Sons. And this is my son, Nathan Sable.' He gives me a sympathetic look. 'So I believe your mother has a terminal illness?'

'Yes. I was hoping she could come too, but I'm afraid she's feeling too ill to travel.' It's not *that* much of a lie. I mean, she is too ill to travel . . . to a funeral planning meeting she knows nothing about.

'I'm sorry to hear that,' the young man says sympathetically. 'So, how about we start by going through the four plans?'

Over the next half an hour, I listen as the two men explain their plans, ranging from incredibly expensive to eye-wateringly extortionate. And that doesn't include the coffins, which are extra. I notice the older man is rather condescending with his son, at times even insulting.

'Any of the plans particularly standing out to you?' the young man asks when they've finished with their spiel.

'I'll have to have a think. Actually,' I say, 'my friend recommended you, Tamsin Lakewell?'

'We have many clients,' the older man says. 'But the name rings a bell.'

I sigh. 'You also arranged the funeral of another friend, Imogen Grayson?'

'Ah, yes,' the younger man says. 'Such an awful tragedy, to have to arrange two funerals.'

'Of course, you must have overseen her brother Matteo's funeral too?'

The young man nods. 'I suspect the young lady was very fragile following her brother's death, hence she took her life.'

His father glares at him. 'Nathan, it is not our place to comment on such things.' His son quickly looks down at the table. 'Now any particular plans that appeal?' the father asks. 'I know the Graysons went for our Platinum plan.'

My fingers flicker over the Platinum brochure selling the most expensive plan. The older man looks excited for a moment. But then I pick up the cheapest. 'I think the Bronze plan would suit us best.'

The disappointment is visible in his face. But the son maintains his composure. 'Excellent. If you sign up for a plan today, you actually get a ten per cent discount.'

I feel like laughing. A ten per cent discount is still 100 per cent more than I could ever dream of affording. 'I really ought to consult my mother.'

The older man sighs. He reminds me of my mother. It's clear he thinks this was a waste of time and frankly, so do I. I'm not entirely sure what I hoped to achieve here.

As I walk towards the door, I see a large-framed picture I hadn't noticed before. It looks like a family portrait with the older Sable in the middle of a group of several men and two women, one older, one younger. They're surrounded by vases of blooming white roses. It's all a bit cheesy. I pause, peering closer. There's something familiar about the younger woman's face though . . .

That's when it hits me: it's Fake Tamsin!

Chapter 19

'Can I ask who this is?' I point to the woman in the picture, trying to hide the adrenaline rushing through me. It's definitely her. Same sharp features, same hard eyes. Sure, she's not wearing her Tamsin wig over her long dark hair, nor fake green contact lenses and all that make-up, but it's definitely her.

'That's my sister,' the young man says. 'She doesn't work here any—'

His father shoots him a look. 'She's taking a career break,' the father quickly says. 'If you would like a female presence at the ceremony, then my wife Carol is available.'

'No, it's not that. I just recognised her.'

'Let me see you out,' the father says abruptly.

I drag my eyes away from the woman's face, head buzzing as I say my goodbyes. When I get out of the place, I put my phone to my ear with trembling hands and call Celia.

'Hey!' she says when she answers.

'I think I've cracked it. I think I know who Fake Tamsin is.'

'Oh yeah?'

'She works at Sable & Sons. I'm outside their offices now.'

A pause. 'I know that name.'

'The funeral directors used for Imogen and Matteo's funerals.'

'No way!' Her shout is so piercing, I have to move my phone away from my ear. 'They're based in London. Where are you?'

'Chelsea.'

'Good, I'm only ten minutes away. There's a cafe around the corner, has black and white stripes on its front. Meet you there.'

Fifteen minutes later, Celia walks in, face alight with drama. She slips into the seat across from me and I tell her everything. 'Wow,' she says, shaking her head. 'Wow, wow, wow. It has to be some kind of scam. This woman reels them in, then . . .'

'. . . Carl butters them up,' I finish for her.

'Exactly.' I frown. But that doesn't explain this woman knowing Gabe. Maybe she doesn't. Maybe it's just an elaborate blackmail ploy after learning what happened with Gabe from Carl, if my theory about the real Tamsin confessing to him is correct.

Celia chews on her lip, her red lipstick staining her teeth. 'So a single grieving woman comes in, the sister clocks them. Somehow finds out they're due to inherit a decent amount of money then gets Carl on to them.'

'He's good-looking, charming . . .'

'Somehow seems to be on their level because he knows a lot about them,' Celia continues.

'Precisely. God, that's sick.'

'So sick. Goddamn inheritance vampires! So what now?'

'Obviously, we have to tell the detective?'

She nods vehemently. 'Totally. Did you get a picture of the family portrait?'

'No, would have been a bit obvious. There might be something online?'

Celia digs her phone out and does a search, smiling. 'Is this the portrait you saw?' I look at the photo she's showing me and nod. She zooms in and her smile deepens. 'Oh yeah, it's Fake Tamsin all right. Same smug face. Interesting, this photo is a cached version, so it looks like it used to be on their website but was taken down.'

'They probably took it down when she went on her "career break",' I say, making quotation marks with my fingers. 'They seemed a bit cagey about that. Maybe they caught on to her, but couldn't exactly report her, because it would mean the end of their business?'

'Or maybe she just ditched them out of nowhere when she realised life was better impersonating a poet. Let me do a search.' She's quiet as she scrolls through her phone. 'Okay, I've found something,' she says, holding up her phone. It's an article from a women's magazine from two months ago. 'A Funeral Director Tried to Steal My Inheritance', the headline screams, featuring a photo of an elderly lady standing sadly by a gravestone:

> *When Ivy Lovestone stepped into the premises of Red Tulip Funeral Homes (name changed in this article for legal purposes) a trusted and well-regarded funeral directors in London, she never dreamed she'd be walking out penniless. But that's what happened when she took out a plan with the funeral home, discovering the £200 a month direct debit she thought she'd agreed to was actually £900 a month.*

My eyes glance down the length of the article which seems to mainly be about Ivy Lovestone's attempts to explain why she didn't pay too much detail to the fine print. At the end, there's a line that catches my eye:

> *When contacted, the funeral directors told us the employee responsible for the fraud has been fired.*

'Well, there we have it,' Celia says, shaking her head in dismay. 'The employee who was fired must be Fake Tamsin. It's all about the money.'

'But I'm still no closer to finding out where the real Tamsin is.'

Celia puts her hand over mine. 'You'll find her. She has a chance . . . unlike Imogen.'

I nod vehemently. 'I *will* find her.' As I say that, I notice a familiar face. 'That's Nathan Sable,' I whisper to Celia. 'One of the sons from the funeral home.'

As he walks up to the counter, he notices me. 'Oh, hello there,' he says, looking slightly uncomfortable. Then he peers at Celia and I can tell from the look on his face that he finds her . . . intriguing.

'Come join us!' Celia declares, clearly noticing too.

He blushes. 'Oh, I don't know . . .'

'My friend was just saying how *fabulous* you were with her. I mean, as fabulous as a man can be when talking about coffins,' she adds with a bat of the eyelids and a giggle. His blush grows even deeper. 'I have *always* wanted to meet a man who works in a funeral home,' Celia continues. 'Haven't I, Liz?'

'Yes,' I say, playing along.

'Please, do join us,' Celia says. 'That's after you order your brie and cranberry baguette, anyway. You're a brie and cranberry kinda guy, I can tell.'

He laughs, visibly relaxing. 'How do you know that?'

'Psychic,' she says, tapping her temple. He laughs again and I smile. Celia really has a way about her.

'I'll just get my order,' he says.

'Fab! I've saved a spot for you,' Celia says, tapping the space next to her.

We wait as he orders his baguette then he comes to sit with us.

'Your father said your sister is taking a career break?' I ask.

He shifts uncomfortably in his seat. 'Something like that.'

Celia leans towards him. 'She the black sheep of the family?'

He shrugs. 'I guess you could say that.'

'Where is she now then?' I ask.

'Don't know, don't care,' Nathan replies. 'If I could take a guess, I'd say anywhere she can roll in a bit of money. Obsessed with the stuff. That's the only reason she agreed to work for the family business a few years back. Dad promised her a share in the company. And yet I've been working at the place since I was eighteen, and he never offered me a share!' Celia and I exchange looks. Nathan is clearly jealous of his sister. He guffaws. 'Funny thing is, my sister had all these plans to be a solicitor. Used to tell us all she wouldn't be seen dead working for the family business.'

'Like the pun,' Celia says. Nathan looks confused. He's not the sharpest tool in the box. That could work to our advantage.

'She sounds like a bit of a snob,' I say, encouraging him.

'Yep.' He picks some Brie out of his teeth and chews it. 'Always thought she was too smart for us all. Mum and Dad couldn't see it of course. She was their clever little princess. Was hilarious when she got thrown out of her law course.'

'Why'd she get thrown out?' Celia asks.

'Got into a fight with one of the other students, some girl,' Nathan said. 'That's the thing with my sister Gwen; has all these hoity-toity dreams but acts like a bloody cage fighter when she loses her temper. Was the same at school. No matter how clever she was, she'd still end up getting into stupid fights over dumb things.' He shakes his head. 'One time, she even got suspended for impersonating one of the teachers. Got a wig and everything.'

Celia's mouth drops open and I shake my head in disbelief. Gwen clearly has form.

'Why'd she do that?' I ask.

'My brother Jeff thinks it was to steal the money they all collected for Comic Relief but I don't know,' Nathan says. 'I don't know if she'd go that far. She was pretty obsessed with money though. That's our dad's fault,' he says with an eye-roll. '*Always* about the money.' He must suddenly realise he's talking to a potential customer and blinks. 'I mean, in terms of helping his client *save* money,' he quickly says.

'Don't worry,' Celia says, leaning close to him and putting her hand over his. 'My dad is *exactly* the same. I get you,' she adds with a wink. He relaxes.

'So you said she got thrown out of uni,' I ask, taking a sip of my coffee, 'then had to return home and join the family business?'

Nathan nods, taking a slurp of his own coffee. 'Was so funny, seeing her in the office every day. Not so clever then, hey?'

'What did she do there?' Celia asks.

'Backroom stuff,' he says. 'Admin, accounts, that kind of thing. She started out at the front, like me. But she got too unpredictable. One minute she was charming clients and bringing in more business and more glowing reviews than any of us, the next she's having a stand-up argument with a client. Dad had to get her away from them. I guess she's clever enough to do all the boring admin stuff.'

'So she'd have access to client details?' Celia asks. I can see she's thinking the same as me.

'I guess,' Nathan replies.

'She got a boyfriend?' Celia asks.

Nathan pauses halfway through taking a bite of his baguette. 'Huh?'

I kick Celia under the table. It's a question too far. 'Oh nothing,' Celia says, biting her lip and examining her long gel nails.

'You said about a boyfriend?' He opens up what remains of his baguette, prodding a lump of cranberry sauce with his finger. 'Yeah, there's this guy she met a few years ago, some Ken Doll type. Dad hated him when he met him, told Gwen to get him to sling his hook. Made us all laugh. She was used to getting her way. She's always been spoilt, only girl out of the seven of us. Plus after what happened with our brother . . .' His voice trails off.

'What happened?' I ask.

'He's been missing twenty years now,' he replies. 'I remember him getting into lots of trouble the last time we saw him though. I was only seven but I still remember him packing all his stuff up super-quick, telling us he had to lie low for a few weeks as some people were after him. I learnt since he used to steal a lot of stuff, shoplifting, items from schoolfriends' houses, sometimes even just walking into someone's house without them noticing and taking stuff. Proper kleptomaniac. I reckon he just pissed somebody off a bit too much and we never saw him again. Proper messed up our sister Gwen; they were the two oldest and very close. She still struggles, twenty years later.'

Twenty years. I find I can hardly breathe. Could it be . . . ? I quickly dig the photo of me and Gabe out from my bag and hold it up to him with trembling hands. 'Is this your missing brother?' I ask.

He leans close and looks at it. 'Yeah, that's Jacob.' So that was Gabe's real name . . . and Fake Tamsin – aka Gwen – is his sister!

Chapter 20

'Wait a minute,' Nathan says, looking at both of us, 'why do you have a photo of Jacob? Do you know him? My parents have spent years searching for him. Where was this taken? When?'

I open and close my mouth, not sure what to say. His poor family, all these years trying to find their son. I ought to tell him, at the very least, that Jacob ended up in Easthaven. But no, that would only lead them to me. I can't risk it. 'I found this photo in your office,' I lie. 'I was going to return it.'

Celia shoots me a confused look but says nothing.

Nathan shakes his head, gathering his phone and keys up. 'You're journalists, aren't you? You're using this picture to make me talk. Dad warned me about people trying to pry into our lives! It's Gwen who swindled them out of money, not us! We don't know where Gwen is, okay? We're as much in the dark as you are. So stop bothering us.' He gives us both an angry look then storms out.

Celia grabs the photo from my hands, staring at it. 'Okay, you just lied, big time. You need to tell me more about this Gabe stroke Jacob dude.'

I sigh. It's probably time I told her *some* of the story, so that's what I do, ending with us discovering him stealing Tamsin's family heirlooms. As I tell her that bit, something dawns on me.

'I bet that's why Gabe came to Easthaven. Tamsin's father passed away only a few months before Gabe turned up. And now I think about it, they had a second house in Chelsea in London. It's where Tamsin's mother was brought up; they'd naturally use the most well-regarded funeral home in the area.'

'You mean Jacob, not Gabe.'

I shake my head. 'I can't bring myself to call him that. He's Gabe as far as I'm concerned.'

'So, what, he and his sister were in on it?'

I think back to the conversations Gabe and I used to have. 'He mentioned he had a sister but she was two years younger than him, just fifteen. So I doubt Gwen was involved, I bet she didn't know anything about it,' I say. 'Nathan mentioned Gabe was a bit of a kleptomaniac and people were after him. I bet Tamsin's mother used Sable & Sons for her husband's funeral; that's how Tamsin knew to use them for her mother's. Maybe Gabe saw a quick get-out after learning about the fortune Tamsin's dad left behind. Maybe he even knew about the ring he eventually tried to steal. So he just followed Tamsin's mother to Easthaven to get his hands on it.'

'So a cute guy scams a teen girl to get her money. Sounds familiar.'

I sigh. 'I don't think it was a scam, as such. Not in the way his sister and Carl are scamming people. I honestly think he was just a desperate kid who used his propensity for thieving and his good looks to get into Lakewell Manor, so he could steal something that would buy his way out of trouble.'

My heart aches as I think of that. Yes, he broke my heart. Yes, he used me and stole from my best friend. But I do sometimes wonder if he loved me in his way. And at the end of the day, he was a messed-up kid running away from trouble. Who's to say Gabe's stories about an abusive grandfather weren't true? I just met his dad; he wasn't exactly the nicest of men.

'I guess that makes sense,' Celia admits. 'I can't imagine Gabe's family knew about the Easthaven link, otherwise their search would have led them to the village, and from what you've told me, that didn't happen.'

'Nope, as far as I know, nobody came looking for a boy called Jacob Sable. I don't think there was anything on the national news back then about a missing boy called Jacob either. I would have recognised his face if there was.'

'Sadly, lots of young men go missing, I imagine. Hard to make national news headlines. With his story.' Celia sighs. 'It's just the way it is.'

I do a quick search for his name, Jacob Sable, and find a few articles about a missing young man. But Celia's right, he's just one of many missing young men. His handsome face looks out at me and I feel my stomach drop.

'So what happened when you confronted him?' Celia asks.

My eyes fill with tears and my heart hammers against my chest as I think back to what happened when Tamsin and I confronted Gabe that evening. 'He denied it at first, then finally he admitted it and . . . well, he just left.' It's a lie, but how can I possibly tell her the truth? 'The next thing we heard, a fisherman saw a body of his description in the sea.'

'Jesus, did they retrieve the body?'

I shake my head. 'Nothing was ever found. I never heard from him again. I – I just have to presume it was him.'

'Then you need to tell the family what happened.'

'I will.' Another lie.

Celia slumps back against the chair, shaking her head. 'My God. I can't believe it. If it *was* Jacob's body do you think he took his own life?'

'Maybe,' I say, voice barely a whisper.

'Maybe Gwen blames you and Tamsin?' Celia says. 'It all kinda makes sense now. So Tamsin falls in love with Carl, she confesses everything about this kid called Gabe and Carl tells Gwen. Gwen puts two and two together, realises Gabe was her missing brother Jacob and . . .'

'. . . turns into the avenging psycho bitch from hell,' I finish for her. 'I don't know, that's quite a few hoops to leap through for Gwen.'

'It makes sense though. It's the only explanation really.'

'True.' As I say that, my phone rings. I frown as I look at the number. 'It's the girls' school, I better take this.' I put the phone to my ear. 'Hello, Liz speaking.'

'Hello, is this Ruby's mum?' a female voice asks.

'Yes, is everything okay?'

'Ruby didn't come into school this morning. We didn't get a call to confirm her absence so I'm just checking.'

I sit up straight, alarm darting through me. 'What? That doesn't make sense. I saw her leave this morning with her sister.'

'Well she's not here, I'm afraid.'

'Thank you,' I say in a trembling voice.

'Is everything okay?' Celia asks as I hang up.

'Ruby didn't turn up at school.'

'Does she often do that?'

'Never.' I dial Ruby's number and put my phone to my ear. But it just goes to voicemail. I jump up and grab my bag. 'I have to go home. I have a horrible feeling about this.'

'Keep me posted!' Celia calls after me.

◆ ◆ ◆

The train back can't go fast enough. I keep trying Ruby's phone but there's no answer. I text Mia and she replies in her break, confirming

Ruby walked her to school. The problem is, Ruby has to drop Mia off at one end of the campus before walking to the sixth form area at the other end. What happened after she dropped her little sister off? I call my mother who confirms Ruby isn't home then promptly begins to bang on about 'youth nowadays bunking off all the time'.

'Ruby has never bunked off, Mother!' I shout down the phone before ending the call.

It kills me to do it, but I call Scott next. When he answers, I explain what's happened. 'Has she been in touch?' I ask.

'No. She's never done this before, Liz.'

'I know.'

'You know what, it doesn't surprise me. The way you all live in that house, the shouting and the lax rules.'

'What the hell are you talking about?'

'I'm just saying. And now I hear from Mia you've been fired.' *Damn it!* 'You better get used to the idea of losing custody of the girls tomorrow,' Scott says with a sigh. 'I hope you've prepared yourself, I know how fragile you can be mentally.'

I slam the phone down before I say something I regret. When I get home, I run into the girls' room. It's a mess, different clothes strewn over the floor, make-up spilled on Ruby's desk. One area of her part of the room is pristine though, a long white sheet hung on the wall where she does her videos. I go to her mirror. Around it are photos of her old friends from Manchester, new ones from her sixth form here. I trail my fingers along the surface of her desk, which she uses as a dressing table too, over the glitter of her black eyeshadow. I pick her perfume bottle up, putting it to my nose and breathing in its grassy scent.

Then I open her laptop but it's password protected and I have no idea what the password is. My eyes alight on a photo of her with Eva as a screensaver. Maybe she knows something? I look through my phone. I have Eva's number from a time when I did an order from the patisserie for Craig's birthday at work. I call her, knowing she'll be on her lunch break at school now. She takes a while to answer.

'Hello?' she says

'It's Liz, Ruby's mum. Sorry to call you while you're at school,' I quickly say. 'You probably know Ruby isn't in. But she's not at home either and isn't reading my texts and taking my calls. I'm really beginning to worry. Did she say anything to you?' There's a pause. 'Eva!' I say. 'Come on, this is serious.'

'It might be nothing,' she says. 'But someone contacted her via her TikTok account with information about the Gabe Artaud imposter thing she's been investigating.'

Terror zigzags through me. 'She told me about that. You don't think she's met up with them, do you? Surely she's too savvy to meet with someone she's met off the internet!'

'Yeah, she totally is too savvy. But she's also totally obsessed with this case.'

'Did she tell you the person's name?'

'She didn't say, but I did see the comment before the video was taken down. It was from someone called Black Rose-something.'

I freeze. *Black Rose.* That's the symbol used by Sable & Sons. I end the call to Eva and try calling Ruby again, pacing her room. 'Ruby,' I say when it goes to voicemail. 'You *must* call me the moment you get this. I'm worried you're meeting with someone very dangerous. Please call me back as soon as you can.'

'What on earth is going on in there?' I hear my mother call out. 'Is that you, Ruby?'

I go to her room. 'It's just me. I'm worried, Mother. Ruby isn't replying to my messages and calls. Did she say anything to you this morning?'

'Nothing.' She scrutinises my face. 'What's going on? I can tell you're hiding something.'

'Tamsin Lakewell is missing. I think she's been conned out of her money and is being held somewhere by the person Ruby might be meeting with.' As I say that, I realise what an awful situation I've dragged my daughter into. Gwen will surely be doing this to get revenge!

'What have you got my granddaughter into?' my mother hisses. 'Let me guess, you've been meddling again and this time, Ruby's going to suffer for it.'

'It's not like that, Mother!'

'Isn't it?' she spits. 'Maybe it's just revenge for what you did twenty years ago. God does work in mysterious ways. You know I'm right, you destroy everything close to you with your meddling. I mean look at me!' she says, gesturing to her leg cast.

'Shut up!' I say. 'Shut up!' I slam her bedroom door and run downstairs, dialling the police. They don't seem overly concerned, telling me Ruby won't be considered missing unless she doesn't return this evening. I explain about Tamsin . . . or specifically, Gwen Sable. I even tell them she wants revenge for something I was involved with in the past and they agree to send an officer over 'later in the day'. Then I leave a message for the detective I spoke with. He knows more about the case after all.

I go to the window and peer out. If Gwen has my daughter, I need to try to track Gwen down. So I head to the manor, buzzing on the gate over and over. But there's no answer. I try the keypad but of course the number has been changed since I met the real Tamsin. I peer at the old tree I once climbed to scale the walls. Dare I do it now? No, I have to do this properly. So I return home and wait for the police, chewing my nails to a stump. They don't arrive and I have to leave the house to pick Mia up from school; I won't dare let her walk back on her own. When I do, I try to question some of the young faces I recognise from Ruby's photos but none of them saw her this morning.

'Where is she, Mum?' Mia asks as I drive us home. 'Is she in danger?'

'No, I'm sure she isn't,' I lie to Mia. 'Try not to worry. I bet when we get back, she'll be home,' I say, more to myself than her.

She frowns. 'Or she could be at Lakewell Manor.'

'Why do you say that?'

'Because of the TikTok video Ruby did? Casper Beashell was saying at school today that he reckons the missing boy's body is buried under the cellar. Maybe Ruby went to find it? I didn't even *know* Lakewell Manor had a cellar, did you?'

Of course I know, I want to say. *That cellar frequently features in my nightmares.*

A thought suddenly occurs to me then. What was it Gwen had said to me about where Tamsin was? *Oh just reliving her nightmares.* That cellar held her nightmares, mine too, of the night Gabe disappeared. Is that where Gwen was keeping Tamsin . . . and now, Ruby?

Of course, it's perfect. No noise could be heard from that cellar, it was so soundproof. I should have climbed that bloody tree! I'm desperate to turn back and head to the manor but we're already drawing up to the house and a police car is parked outside. The sight of it makes me weak with terror. It all feels so horribly real now. I park and jump out of the car, noticing four police officers standing outside my door. One is a tall man with a smart black suit on. The other is a young uniformed woman with red hair. Then behind them are two uniformed men who almost look like twins. 'Sorry,' I say when I reach them, getting my keys out. 'My mother's inside but she's unable to move properly. I had to pick my daughter up. I think I know where Ruby is!'

'Okay, let's do introductions first,' the man says. 'I'm Detective Clarke.'

I pause. 'You've come all the way from London?'

'Yes. You mentioned a Gwen Sable in your voicemail.'

'Yes, she's the one who's been pretending to be my friend Tamsin and now I think she has my daughter at the manor *with* Tamsin.'

Mia looks up at me with worry in her eyes and I quickly open the front door. 'Go upstairs to your grandmother, darling,' I say to her, feeling desperate and disorientated. She nods and runs upstairs. I turn to the officers. 'So, shall we try the manor then?'

'We already have after your call earlier,' one of the police officers says, 'and nobody's answering.'

'Then barge your way in!' I say.

The detective holds his hands up. 'Slow down. First, let's establish why you think Carl de Leon and the woman you claim to be Gwen Sable have your daughter?'

'Gwen is trying to get revenge for something that happened to her brother.'

'And her brother is . . . ?' the detective asks.

'Jacob Sable. I knew him as Gabe.'

'You *knew* Jacob Sable?' the detective asks.

'Yes, he was here in Easthaven twenty years ago.'

The detective takes a deep breath. 'I think it's time you told us everything, Liz.'

'But we need to find my daughter!'

He sighs. 'Fine.' He looks over his shoulder at the two local officers. 'Try the manor again. Maybe see if you can get a drone up to check inside the grounds.' The two officers nod, then head to the police car. I watch as the car skids off into the distance, then reluctantly let the detective and young officer inside, leading them to the kitchen. I don't want to offer them a drink. I want this over with quickly so I can head to the manor too.

The detective turns to me. 'So?'

I take in a deep breath. Is this it? Is this when I'm going to be finally telling the truth to the police? I realise in that moment it's what I must do, for Ruby. So that's what I do, I tell him everything, memories from that awful night flooding back in the process as though I am reliving them right there and then.

Chapter 21

20 Years Ago

There is a fleeting moment of surprise on Gabe's face when he sees Tamsin and me together in that cellar. But he quickly recovers himself by throwing us his big, beautiful smile. It shatters me again, and I know I am crying now because his smile falters slightly.

'What's wrong?' he asks.

'Why are you down here, Gabe?' Tamsin's voice is laced with fury.

'I just needed to get out of the heat,' Gabe replies, eyes still on me. 'You know this is the coolest part of the house.'

'Liar,' Tamsin snaps. 'I know you're stealing from me.'

Gabe pretends to look shocked. 'Stealing? What are you talking about?'

Tamsin marches up to him and grabs his rucksack off him. He tries to wrestle it back off her and in the process, an array of items tumble out of the rucksack . . . including the ring that clatters from the cheap cardboard box he placed it in and scoots across the floor.

We all go silent, Gabe's face paling. I hate myself for it, but my heart goes out to him. To be caught in such a humiliating way! He raises his eyes to meet mine and I find myself trying to read the message in his eyes. I want to think it's a message of love. *I loved you more, Lizbeth. I loved you more than Tamsin. I loved you more than these trinkets and heirlooms.* But now my anger is beginning to paste the pieces of my heart back together and I feel a boiling rage.

'I will *never* forgive you for this,' I say simply.

'Lizbeth, let me explain.' He goes to reach for me but Tamsin stands between us, shoving his hand away.

'There's nothing to explain,' she says, crossing her arms as she glares at him. 'You stole my grandmother's ring. You *know* how important that is to me.'

'Exactly!' Gabe says, Adam's apple bobbing as he swallows nervously. 'I – I was getting it so I could propose to you with it, Tamsin!'

I put my hand to my mouth before I let out a cry. I know he might be scrambling for excuses but part of me can't help but wonder if it's true. Have I got all this wrong? Was that why he took the ring? But why replace it? And what about all the other stuff that spilled out of his rucksack?

'You lying bastard,' Tamsin says.

'It's true. I love you, Tamsin!' He has the same look in his eyes that he gives me when he tells me he loves me. I hate him. I hate him. I hate him!

Tamsin leans down, picking up an ornate clock that has fallen from his rucksack. 'So why do you have this?' she asks. 'Were you going to propose with this as well?' Gabe opens his mouth, then closes it. He knows there's no convincing us, no matter how many charming lies he weaves.

'Fine,' he says with a weary sigh, 'the game's over, I get it. Just let me leave, and you never have to see me again.'

'You are *kidding* me, right?' Tamsin says.

'Did you ever love me?' I find myself asking Gabe. I feel pathetic but I have to know.

'Of course he didn't,' Tamsin spits. 'He's clearly not capable of love. It's just been an act so he can steal off me.'

'*Did* you love me?' I ask again.

Gabe frowns, his eyes dropping from mine. 'I definitely like you.'

So there we have it. It really was all an act. 'You took my virginity, Gabe.'

Tamsin looks at me in shock. '*What?*'

'We – we slept together,' I say.

'You initiated it!' Gabe whines.

What happens next happens so quickly, I can barely make sense of it. Tamsin lifts her hand then throws her father's heavy, antique clock right at Gabe's beautiful face. He tries to duck out of the way, but the clock's corner catches him right on his temple. Gabe lets out a grunt then falls to the ground. Blood pools around his head and Tamsin stumbles away with her hand to her mouth. 'I – I didn't mean to do that,' she whispers.

I run to Gabe. His eyes are closed and the blood, Oh God, so much blood.

'Gabe!' I shout, shaking his shoulder. No response. I reach out a trembling hand and place it on his cheek. 'Gabe?' I whisper, feeling his warm blood beneath my fingertips.

'Is, is – is he dead?' Tamsin asks, voice trembling.

Dead. Gabe, dead? I place a shaking finger to his neck, the same neck I have kissed a hundred times. I feel for the pulse too but there is nothing. I snatch my hand away, staring in horror at his pale face and the blood around his head. I look over my shoulder at Tamsin. 'I – I don't know if he's breathing,' I admit, heart pounding with fear.

Tamsin's eyes widen. 'Oh no, oh no.' She suddenly scrambles up and runs from the room, fleeing up the stairs.

I stay where I am for a moment, looking down at Gabe. Can he really be dead? I realise with horror that a part of me is pleased. How awful is that? How evil! How could I even *think* that? I quickly stand on shaky legs and back away, before letting out a sob and running upstairs too, slamming the cellar door behind me and leaning against it with my eyes closed, gulping in deep breaths to calm myself. When I open my eyes, I feel more clarity. 'We have to call an ambulance.'

I go to the phone in the hallway and pick it up, but Tamsin rushes towards me, slamming my hand down. 'No.'

'But we *have* to. We can't just leave him there. He might need help.'

'He's dead. It's obvious. You couldn't feel a pulse.'

'I'm no bloody doctor, Tamsin! He could be alive, bleeding to death down there.' I go to the cellar door again but she blocks my way. 'Tamsin, come on, what is *wrong* with you?'

'I'll get arrested.'

'We'll say it was an accident. I – I won't say it was you. We'll say he fell.'

'Don't you watch crime dramas? They'll *know* he was hit with something. And this time, they really will lock me up.'

I frown. '*This* time?'

She blinks, looking away from me. 'It's why we left London. I – I get so angry sometimes. I kind of blank out and the next thing I know, someone's hurt.'

'I don't understand.'

'I pushed a girl down the stairs at school after my boyfriend cheated on me with her. She – she's paralysed because of it.'

My hand flies to my chest in shock. 'Tamsin, why didn't you say?'

'I was ashamed. And now this.' She peers towards the cellar door. 'It's not just Gabe's life that will be over, it'll be mine too. My family's money might be able to buy me out of an accident at school but murder?'

We both freeze when the front door suddenly opens and Dorothy appears. I quickly put my bloody hands behind my back, my heart racing as I try to compose myself.

'Girls!' Dorothy declares when she sees us. 'I thought you'd still be out by the pool, it's so *warm* this evening.'

'We – we thought you were staying overnight, Mum?' Tamsin asks, her eyes darting to the cellar door then away again.

'Oh so did I!' Dorothy says, placing her bag on the side, 'but my friend started feeling unwell so we called it a night and now I just want to draw myself a lovely luxurious bath and have a *very* expensive bottle of wine.' She starts heading to the cellar where the wine is and I almost faint with panic. Luckily, Tamsin gets to the door first, pressing her back to it as she smiles at her mother.

'Let me get you a bottle, Mum. You go and get your bath sorted. Let me guess, a bottle of the Pahlmeyer Jayson Red?'

Dorothy smiles, stroking her daughter's face. 'You know me so well.'

Tamsin slips inside the cellar door, leaving me alone with her mother.

'Are you okay, Liz?' Dorothy asks me. 'You look terribly pale.'

'I'm fine,' I say in a voice I realise is unnaturally high.

'How's Tamsin been?'

'Fine,' I say. 'Totally fine.'

'Yes, she has seemed more – how shall I put it – *sprite* of late. I was wondering if she and Gabe . . .' Her voice trails off and she raises her eyebrows.

'No,' I lie, pain a drum in my head. 'They're just friends. We're all just friends.'

She glances around the back of the manor. 'Where is that handsome boy?'

'He's fine, he, erm, his grandfather said he could come back. He's actually gone there tonight, to chat.'

She frowns. 'Oh, really? I'm not sure how I feel about that; his grandfather sounds like a tyrant.'

'It's fine.' Fine, fine, fine, why do I keep saying fine? 'They're going to get family therapy,' I add. 'It's all good.'

'Therapy *is* good, it's been a godsend for Tamsin.' Her green eyes, so much like Tamsin's, settle on me. '*You've* been a godsend for her too, Liz. I have honestly not known a year in my daughter's life when there hasn't been some drama or another. You clearly have a calming influence on her.'

I have to draw on all my reserves not to let out a sob. 'I'm pleased,' I say instead. 'She's – she's been good for me too.' *Apart from the dead body down in the cellar, of course.*

Dorothy yawns. 'Your bath clearly calls to you,' I say with a nervous laugh.

As Dorothy disappears from sight, Tamsin slips out from behind the cellar door, the bottle of wine in her hands. 'He's definitely dead,' she whispers in horror, her green eyes haunted.

I grab her arm and pull her into the living room, shutting the door. 'Keep your voice down, your mum might hear.'

'Seriously though,' Tamsin says, her voice trembling. 'He's properly dead.'

I wrap my arms around myself, my teeth chattering. 'We need to figure out what to do.' As I say that, we hear the front door slam. We both go quiet.

'Maybe your mum forgot something from her car?' I suggest.

'No,' Tamsin says, shaking her head. 'Listen, you can hear her walking around upstairs.'

We run to the window, peering out into the semi-darkness to see a figure stumbling towards the swimming pool.

'It's Gabe!' I say, relief flooding through me. 'He's alive! Look. He's heading for the steps that go down to the beach from the clifftop.'

'Or he'll go to the police!' Tamsin says. 'He'll tell them I assaulted him.'

I try to gather my thoughts. 'Okay, you go and give your mum her wine. I'll go after him.'

Tamsin grasps my arm, face desperate. 'Tell – tell him it was an accident. He – he can take the bloody clock and sell it if he wants to, it's worth tens of thousands. He just *can't* go to the police.' I nod and we step out into the hallway. There is a trail of blood across the floor. 'Shit, my mum will see.'

'Then clean it up!'

'But . . . how?'

I roll my eyes and run into the kitchen, going to the cupboard where I know Simone keeps her cleaning stuff. I find some cleaning spray and kitchen towels then run back out.

'Do this,' I say to Tamsin, getting on my knees and wiping the blood up with kitchen towel then spraying it and wiping it again. 'If your mum comes down, tell her it's ketchup.'

Tamsin nods, so placid now. 'Go, before Gabe gets away.'

I take a deep breath then head out into the night, the wind thrashing my hair about. The moon is so high and so bright, it illuminates the gardens. But I can't see Gabe anywhere. I call his name as I walk around the edge of the swimming pool, but my voice is carried away by the wind. What will I say to him when I see him? I'm feeling such a storm of emotions right now. Relief he's alive. But anger at his betrayal too, so much anger. Worst of all, heartache.

At least it's not grief. At least he *is* alive.

My eyes scour the gardens at the back as I continue walking, then I approach the steps going down to the beach. Has he gone already? I peer over the edge of the cliff towards the small curve of beach below. Then something catches my eye in the sea directly below the cliff to the right.

There's something in the waves. Not just something but . . . a body. The moon is shining right on it and it's unmistakable. It's Gabe. I can tell from his dark hair and those distinctive red shoes. Did he jump? Or did his head injury confuse him, making him stumble and fall over the edge?

I go to run down to the beach, but find I am paralysed all of a sudden. There is something almost hypnotic about the sight of Gabe's body being carried away by the sea. Is he dead, truly dead? I double over with the pain of it. How can this be happening?

Eventually, I run back to the manor, tears streaming down my face. Tamsin is waiting for me at the entrance now, a bloody kitchen towel in her hands. 'What happened?' she asks.

'Gabe is gone.'

'What do you mean?'

'In the sea. He's in the sea.'

Her eyes widen in shock. 'I – I don't understand.'

'I saw his – his body down there, he must have fallen over the edge of the cliff.' Tamsin's face fills with horror and I grasp her hands. 'Or maybe he did it himself. Maybe he felt *so* terrible about what he did, he jumped.'

'No,' Tamsin shouts out, shaking her head. 'I killed him. My mum will never forgive me. She'll – she'll definitely see me for the monster I am now. How can she love me?'

'Your mother will always love you, no matter what you do.'

'No, no, this is a step too far, the worst possible kind of step, even for her.'

'But it was an accident, remember? He was injured. You did *not* kill him, you hear me?'

Her eyes flicker up to me. 'But I did. I – I wanted to. In that moment, I did.'

'What the hell is going on, girls?' We turn to see Dorothy watching us from the top of the stairs.

Chapter 22

Now

'You should have shared this from the start,' Detective Clarke says when I finish telling him. 'It would have helped me a great deal. The Jacob Sable case was one of my first cases when I joined the force.'

I look at him in surprise. 'It was?'

'When his family reported him missing, we spent a great deal of time trying to find him to no avail. An uphill struggle when so many young men go missing, especially one with his troubled past.'

'What do you mean by troubled past?'

'The kid had a thing for stealing. Seems he was pretty good at it until he was caught trying to steal a bag of money from a friend's house. His friend whose dad was a known criminal. When Jacob learnt the father was trawling CCTV footage from when the bag disappeared, he knew he was in trouble.'

'That was why he left London?'

The detective nods. 'What happened to him after has always been a mystery. It was presumed his friend's father harmed him in some way, but he always had a solid alibi. It's a relief to finally know what happened.'

'I'll be relieved too when you find my daughter safe and well,' I say. 'Can you check if your officers have managed to get into the manor? It's only a couple of minutes' drive.'

The detective nods at the police officer with him. She leaves the room with her walkie-talkie.

'You can see why I'm so worried for my daughter, can't you?' I say. 'The woman I've been telling you has stolen Tamsin's identity; she is Gwen Sable, Jacob's sister. She wants revenge. God only knows what she's capable of.'

The young officer walks back in then. 'They're there, but they can't get in,' she says. 'They're trying to get the combination for the gate from the security firm.'

'They can just scale the walls!' I say.

'No they can't, Liz,' the detective says.

'But surely you know now how unstable Gwen Sable is? How *urgent* this is?'

'All we know,' the detective says sadly, 'is that Tamsin Lakewell's actions may have caused the death of a young man. And that you, Liz Barrowman, conspired to conceal the truth.' He sighs very deeply. 'I'm afraid I have no choice but to arrest you.'

I look at him in shock. 'Arrest *me*?'

'I'm sorry, I really am,' the detective says, gesturing to his colleague, who pulls out some handcuffs and heads towards me.

I back away, shaking my head. 'No, this is ridiculous. My daughter is in danger, *Tamsin* is in danger. You have to find them.'

'Rest assured, we will do all we can to find them,' the detective says, 'especially now Tamsin is a person of *extreme* interest to us.'

The police officer goes to cuff me, but I jump back. She sighs. 'We can do this the hard way or the easy way.'

I close my eyes. Of course, this was always going to happen, ever since that fateful night twenty years ago as I looked down at Gabe's body.

'Can I first say goodbye to my daughter?' I ask, eyes pleading with them. 'And ask my mother to get my ex-husband to come down? My mother can't move without assistance so I can't have just her in charge of Mia.'

The two officers exchange looks. 'Fine,' the detective says. 'We'll wait here.'

I give him a grateful smile, then jog upstairs. 'Darling,' I say as I walk into the girls' room. 'I need to pop out to help the police find Ruby, but your grandmother's here and I'm going to get her to call your dad to come down to look after you, in case I'm longer than I think.'

She frowns. 'What will Dad think about all this, Mum? Will it be mentioned in the custody case tomorrow?'

I can't tell her that of course it will. I can't tell her the reason I know that is because I'm about to be arrested. I can't worry her more than she already is. I feel tears flood my eyes and quickly stand up, going to the window so I can hide my tears from her. What a mess! And all because of that bloody manor. I look towards it, then freeze: there's a huge crane protruding from the grounds of the manor in the distance. Or is it just a crane?

Mia follows my gaze. 'Oh, that must be happening today then.'

I turn to her. 'What's happening?'

'Our teacher said Lakewell Manor's being knocked down so they can build new houses on it. The poet lady's done a deal with Mr Gold, it's in the news and everything.'

I can barely breathe. It's not a crane that's out there, it's a wrecking ball! If Ruby is in the manor then she's in even more imminent danger. In fact, that might be exactly why Gwen took her today! I go to run downstairs to tell the police, then pause. I know a way in.

'Mum?' Mia asks in a worried voice.

I take a deep breath and go to her, pulling her close to me. 'It'll all be okay,' I lie. 'It will all work out.' Then I walk from her room and head to my mother's room. 'I need to go out,' I say. 'Can you call Scott to come down for Mia? And in the meantime, make sure she's okay? I'll get Lester to drop off some dinner for you both.'

My mother narrows her eyes suspiciously at me. 'Why is there a police car outside? I can see it from here.' I don't answer. 'You're finally getting arrested, aren't you?' she says, almost triumphant.

I peer over my shoulder and lower my voice. 'I had to tell them everything, for Ruby's sake.'

'I always knew it. I always knew it would be your downfall. From that first moment you climbed into that girl's house, you began your downward spiral. Curiosity killed the cat, you know.'

'At least I *am* curious,' I snap. 'I want to know about the people I love. I want them to be happy. I want to show them my love. I want to be *loved* because God knows, you've never given me any love or shown an ounce of curiosity and interest in me.'

She looks at me in shock. I shake my head then jog to the bathroom, closing the door behind me. Outside, the branches of the old oak tree in the front garden thrash and turn in the wind. I open the window as wide as I can. Then I clamber on to the windowsill and step out on to one of the tree's sturdy branches. Time to find Ruby and Tamsin.

Chapter 23

The landscape is eerily beautiful as I run towards the manor, the sun half shrouded by clouds, pitching long shadows across the lawn. But all I feel is a sense of menace as I approach. I am risking *so* much to do this: evading arrest being the worst, giving Scott yet more reasons to have the girls taken away from me tomorrow. But my gut tells me Ruby and Tamsin are inside Lakewell Manor and that wrecking ball is readying to knock the place down around them. In fact, I can see it right now, by the side of the manor, no workers anywhere to be seen. At least that's something. At least that means it's not ready to be used right now. As I draw closer, I see the two local police officers peering through the gates, one of them on the phone to someone. I know they won't be able to force the gates open, nor scale the walls. They won't want to break the rules for a girl who's only been missing a few hours. But I will.

I run to a familiar tree at the side of the manor and peer up at it. It's even taller than it once was, its branches golden beneath a column of sunlight that shines through the cloud above. I take a deep breath then haul myself up on to the first branch, just as I did all those years ago. I feel a mixture of exhilaration and deep sadness. So much good happened from the moment I climbed this tree all those years ago. So much bad too.

'Pssst, what are you doing?'

I look down to see Lester peering up at me. *Shit.* 'I was walking by and saw you up the tree,' he says. 'What *are* you doing?'

'I haven't got time to explain,' I say. 'I have to get in there.'

'Fine,' he says, wrapping his arms around the tree trunk. 'I'm coming with you.'

'No, Lester!' But it's too late, he's swinging up on to the branch below me. I shake my head. I don't have time for this.

I rapidly climb up the tree, branch by branch as Lester follows below, huffing and puffing all the way. 'Jesus Liz,' he says, 'what are you, a monkey?'

'I did lots of tree climbing as a kid.' I haul myself on to the wall and the memories of doing the same all those years ago accost me. I take a deep breath as I look at the wrecking ball. Men in hardhats are now walking out from the back of the garden. Could Gwen really have planned for this? A wrecking ball through the very place that took her brother from her . . . and through the woman she knows caused his death. What about Ruby? A taste of my own medicine to feel the pain of a loved one gone? As I think that, one of the workmen hops into the carriage of the vehicle operating the wrecking ball. Horror rushes through me. I look towards the front of the manor. The police have gone!

'Wait!' I shout to the workmen but they can't hear me. The wrecking ball starts up, its mechanical arm beginning to rise. 'I have to get down there!' I say to Lester as he pulls himself on to the wall beside me, out of breath. 'The tree I used to climb down this side isn't here any longer. You'll have to lower me down.'

The wrecking ball begins to roll towards the manor. 'Stop!' I shout, even though I know it's of no use. I lower myself off the wall until I'm holding on to the ridge with my hands, my feet dangling about six foot off the ground. I could jump but chances are, I'd break my ankle. I peer up at Lester. 'Quick, take my wrists, grip them hard and help me lower myself down.' He does as I ask, his large, warm hands around my wrists as he lowers me to the ground until I can jump of my own accord. I don't even stop to breathe. The wrecking ball is about to swing into the wall.

'No!' I scream. Two workmen standing by the wrecking ball turn, catching sight of me. I run over, waving my hands. 'Stop, people are in there!'

'Shit,' one of them says. He jumps on to the cabin of the wrecking ball and smashes his fist at the glass to get the driver's attention. The giant arm holding the ball pauses and I let out a breath of relief.

'But the woman told us it was empty,' the workman driving the machine says.

The woman. Gwen. She *did* mean for this to happen.

'Well, it's not,' I say, trying not to show the fury I'm feeling. I pause and look up at the manor. It looks just as it did that night twenty years ago, standing high above me. There are no lights on inside. It really does give the impression of being empty. Have Carl and Gwen just left it to be knocked down, running off to safety?

'Hey, you've left someone behind!' I turn to see Lester sitting on the wall.

I roll my eyes and jog back over. 'Stand on my shoulders.' He does as I ask, clambering on to my shoulders before lowering himself down. Then we head to the front door but when I try the handle, I see it's locked. So I run around the other side of the house as Lester jogs to catch up with me.

'I know another way in. Tamsin and I used it to sneak out to meet Gabe during sleepovers.'

I lead Lester towards a large sash window that I know used to have a dodgy latch. Just as I predicted, it slides up when I try it and we quietly slip into the manor's dark hallway. Though it's daylight, all the curtains are drawn so it feels vast and oppressive, shadows crawling up the walls.

'This place is creepy in the dark,' he whispers.

I move in closer to Lester, pleased he's here now. 'Tell me about it,' I whisper back, turning the torch from my phone on and shedding some light around the room.

'So where's the cellar?' Lester asks.

'There,' I say, gesturing to the doorway that is just visible in the corridor that leads from the hallway to the kitchen. I go to it, heart thumping, and clasp the handle, turning it. But it's locked! I'm about to start looking for the keys, but then there's a noise. Lester and I turn around just as a figure darts away in the distance.

'Hey!' I call out.

'Liz, wait,' Lester says, but it's too late, I'm running in the direction of the figure. As I do, I trip over something and am sent sprawling. As I try to pick myself up, there's the sound of commotion, a shout of pain and I turn to see Lester standing with his foot on Carl's chest.

'Where's Ruby?' I shout at Carl. 'And Tamsin. They're in the cellar, aren't they?'

He looks at me with surprise in his eyes. 'What on earth do you mean? And will you get your bloody foot off me,' he says to Lester.

Lester reluctantly removes his foot and Carl gets up, brushing mud from his crumpled shirt.

'Are they in there?' I ask. 'Where are the keys?'

'I don't have the keys and I have no idea what you mean,' Carl says.

'Don't lie,' I say. 'You know what *Gwen Sable* is up to,' I say, emphasising the name so it's clear I know who she is now.

Carl looks at me in shock. 'You – you know about Gwen?'

'I know *everything*, Carl,' I say, crossing my arms as I look at him. 'Now where's my daughter, and where's Tamsin?'

'I have no idea, I swear to you.'

'Bullshit. Oh and I've stopped the wrecking ball by the way so your little plan won't work.'

215

'My only plan was to be in here when the wrecking ball took the manor down, so I could go down with it.' His shoulders slump and he sinks on to the first step of the manor's grand staircase. He really does look broken, his eyes red-rimmed and distraught beneath the light of my phone. 'I can't lie any more,' he whispers. 'I just can't.'

'Then tell us the truth,' Lester demands.

Carl peers up at him. 'Tamsin is dead.'

Chapter 24

20 Years Ago

Dorothy is wearing a thick blue bathrobe and her hair is wet. She marches down the stairs and grabs the bloody kitchen towel from Tamsin. 'What is this, are you hurt?'

'I cut myself,' I say, holding my shaky bloody hands out to her. 'Tamsin was helping me.'

Dorothy examines my face. 'I know you're lying, Liz.' She turns to Tamsin. 'What did you do?'

'We both did it,' I quickly say. 'Both of us, right?' I say to Tamsin, giving her a look.

She slowly nods. Dorothy quickly searches the darkness outside, then pulls us both into the hallway, closing the front door.

'I need to know everything,' she says. '*Everything.*'

So that's what I do. I tell her everything. Gabe's deceptions and manipulations. How I caught him stealing their family heirlooms.

'We confronted him,' I say. 'He eventually admitted it. He was so . . . arrogant about it. He never cared about us.'

My voice catches in my throat then and Dorothy squeezes my hand. 'Go on,' she says softly.

'He said he was going to take all the stuff,' I lie, 'and we could do nothing about it, right Tamsin?' Tamsin nods, eyes vacant. 'He went to leave the cellar with it all, so the two of us,' I say, gesturing between us, 'we ran after him and grabbed the rucksack, but we ended up accidentally pulling Gabe down the stairs and he – he hit his head. *Badly.* Then he stumbled outside and – and he fell from the cliff.'

Dorothy is quiet as I say that, looking at me, then at her daughter. 'Is this true, Tamsin?'

Tamsin raises her eyes to her mother. 'Yes.'

Dorothy sighs. 'I always know when you're lying, remember?' She turns to me. 'You're a good friend to Tamsin, Liz, such a good friend, lying like this.' I go to protest but Dorothy puts her hand up. 'I know my daughter and I love every part of her. She will be fine, I'll make sure of it. But I will *not* have you dragged into this. If people come looking for the boy, we will say nothing. It will be assumed he took his life.'

'But his head injury!' Tamsin whines.

'The sea can be very violent. Head injuries are inevitable.'

'Do you hate me?' Tamsin whispers to her mother.

Dorothy smiles sadly. 'I could *never* hate you. You are my love, my everything.' She pulls Tamsin into her arms as Tamsin begins to cry. 'There, there, my sweet, it will all be okay. We'll move away again, as soon as tomorrow if need be.'

Tamsin peeks at me and I can see she is as sad as I am at the prospect of her leaving Easthaven.

I watch them for a while, wishing with all my heart I had a mother like Dorothy. Then I go to leave. Dorothy looks up at me, mouthing a *thank you*. I nod, then walk out. I don't remember the walk back home, I'm still in shock. I just place one foot in front of the other. When I get home, my mother is in the living room and I think of that image again, of Tamsin being comforted by her mother. Maybe something like this is all that's needed to finally feel my mother's arms around me and her comforting words?

She looks up from her TV show when I walk into the living room. 'What's up with you? You look a right state.'

'Something terrible happened.'

'What now?' she asks, like she's always having to ask such things when the truth is, I am no trouble to her, none at all . . . unlike Tamsin is for Dorothy.

I sit on the sofa next to my mother. She shifts up, uncomfortable by my proximity. I ignore how that makes me feel.

'So, spill your guts,' she snaps.

'A boy lied to me. He – he broke my heart.'

'Oh Jesus, you're pregnant, aren't you?'

'No! He lied to me, he used me, and Tamsin too, to steal stuff from the manor.'

'Well, that's men for you,' Mother huffs. 'Haven't I told you enough over the years? I have no sympathy. It's not like I didn't warn you.' She goes to turn her attention back to her TV programme.

'It's not just that!' I shout. 'Something happened. Something really bad.'

She sighs, turning the TV down. 'I'm not going to want to hear this, am I?'

'I need you to.'

'Fine, go on then, it's not like you haven't ruined my life already.'

I close my eyes, blocking her hateful words out. Then I tell her the version of Gabe's death that I told Tamsin's mother. I don't want to risk Tamsin getting into trouble. When I'm finished, I start crying. I can almost feel my skin tingling at the need to feel my mother's arms around me. But instead, she just shakes her head.

'What a sorry mess you've got yourself into. And let me guess, Dorothy Lakewell will be moving her daughter away again.'

I nod. It really hits me then. Tamsin is leaving Easthaven. My only friend, gone. The grief is unbearable and I sink my forehead on to my mother's plump shoulder, sobbing.

But she jerks her shoulder away. 'Always knew you'd end up in trouble. Lucky you have a friend rich enough to cover your tracks. Don't expect any sympathy from me though.'

'Can't you see I'm upset?' I shout. 'Why can't you just comfort me for once in my life? I'm grieving.'

She laughs. 'Grieving a cheating scoundrel, so what? As for Tamsin Lakewell, she's never been good for you. That's not grief, that's a godsend, her leaving.'

I stand up, wiping my tears away. 'I don't know why I bother.'

'No, I don't know why you do either.'

Then I run upstairs and slam the door, looking out towards the sea.

'Oh Gabe,' I whisper. Then I take in Lakewell Manor in the distance. 'Oh Tamsin.'

Chapter 25

Now

I shake my head, backing away. 'No. No no no, Tamsin can't be dead.'

'It was an accident,' Carl quickly says. 'Gwen turned up at the manor. She argued with Tamsin. Tamsin can get pretty . . . wild when she argues. I think Gwen got scared, she pushed Tamsin, and – and she fell.'

'And Ruby?' I say, voice desperate. 'Where's my daughter?'

'I really don't know. I haven't even seen Gwen all day. I have no idea why you think she took your daughter.'

'You're bloody useless,' I shout at him. I run to the cellar door, yanking at the handle. But it's locked. I turn back to Carl. 'Where's the key?'

'I have no idea, I've never been down there.'

I slam my fists on the door. Lester comes over, putting his hand on my shoulder. 'I'll see if the workmen can help us get in.'

He leaves the manor and I turn to Carl. 'How did Tamsin die?'

'A knock to the head,' he says, flinching at the memory. 'Gwen turned up at the manor in the night on the Monday after we first arrived in Easthaven, went ballistic, throwing stuff about, telling

Tamsin I was just using her.' He looks up at me with pleading eyes. 'I wasn't though, Liz, not by then. I'd really fallen in love with her.'

I shake my head as I continue trying the cellar door. 'Some way of showing it.'

'Fine, if you don't want to believe me, but at least I know in my heart it is true. When Tamsin ran upstairs to get her phone, threatening to call the police, Gwen followed her and tried to pull her back down.' He puts his hand to his mouth, shaking his head as his eyes fill with tears. 'That was when Tamsin fell down the stairs and – and hit her head on this very step,' he says, looking down at the step he's sitting on. 'That's where I was planning to die tonight too, before you stopped that wrecking ball. I decided to return and crumble with the manor, in the very place the love of my life died. I just can't live on without Tamsin. I've tried, I've really tried.'

'Jesus,' I whisper, slumping against the wall, the reality of what he's saying truly sinking in. 'So Gwen killed Tamsin?'

Carl rakes his fingers through his dark, dishevelled hair. 'Not purposefully. It really was an accident. When I tried to get near Tamsin to check on her, Gwen wouldn't let me.' His eyes fill with anguish. 'She was like a wolf protecting its dead prey. She started to blame me, said the police would of course think I was responsible, considering the time I'd already spent in prison. She told me to get out if I wanted to have any chance of avoiding prison again and she would sort it. So – so that's what I did.'

'You just left Tamsin's body here with her?' I say, tears streaming down my cheeks.

He nods. 'I couldn't look at Tamsin like that. I – I couldn't face it. You have to believe me when I say I really did love her.' So that's it. My friend is dead. All this time she's been dead. And what does it mean for Ruby, my darling Ruby? Terror shoots through me as I peer towards the cellar door.

Lester comes back in then, out of breath. 'The workmen are refusing to get involved. But I did find these on the bistro table outside.' He hands me a bunch of keys. 'Recognise any as the cellar key?'

I nod. It's unmistakable with its distinctive bird motif. I run to the door with Lester and use the key to unlock it, heart thumping as I fling the door open and run down the stairs. It's so dark, I can barely see. The smell of the cellar – that old musty smell – hits my nostrils, bringing back a flood of memories, good and bad. Even the creak of each step beneath my feet brings back a new memory: how I quietly crept down to see Gabe stealing. How I slowly walked down with Tamsin to show her.

Oh Tamsin.

When we get to the bottom, my eyes search the darkness. I feel like I'm all of a sudden transported back to that night again, with Gabe lying on the floor before me. Will I find Tamsin's body here? Or Ruby's?

Something moves in the darkness and brushes against me. I let out a scream.

'Mum?'

It's Ruby's voice. 'Ruby!' A light comes on and she's standing before me, shining her mobile phone at me. Behind her is someone else huddled on a sofa, white cloth bandages around her head stained with blood. 'Tamsin!' I shout in disbelief.

Ruby runs into my arms as I look at Tamsin, unable to believe she's alive.

'Thank God,' I hear Lester whisper.

Behind us, Carl appears ashen-faced on the stairs. 'Tamsin?' he whispers. 'But – but how?'

I'm wondering that too, but I have to check Ruby's okay first. I hug her close, relief flooding through me.

'Are you hurt?' I ask, examining her face.

Tamsin stands and under the lamp light in the room I can see how awful she looks: skinny, bruised, a gauze on her head sticky with old blood.

'I'm fine,' Ruby says. 'Honestly. Just feel like an idiot for falling for that fake cow's trap.'

'You're alive!' Carl says to Tamsin. 'My darling Tamsin, you're alive!'

He runs towards a fragile Tamsin and tries to take her into his arms, but she shoves him away. 'Get away from me,' she says in a trembling voice.

'You heard her,' Lester hisses at Carl as I stride over with Ruby and put my arm around Tamsin's shoulders.

'Gwen told me you were dead,' Carl says, voice desperate. 'She – she said she checked your pulse and everything. I swear I didn't know. I was devastated, a mess.'

'You *used* me for my inheritance,' Tamsin says.

'At first, yes, but then I fell in love with you.'

'You don't know what true love is. I never want to see you again.' She turns to me, eyes red and filled with tears. 'Please, can we get out of here? I'm scared Gwen will come back. She is *completely* unhinged.'

Fear traces a line down my spine. 'Of course.' I turn to look at Carl. 'Don't you dare follow.'

Carl's shoulders slump as Lester and I help Tamsin limp out of the room and up the stairs with Ruby. When we get to the hallway, Tamsin searches it with scared eyes. 'Do you think Gwen is gone?'

'I haven't seen her. What did she do to you?'

She looks up at me beneath tear-drenched eyelashes. 'She's Gabe's sister!'

'I know. You're so skinny,' I say as I help Tamsin sit down on a nearby chair. 'Did Gwen even feed you?'

'She brought down food, twice a day,' Tamsin says. 'I just found it hard to eat.'

'Me too,' Ruby says, frowning as she wraps her arms around herself.

'What was she planning to do with you both?' I ask them. 'Did she say?'

'At first, she just wanted to talk to me about her brother,' Tamsin says. 'Did you know his real name was actually Jacob Sable?'

I nod. 'I do. But how did she find out about Gabe?'

'I told Carl when I got to know him better and he told Gwen. They had no idea Gabe was Gwen's brother, of course. When Gwen tracked us down here,' she says, looking around her, 'she still knew nothing of my connection with her brother. She was angry with Carl for leaving her for me and turning his back on their awful scams. The fight Gwen and I had.' Tamsin shudders. 'I know I get angry, Liz, but the way she was. I saw the red mist and she saw it harder. I don't remember what happened after I smacked my head. She told Carl I was dead, ultimate punishment for Carl and something to hang over his head to get him back. She dragged me down to the cellar while I was still unconscious and decided to keep me there until she figured out what to do with me.'

'So how did she find out that Gabe was really Jacob?' I ask.

'She found a photo of him. It was in one of Mum's old boxes in the office from the luncheon that year. Gwen was going through documents trying to find proof of address to get some money of mine. When she saw the photo of Gabe with us and recognised him as her brother, she put two and two together and realised that I killed her brother.' Tamsin hangs her head. 'She lost her mind in the cellar that day; I honestly thought she would kill me but in the end she decided to torture me by getting me to tell her about that night over and over, while disguising herself as me to strip me of my money in the process too. She'd even wear that stupid wig of hers

225

and read my poetry to taunt me.' She shudders. 'Then she started talking about getting the manor bulldozed with me in it.'

I shake my head. 'She's a monster.' I turn to Ruby. 'How did you end up here, darling?'

Ruby sighs. 'Gwen got me here under false pretences, pretending to be some maid from the manor who knew all about what happened to Gabe.'

'The comment on your TikTok video?' I ask.

Ruby nods. 'Yeah, but then she messaged me direct too last night. She told me to meet her here, at the manor. She didn't have her lame red wig on when I got here, so I didn't recognise her. I'm *such* an idiot.'

'You *were* silly to come here,' I say. 'But you're no idiot.'

'She then tricked me into going down to the cellar and locked me in there with Tamsin. She's a proper psycho, Mum.'

'Oh I know,' I say.

'That's not a very nice thing to say,' a voice says from the open front door. We all look over to see Gwen standing outside, a suitcase in her hands.

Chapter 26

Gwen still has her Tamsin wig on and is wearing a khaki-green jumpsuit with an extravagant red scarf around her neck. Tamsin cringes away from her as Ruby clasps my arm. Carl reappears from the cellar, looking forlorn as he stares at Tamsin. Then he notices Gwen and fear flashes in his eyes. He's scared of her.

My own heart beats with terror, but then overwhelming anger cuts through me and I find myself storming towards her, grabbing her arm. Her suitcase falls, landing open on the marble floor, her clothes spilling out.

'How dare you kidnap my daughter!' I scream in her face.

'And how dare you kill my brother?' Gwen shouts back. *'I'm* the one who ought to be angry.'

'It was an accident, how many times do I have to tell you?' Tamsin says from behind us.

'Throwing a heavy clock at his head? I wouldn't call that an accident. And what about you?' Gwen says, turning her cold stare to me. 'From what I hear, you were quite happy to watch his body float out to sea, weren't you?' Her eyes fill with tears. 'If you'd alerted the authorities, Jacob may have been saved.'

'Yes, I regret that,' I admit. 'But it doesn't excuse you kidnapping my daughter, and Tamsin too. And what about the wrecking ball?' I ask, gesturing outside.

She follows my gaze. 'Oh yes, that. It's only fitting after what you did to my darling brother, Jacob.'

'But Ruby had nothing to do with it!' I shout.

Gwen shrugs. 'I wanted you to understand how it feels to lose someone so special. And Jacob was special. He was the only one who understood me – but *you*,' she screams at Tamsin, 'you took him away from me!'

'You can't blame Tamsin for his death,' Lester says.

'She can, Lester,' Tamsin says with a sigh. 'She can blame me.'

'No, Tamsin, you don't understand,' Lester says. 'Gabe – Jacob – he was pushed.'

We all look at him in surprise.

'Pushed?' Gwen says, shoving past me to look directly at Lester. 'What do you mean, *pushed?*'

'I was sitting at the cliff edge at the end of the road, by the manor. There used to be a bench there,' Lester explains. 'I'd go there sometimes with my girlfriend at the time. That night, we heard arguing, so I looked through the manor gates to see Gabe inside the manor grounds, right on the edge of the cliff with someone.'

'Someone? Who?' Gwen and I ask at the same time.

He sighs. 'Douglas Gold.'

My mouth drops open. 'You're saying *Douglas* pushed Gabe?'

Lester nods but Gwen shakes her head. 'I don't believe you. How could you even tell from that distance?'

'The moon was crazy that night, huge,' Lester says.

'Yes, I remember,' Tamsin says.

'It was shining right on them and you know how long Douglas's hair was back then?' Lester says to us. 'You couldn't mistake him, really. He was angry and shouting at Jacob. Douglas accused him of stealing his watch right off his wrist while he was distracted at the Lakewell Manor luncheon. The watch belonged to his late grandfather and was worth a fortune. Honestly, Douglas was fuming.' He turns to Gwen. 'He said he'd overheard Tamsin and Liz talking in the living room about your brother stealing stuff in the cellar and realised what was going on.'

'But Douglas wasn't there!' Tamsin says.

Lester sighs. 'Maybe you didn't see him, but he was up to his voyeurism tricks again. I'd actually caught him spying on you and Tamsin once, during my paper round, watching from the tree as you guys sunbathed by the pool in your swimwear. I think he was enjoying it a bit too much. Clearly, he was doing the same that night.'

'Bloody pervert,' Ruby says.

'He punched Gabe,' Lester continues, 'and – and then just pushed him, right over the edge.'

I look at Gwen. She's blinking, trying to compute what Lester is saying.

'My God,' Tamsin whispers, putting her hand to her mouth. 'All this time . . .'

'Why didn't you *say* anything?' I ask Lester.

'I confronted Douglas,' he replies. 'When he let himself out of the manor gates. He didn't care, he admitted it all to me. Said Gabe deserved it.'

Gwen is still quiet, looking at the Golds' villa in the distance as her eyes swirl with anger.

'Did you not call the police?' Tamsin asks Lester.

'Did *you*, after what happened?' Lester asks.

Tamsin sighs. 'No.'

'I threatened to,' Lester continues. 'But then Douglas reminded me my mum cleaned for him, and other families in Easthaven too. He said he could easily get my mum fired from all her cleaning jobs. You know how difficult it was for us then, Liz. We were skint. It would have been a disaster.' He swallows, looking down at his hands. 'I was a scared, stupid kid.'

'What's your excuse now then?' I ask, frustrated that he's kept the truth from me, his friend. But then hadn't I kept so much from him, too?

He looks up at me. 'I swear I've been planning to tell you *and* the police, Liz. The thing is, Douglas still has so much power over me. I rent the building with the patisserie and the flat off him, remember? That's why I've been trying to find out if it actually does legally belong to him. The moment I don't have that threat hanging over my head, over *Eva's*, I was going to go to the police, I swear.'

So *that* was why Douglas wanted me to intercept a letter. If he lost that building, he'd lose his hold over the one witness to what he did to Gabe.

'So . . . I didn't kill Gabe,' Tamsin whispers.

'No,' Lester confirms.

She slumps down on to a nearby seat. Carl goes to walk towards her, but I shoot him a warning glare and he stops. I turn to Gwen. 'So, you've heard it all now,' I say.

'I certainly have,' a voice says. We all look up to see Detective Clarke stroll into the manor with the young police officer, the two other officers behind him. 'Go to the villa next door, arrest Douglas Gold for the death of Jacob Sable.' Then he strolls up to Gwen as Carl backs away, face going pale. 'Gwen Sable, I'm arresting you for false imprisonment, fraud by false representation and assault.' Gwen struggles against the officers as they try to arrest her, her wig falling off in the process to reveal her dark hair beneath.

Another officer approaches Carl, handcuffing him too. As he's led past Tamsin, his face falls. I can see from the look in his eyes that he really did love her in his own pathetic way.

'The thing is,' Tamsin says as she watches him being led outside, 'I still feel something for that bastard.'

'You loved him,' I say. 'Just like Imogen did.'

'Who's Imogen?' Tamsin asks.

'Another woman he duped. I'll tell you all about it later. But she loved him too.'

Tamsin nods. 'I did love him.' As she says that, we notice Gwen has lost all her bravado as she begins crying, mascara crawling down her cheeks, her thin brown hair making her look like a completely different person.

There's the sound of shouting from the villa next door. I recognise Douglas's voice.

'Aubrey, son, call my solicitor!' I hear him shout.

I stand on tiptoes to see Aubrey at one of the windows, watching his father being led away.

'Aubrey!' I hear his father shout again. 'Make the call, now!'

But Aubrey doesn't do as his father asks for once. Instead he just continues to watch him.

'Looks like the right people finally got their just rewards,' Lester says. 'I just wish it had happened sooner. I really should have said something.'

'I understand why you didn't,' I say. 'You couldn't lose your house, your business. Our kids always come first, right?'

'But still,' he says, shaking his head. 'All these years you've suffered, Tamsin, thinking it was you who caused his death.'

'Don't let it torment you, Lester,' Tamsin says. 'What's done is done. You're a good man, don't let all this make you think otherwise.' She turns to me. 'And you're a good woman, Liz. The best kind of friend, just as my mother said. And Ruby, wow. Like mother, like daughter.'

We all look at Ruby who is being interviewed by Detective Clarke nearby and smile. But then the smile disappears from my face. The custody hearing is tomorrow. I may have saved Ruby today, but will I lose her tomorrow?

Chapter 27

I take in my reflection in the mirror. I'm wearing a smart navy-blue suit which I'd bought for my job interview for the Easthaven postie job. It doesn't fit as well as it once did, I've lost weight in the past two weeks. I lean in close to the mirror, applying more blusher and hoping the circles under my eyes don't look so bad. I am so tired; I didn't sleep a wink last night. How could I with what happened the day before and what I'm about to go through now?

Outside, the taxi beeps its horn. I don't want to drive us to the custody hearing. I worry my hands will shake too much on the steering wheel. I take a deep breath and head out into the hallway, surprised to find Ruby and Mia already waiting for me. Ruby is wearing a pair of black trousers and a black blouse with cherries over it, and Mia is wearing a cute navy-blue dress I got her for Christmas. It's so unbelievably sweet. They've already given written statements to the judge, so they're not going to appear in court. But they've insisted on coming along as support and Scott was fine with that. After all, he believes he'll be taking them home with him anyway . . . and I believe that too.

Ruby looks me up and down, then nods. 'Perfect.'

Mia quickly runs into her room and I think she's upset, but then she reappears with some lip gloss. 'Just a teensy bit,' she says, applying it to my lips.

'Thank you, darlings,' I say, hugging them both close and trying not to think about the fact that it's unlikely they'll be coming back with me. We go to head downstairs, but first I pause at
my mother's doorway. She knows what happened yesterday and as
always, doesn't seem to care. I make a decision then: I will do all
I can to move out of this place. I can't bear the thought of living
alone with my mother after the girls have gone.

The three of us walk downstairs and get into the taxi. The half-
hour journey is silent. Ruby doesn't even look at her phone and
Mia's ears aren't filled with her AirPods. Instead, they sit either side
of me, hands clutched in mine. When we get to the courthouse,
I'm pleased it's nothing grand. Just a plain brown-bricked one. We
all walk in, still holding hands and I am grateful for that. For my
girls. I feel like sobbing. How will I be able to cope not having them
with me? It's bad enough on the weekends when Scott has them.

I give them quick hugs, then walk alone into the courtroom
with my solicitor. I see Scott right away, sitting at the front on the
left-hand side with his solicitor. My tummy turns over. In front is
the judge, a man in his sixties with a stern-looking face. My solicitor and I go to sit in the front row on the right-hand side. I try to
catch Scott's eye, but he's staring straight ahead, looking as nervous
as I feel. Determined too. All that happened yesterday must have
made him even more set on getting custody of Ruby and Mia. Sure,
Detective Clarke decided not to charge me or Tamsin in the end,
but Ruby was in danger and it was all because of me. I'd explained
it all to Scott in a long email so he had all the facts. I'm not sure if
it will help or hinder things, but I wanted him to know the truth.
From what I can see by the look on his face now, my past is about
to catch up with me.

A clerk sitting in front of the judge turns to him. 'Judge
Matthews, this is case 13565, Thomson versus Barrowman resi-
dency order.'

The judge nods, then turns to Scott's solicitor. 'You can begin.'

I take a deep breath and hold it. What's he going to say?

Scott's solicitor stands. 'Your Honour, we are here today because Scott Thomson asked me to enter a motion seeking custody of Ruby and Mia, his two children with Elizabeth Barrowman. Mr Thomson would like to make a statement to the court.'

I continue holding my breath as Scott stands up. He smooths his suit down, and opens his mouth. I let out my breath and close my eyes. Here it comes . . .

'Your Honour,' he says, 'I want to begin by stating I have the utmost respect for you and this court.' I try not to roll my eyes. Typical smarm. 'It's important for you to know that a great deal of additional information has come forward in the past twenty-four hours.' I clench my fists. I *knew* this would happen. 'Information that has persuaded me to ask for these proceedings to be stopped.'

I let out a gasp. Did I just hear that right?

'My ex-wife, Liz,' he says, turning to me, 'has proven to us all what a brave person she is, risking her life to save our daughter Ruby.'

I put my hand to my mouth, tears filling my eyes.

'I made a mistake applying for custody,' Scott continues, 'putting my anger above the facts, when the fact is, Liz is an amazing mother and our children would suffer from spending more time apart from her.'

The judge lets out a long sigh. 'I'm not happy about you wasting our time, Mr Thomson. But from the evidence I have already read, I agree.' He smacks his gavel on to the pad. 'Proceedings now ended, next case please.'

I put my head in my hands, sobbing in relief. Scott comes over to me, placing his hand on my back. 'Sorry to put you through all this, Liz.'

I look up at him. 'I don't care, I'm not losing my girls. Did yesterday really change your mind?'

'Yes, but Ruby and Mia sent me an email last night too. It was very persuasive.'

'My girls,' I say with a smile and suddenly, that's all I want to do: see my girls. I run from the court, finding Ruby and Mia outside with Scott's mother. The looks on their faces show me they are as surprised and delighted as I am. I run to them and pull them into a hug.

Now it *is* really over.

Epilogue

THREE MONTHS LATER

I park my Royal Mail van in Easthaven's promenade car park, then walk up the cobbled path, legs pumping. When I get to the top, I take a photo for my Instagram account. It's autumn now, so there's a mist lying over the sea, the promenade and white villas almost shadows in the early morning sun. When I upload my photo to my account, I smile. I've changed the name to 'Jolly Journalist'. I'm a freelancer now, writing articles for local papers and online magazines. It helps that after the news articles about the 'Postie Who Saved The Poet', my follower count has climbed into the tens of thousands. Celia is rather jealous and likes to remind me of it with regular texts telling me to 'Stop being so popular or you'll overtake my follower count'.

'Lovely view today, isn't it, Liz?' a voice calls out.

I look up to see Tilda Beashell leaning over her balcony. Funny how her tune has changed since the truth came out about Gwen and Douglas. She's so fake, able to pretend more readily than others if it suits her. I don't respond to her. I just nod. I can't be fake like her.

'I bet you get an even better view from your place,' she adds, gesturing to my new house a few rows down. It's pale blue with a balcony just like Tilda's, which I sit on after each postal round, eating my lunch. Thanks to selling my story to an upmarket newspaper, I was able to afford the deposit and a few months' rent on the place. The girls love it, waving down at passers-by like royalty. I even let Scott come in to have a look once and he was impressed. Things are better between us. How can they not be after what he did in the end? Sure, he's done a lot to hurt me too, but he's my girls' father. He even offers to pick them up now and sometimes stays in Easthaven if they have something going on at school. I think he visits my mother in her new care home a few miles away. I visit her too at least once a week. They're not exactly what I'd call the most joyous of visits. Still, she is my mother and we care for our own, don't we?

I pull some parcels out for Tilda.

'More dresses, naughty me!' she says as she looks down at them. 'Just leave them there in my garden, I'll come and get them in a minute.'

I place the packages on Tilda's doorstep. 'Best I don't trespass,' I say. I don't hang around to see her response. I promised Tamsin I'd pop by for a cuppa anyway. She's decided to keep Lakewell Manor and renovate it with her mother's inheritance. Now she knows that Gabe's death – I still struggle to think of him as Jacob – wasn't directly her fault, her love for the place has returned.

I do the rest of my round quickly, striding to the patisserie with a smile. Lester is at his usual place by the counter. His face lights up. 'Hey you.'

'Hello!' I hand his post over, noticing one letter from his solicitor. 'So you'll finally own this place soon,' I say, smiling as I look around me.

'Yes, we're due to complete next Friday.'

'Amazing!' With Tamsin's help, he'd managed to prove the transfer of deeds between her father and Douglas's father was illegal, landing the property back in the Lakewell estate's hands. And as sole owner of the Lakewell estate, Tamsin was able to offer the space at a ridiculously reduced rate for Lester to buy.

'Cuppa?' he asks.

'I can't stay today, I'm meeting Tamsin.'

'Ah, nice, say hi for me.' He looks me in the eyes. I can see he's nervous. 'I was thinking. Maybe we should go out for dinner sometime?'

I hesitate. I want to say yes, but it scares me. After everything that happened with Scott, the idea of another relationship evokes complicated emotions. 'I'll message you,' I say. I know he can tell I'm fobbing him off. He hides his disappointment well. I give him a wave and head out of the cafe, feeling bad. A little while later, I'm walking towards the manor gates, finding Tamsin within, sitting at that rusted bistro table and writing poetry.

It's taken her a while to get over her ordeal. She collapsed when she was eventually taken to hospital and there were weeks when I wondered if she'd ever recover. But gradually, she's getting there. It's good to see her back where she belongs, in her garden writing poetry as she looks out to sea. She looks up, waving when she sees me. I press in the gate code and walk through as the gates slide open. We give each other a big hug.

'Hello Liz with an L,' she says. 'What delights do we have here?'

I hand over her post. There's a big package from her publishers and I can tell it's yet more gifts from them to celebrate her winning the T. S. Eliot Prize for poetry. The whole experience seems to have brought Tamsin out of her shell. She even did a media interview. It was important to her that other women were warned how easy it is to be conned by a handsome face.

There is another letter, too. One with a postmark from the prison where Carl is awaiting trial for fraud, a few miles from where

Gwen is awaiting her own trial for kidnapping and fraud. They should count themselves lucky compared to Douglas, who faces many years in prison for murder. I sigh as I look at the letter. These letters from Carl arrive about three to four times a week. I sometimes see a wistfulness in Tamsin's eyes when she looks at them. It's not easy to turn off love and she *did* love him . . . like I loved Scott and yes, Gabe too. But sometimes the people you love let you down. She smiles at me now and places the packages on the table, gesturing for me to take the seat across from her.

'So,' she says, taking a sip of her peach juice, 'any gossip?'

'Lester asked me out for dinner.'

Tamsin can't stop herself from smiling. She adores Lester. 'Interesting. And . . . ?'

'Annnnd . . . I'm not sure.'

'Fair enough. You shouldn't feel rushed.'

'No, I shouldn't.'

We both look out to sea. The mist is clearing, exposing the horizon. I watch a heron swoop over the sea, wings sweeping away the mist.

'But then again,' Tamsin says, 'maybe that heron shouldn't be the only one spreading her wings. Maybe it's time for you to as well.'

I smile and get out the brand-new notepad the girls got me for my birthday last month.

'Can I borrow your pen?' I ask Tamsin.

She nods and I pick it up, scribbling a note inside. *Say yes to dinner with Lester.*

Then I close my notepad and tuck it into my pocket, leaning back to luxuriate in our own little sunny spot.

ACKNOWLEDGEMENTS

This novel wasn't an easy one to write as I struggled with the grief of losing my darling mum. So more thanks than ever to those who supported me along the way. To the team at Lake Union, especially Victoria and Ian. Thank you for your patience and handholding through multiple revisions! To my agent Caroline as always for her constant guidance and support. And to my family and friends, especially my husband Rob, my brother Paul, my aunt Laura and my stepdad Vic who have helped me hold it together. And I must mention my amazing daughter Scarlett, as she always looks for her name in my books. So here you go Scarlett, big cuddles and thanks to you for keeping me smiling.

BEFORE YOU GO!

I'm so pleased you've read my novel and I very much hope you enjoyed it. Here are four things to continue your journey:

1. Want to read a FREE novella set in the same location, filled to the brim with twists, drama and romance? Sign up for my newsletter by visiting www.tracy-buchanan.com/novella.

2. I honestly love hearing from readers! You can find multiple ways of contacting me by visiting my website at www.tracy-buchanan.com.

3. If you like joining Facebook groups, come join me and two other AMAZING authors, Kerry Fisher and Kelly Rimmer, in The Reading Snug where you can get even more book recommendations, freebies and exclusive insights.

4. I'd be so grateful if you could leave a review on all the usual channels. Reviews mean so much to us authors and the good ones always bring a smile to our faces.

ABOUT THE AUTHOR

Photo © 2018 Nic Robertson-Smith

Tracy Buchanan is a bestselling author whose books have been published around the world, including chart toppers *My Sister's Secret*, *No Turning Back*, *Wall of Silence* and *Trail of Destruction*. She lives in the UK with her husband, their daughter and a very spoilt Cavalier King Charles Spaniel called Bronte.

Before becoming a full-time author, Tracy worked as a travel journalist, visiting and writing about countries around the world. She has also produced content for the BBC and the Open University, and rubbed shoulders with celebrities while working for a London PR firm.

When she isn't spending time with her family and friends, Tracy spends her days writing with her dog on her lap or taking walks in forests.

For more information about Tracy, please visit www.facebook.com/TracyBuchananAuthor and www.tracy-buchanan.com.